Breaking News

A Finnerty and Liccione Mystery

Mary Rae, MD
&
Wanda Venters, MD

Praise for Breaking Apart

"Rae and Venters have once again spun a medical murder mystery with precision, passion, and complexity. Breaking Apart takes you on a sexy and high-stakes ride."
-Patty Dann, Author of Mermaids, which was made into a movie with Cher, Winona Ryder, and
Christina Ricci

"Breaking Apart...features the two physicians teaming up again, this time to explore the cruel
reality of Post-Traumatic Stress Disorder...the reader is taken on a journey full of twists and turns
to arrive at the truth. It's a great read!"
-Deven Greene, Author of the Erica Rosen, M.D. trilogy

"Unbelievably Addicting and Surprising! The first book in this series was incredible, but this second installment left me absolutely reeling! It was an emotional rollercoaster and threw in unexpected twists and turns. I truly appreciate that it highlights PTSD as I don't feel like it is talked about enough, and these authors captured the heartbreaking points that some experience. There are some steamy romance scenes woven in as well, and the entire story flows flawlessly. Both authors are definitely on the top of my list of books to pick up, so I can't wait to

"Break Bone Fever is a fast-paced, page-turning medical
mystery that will keep you reading late
into the night. I enjoyed reading about the world of
hospitals and research labs just as much as I
liked reading about the unique landscape of Galveston.
This is a timely, wonderfully written
book that is impossible to put down."
—Caitlin Cieslik-Miskimen, Assistant Professor,
University of Idaho

"So So Good! The co-authors of this murder-mystery are
MDs, so it only makes sense that it is
so well-written that I had white knuckles gripping it while
my eyes soaked it in. These lead
female characters are strong, well-rounded, intelligent,
and pretty awesome. This story involves
intriguing conspiracies and is very relevant to the things
we face in real-life these days. I highly
recommend this book to anyone looking to get lost in a
good, gripping, interesting read that also
makes you think." Chrissy Spulak

"Engaging Story with Characters to Love and Loathe I
picked up a copy of BREAK BONE
FEVER to just flip through it and check it out, and I
pretty much didn't put it down until I
finished the book. Timing was perfect with a long plane
ride ahead, so I was able to really settle
into the story and stay there." Hall Ways

Praise for the Finnerty and Liccione Mystery Series

Praise for Break Bone Fever

"**Break Bone Fever** has many layers of intrigue—I was hooked before the end of the first page!
This murder mystery is relevant to current events on so many levels and interwoven nicely.
Having gone to school in Galveston, the authors capture the unique essence of the city known
only to those who have lived there."
—Natalie Dryden, M.D.

"**Expertly** crafted with intriguing characters, Break Bone Fever is a page turner."—William Maikovich, Esq.

"**Drs. Rae and Venters** have laid out several suspenseful story lines which will eventually
converge on the main narrative of Break Bone Fever. For the reader, they generate interest
because they are well written and have a ring of authenticity insofar as they reflect the combined
expertise of the two female physician/authors."

see what they have in store for us next!" Shannen Kern

"Even Better than the First Book- I highly enjoyed Breaking Apart and cannot say enough good things about it! I accidentally read this book before the first book in the series, Break Bone Fever, but I was able to follow the story with no problem. The pacing and suspense were perfect. The characters are all fleshed out with backstories and felt real. The multiple points of view kept me guessing until the end what really happened with Josh's death. It also touched on multiple difficult topics such as PTSD, suicide, and drug addiction. I cannot wait to pick up the next book in the series since there is a nice little cliff hanger at the end." Callie Luna

"Intense Medical Thriller- This is the second book in the series. I was drawn into the plot in the first chapter. This medical thriller is right on target about the PTSD and traumatic brain injuries our veterans face. The characters were flushed out well and made the reader invested from the beginning!" Brandy Vaughn

"Page Turner-I absolutely could not put this book down once I started it! It is an extremely well written medical crime drama that hooks you immediately and keeps you reading until the very last page. I thought that they did an excellent job in exploring the mental health system in conjunction with our Veterans and the complex issues they are facing daily." Amanda Haller-Dor

Breaking News

A Finnerty and Liccione Mystery

Mary Rae, MD
&
Wanda Venters, MD

Publishers: Wanda Venters and Mary Rae
Editor: Caitlin Cieslik-Miskimen
Copy-Editor: Mary Rae
Cover Art Designer: Tatiana Vila
Interior Layout Designer: Wanda Venters
eBook Layout Designer: Wanda Venters
Category: Medical Thriller/Mystery
Description: Marnie Liccione and Louise Finnerty are
together again to solve a mystery of a cold case murder.

Breaking Apart: A Finnerty and Liccione Mystery
Wanda Venters, M.D. and Mary Rae, M.D.,

Paperback ISBN: 9798300114794

DEDICATION

To my grandchildren, Alachi, Theo, Sasha and Andrew.
May you always follow your dreams
Wanda Venters, MD.

To: Nancy
Mary Rae, MD.

Table of Contents

Chapter 1

Tuesday, January 21, 2020

To: Chris Hill, Editor, Bay City Daily
Re: 18th anniversary
January 18, 2020

I wish this were a happy anniversary. But, as you know, since you're reading a letter from the family of Luther Wood, it's not. My father has been gone for eighteen years. My mother wrote to this newspaper yearly for the last seventeen years. Now she's gone. The duty falls to me. Let me remind you of the facts.

1. In January 2002, my father's body parts were discovered, washed up by the jetty at East Beach.

2. The Galveston Police Department investigated the case.

3. The cause of death was determined to be a shark attack.

4. My mother was "encouraged" to leave town.

My father's horrific death on January 11, 2002, occurred two months after Morris Black's body parts were found and Robert Durst was suspected of his murder. Both murders involved dismemberment. I'm sure I do not need to remind you or your readers of the details.

Our family's concerns are that my father's death and mutilation had the characteristics of a copycat murder. A shark attack was highly unlikely since my father was not a fisherman, nor would he take a swim in the Gulf in January.

As explained, perhaps poorly by my mother, the Galveston Police Department refused to thoroughly investigate his case. I have theories regarding the motivation for a quick resolution and subsequent cover-up. I'm sure that the Galveston Hospitality Consortium didn't want another lurid murder investigation. I am now asking for your intervention. I've been following your work. Your investigative journalism has garnered national attention.

Mr. Hill, it's time to put this matter to rest.

Respectfully,

T. Wood
TWRE6837@gmail.com

Chris reread the letter. *I've had five of these letters about Luther Wood since becoming editor. No expletives in this one.* I can print it. He walked over to the picture window and sighed. Since taking over The Bay City Daily, Chris had never had an easy year. Nor had the paper itself. The Daily gave up its historic and beautiful downtown building for this spit of land obtained at a fire sale price in 1965. A power broker in Texas journalism purchased the paper and quickly sold it for a profit. Throughout the turmoil and subsequent changes in management, The Bay City Daily continued to publish in print and now, online. Chris's daily mantra since joining the paper twenty years ago: *We've got to keep it up.*

He left his office and joined Willa Owen, his assistant, and Tom Assan at the worktable. After several years, Tom had risen through the ranks to become Chris's assistant editor. Having been at the paper longer than anyone on the staff, including Chris, Willa was also the unofficial historian and archivist.

"Looks like 'The Letter' arrived," Chris said.

"Yup. Right on schedule," said Willa. "But this one's different. Really different."

"You two are going to have to enlighten me about the history of this letter. Different from what?" asked Tom.

Willa flipped open one of her innumerable spiral notebooks and glanced at her handwritten notes.

"In 2002, we had our first letter from Janelle Wood. She alleged that her husband, Luther, had been murdered. The problem was that she also said that the perpetrator was the spawn of Satan. She used language that was very colorful about our Galveston County DA, the medical examiner and the detective assigned to her husband's case."

Chris looked up and added, "In other words, it was unprintable. Crazy and obscene. Plus, she never provided a phone number or address to verify her existence. Those letters continued yearly until now. This letter looks like a lawyer wrote it. It meets our guidelines for publication. T. Wood has a point. Galveston's hospitality businesses had reasons for squelching the story."

"How many of these yearly letters have you seen, Chris?" Tom asked.

"Around five. Does that seem right, Willa?"

"Yes. I have copies of those five. I filed them, like you asked me to." Willa paused, "Before that, I think they got tossed."

"If we print this letter, we better give the police a heads up," Tom said.

"I've got Detective Iliana Sudhan's number under my thumb. Let's print the letter and ask for tips. Let's also get a dedicated line for anonymous phone calls—order one for two months."

***

As she heard Chris's car pull into the driveway, Marnie slowly came downstairs. "Stop tripping me," she said to the two dogs whirling around her ankles. "I'm off balance enough with this bump in front of me."

"How are you feeling?" Chris asked as he came in the door.

"Like a blue whale. When I was twenty-three and pregnant with EJ, I did a twelve-hour-shift in the ICU before going into labor. Now it takes me an hour to get up from my nap."

Worry creased Chris's forehead. "Just a few more

months to go."

"Thanks for the pep talk. I've always said that the last month of pregnancy was so that the delivery seemed like deliverance. I now think that it's the last two months." She didn't add that, after her last delivery, she almost died. She was scared that, this time, she might. *That thought is more appropriate for my therapist—or my obstetrician. Chris has enough to deal with.*

"Are you taking it easy?" he asked.

"Yes. Mild activity only." Looking at her swollen ankles she said, "I couldn't fit in my running shoes anyway."

Chris smiled and gave her and her huge belly a bear hug. "I promise that once the baby's here, I'll take over half the responsibilities."

Marnie wanted to say something snarky, like he could take all the responsibility for the next nine months, but she was saved by his phone buzzing.

"Hi Iliana," Chris said. "Thanks for calling me back. I just wanted to give you a heads up about a letter we're printing in the paper tomorrow. It accuses the Galveston Police Department of botching the investigation of Luther Wood's death in 2002. The family doesn't buy the official explanation that the cause of death was a shark attack."

Chris paused, listening to Iliana's question. "Yeah, a while ago. We've been getting the letters for seventeen years, but this is the first one that we can print. We thought we would just toss it out there and ask for any leads. We're going to have an anonymous tip line for the paper. But the police department might get calls as well. We wanted you to be aware of the situation."

Another pause. "She's right here."

He handed Marnie the phone. "Hi Iliana."

Marnie paused. "I'm hanging in there. I haven't killed Chris yet." She shot Chris a smile. He took the opportunity to go upstairs and change clothes. "We would love to come to dinner. Our social calendar is open. EJ said that she likes working with Ben. I know Chris is planning to start the interns at the paper on some new assignments." Another pause, "Yes, February first works great. See you then." Marnie hung up.

Marnie went to the kitchen to check on the chili relleno casserole. Rosa, Chris's long-term housekeeper and friend, insisted on doing most of the cooking. Marnie had no complaints. After moving to Galveston last fall, Marnie had traveled multiple times to Denver to work on her research program. It had been a grueling schedule. The study was now set to run efficiently during her upcoming maternity leave.

I think one of the most rewarding things that I did last fall was to help Rosa get her GED. The story of her missing her senior year of high school was heart-breaking. The time spent with Rosa made it easy for them to agree on a new division of responsibilities. Rosa and Chris had been a team for the last eight years. She had worked for his parents before that. Chris was not interested in taking on the domestic responsibilities that Rosa had handled for years. He was eager to make more time for his new role as Dad. In a three-way conversation, Marnie, Chris, and Rosa discussed changes that they would make with Marnie's addition to the household.

Rosa had been excited to reduce her work week to four days, Monday through Thursday. Having a GED gave

Rosa the confidence to teach a cooking class elective, focused on traditional and regional Mexican cuisine, at the high school.

Marnie inhaled the delicious aroma of the casserole. *What a luxury to have dinner prepared at least four days a week.* Rosa often made extra meals and left them in the freezer or refrigerator. Cooking was her passion.

Having passed the thirty-week mark in her pregnancy, Marnie was beginning to believe that this pregnancy would result in a baby—not another loss. Episodes of bleeding early in the pregnancy caused her to fear that she would miscarry again. Now in her early forties, she was going to have an infant to care for after a twenty-year break. *That was scary.*

She fed her dogs who acted as if they hadn't eaten in weeks. *That's the lab in the labradoodle.* Harlee was a red miniature doodle and only weighed twenty-five pounds. But she was the alpha dog and kept Jack, a solid brown pup of sixty pounds in line. Marnie was glad that the poodle half of their genetics kept them from shedding.

Chris entered the kitchen and put his arms around her from behind. She leaned back into him. They were going to do fine as parents—even if by the time the child was playing soccer everyone in this south Texas town would think they were the grandparents. *Stop it* she scolded herself.

As they ate dinner, Chris told Marnie the details of the letter and what was known about Luther Wood's death. He mentioned that he planned to put his interns to work on the case.

"This sounds like a great distraction for me,"

Marnie said. "Can I become an intern with EJ?"

Chris laughed. "It's enough that I have your daughter on my staff. I'm afraid that you're going to have to participate vicariously. How's the neurofeedback study going in Aurora?"

As Dr. Liccione, a new physician on staff at the Front Range VA hospital in Aurora, Colorado, Marnie had started a neurofeedback study on the treatment of PTSD in vets—and helped solve a murder case involving a young veteran. Because of her pregnancy and Chris's job, she had moved to Galveston in September and was working remotely.

"It's running smoothly. Allison said that Esther was keeping the study on track. They should have some new data for me to crunch before my maternity leave. I'm glad that I was able to go up in person before the holidays and check things out. My OB says I can't fly anymore."

"I'm glad she said it," Chris said. "Keeps me from being the bad guy. After all the trouble last summer, I'm sure Allison is keeping a close eye on every detail. It's great that you can work remotely."

Marnie smiled. "I'll stay in my lane, but you have to let me know how the case develops. This study helps me maintain a professional life, but I do love a good mystery. Keeps my mind from worrying about the bump."

Chris stood up to do the dishes. "Let's take 'Junior' and the pups for a walk in a few minutes. We can discuss baby furniture."

Chapter 2

Wednesday, January 22, 2020

The next day, Marnie was in the kitchen before Chris. She could tell by Chris's expression that her early rising had worried him.

"I'm fine," she said with a smile. "Just woke up and wanted some breakfast."

She passed Chris a plate of huevos rancheros. She was glad that she was past her morning sickness which had lasted into her second trimester. In the first months of pregnancy, she had lost ten pounds. But she was up twenty pounds now and her OB had said she was no longer worried.

"What's on your schedule for the day?" Chris asked.

"I think I'll try to meet Louise for lunch and do a little online shopping for things we need. Anything you want added to the list?"

"Not that I can think of before work. I can't switch roles easily."

"Better get used to it," Marnie teased.

***

When Marnie went upstairs to get dressed, Chris sat in the kitchen scanning the morning news. He looked up from his tablet toward the large window over the sink. The view was dominated by an ancient live oak tree. It must have been planted by the original owners of his Victorian home. Although it had lost some enormous branches during Hurricanes Harvey, Ike, and numerous preceding storms, it was still standing. Like the house itself. The live oak shed its leaves every winter like clockwork. The new greenery would already be coming in, so it was never completely bare. The crispy, brown leaves filled the driveway and skittered in the breeze. The driveway led to the garage apartment where he had lived until recently. The light was on. EJ was up.

Those years in the apartment were the last of his bachelorhood. He lived out there as he slowly renovated the crumbling 'mansion' he had bought from his cousin. At the time, he thought it was a steal. The never-ending renovation made him reconsider. *It must be part of my nature to want to preserve old things of value. That's why the newspaper means so much to me.* Rosa had been the foreman of the renovation, and now that the job was finished had decided to move from her guest room in the big house to her own bungalow a few blocks away. Chris watched Rosa come through the back gate, pick up a rake and get to work on the live oak leaves.

Chris turned as the kitchen door flew open, and EJ strode to the refrigerator. She grabbed a yogurt, then poured some coffee into her traveling cup.

"Gotta go. My boss is a real jerk, and I can't be late," she said with a smile. She was out the door as fast as she had come in. Chris watched her greet Rosa before pulling out of the driveway. He was glad those two had hit it off.

He wished his own relationship with EJ was that easy. She wasn't technically his stepdaughter since he and Marnie hadn't gotten around to getting married. *Not yet? Not ever?* EJ was about to become the half-sister of Marnie's and his baby. In the last two years, she had lost her father in a rafting accident and almost lost her mother in an attack that had put Marnie in the ICU. He couldn't blame her for keeping her distance while she sorted things out.

When Marnie came back down, Chris said, "I've got to run. Should I try to come home for lunch?"

"Please don't. I feel like you're hovering." She came to his side and took his hand. "This pregnancy has been hard, uncomfortable, and scary. I know you'll be here when I need you."

"You can count on it."

"Louise said she could meet me for lunch. Give EJ a hello from me. I think she's trying to avoid me, and I totally understand. I've been tense these last few months. Work hard and come home missing me." Marnie gave Chris one of her real smiles.

Chris grinned back, grabbed his keys, and headed out.

***

Marnie watched him drive off. She was envious. She

wished that she could split herself into two parts. One part could relax around the house growing a baby and the other part, a twenty pounds lighter part, could whisk off to work.

Taking a deep breath, she pushed back against 'Junior' trying to kick his way out under her diaphragm. Once again she thought of the movie "Alien" with a lifeform bursting out of its victim's chest. She wondered if a woman had suggested the scene to the script writer.

"If I can wait a few more weeks, so can you," she said to her bump.

She didn't remember when she started to call him Junior in her head. She was glad that her baby was a boy—though she did catch herself and say probably a boy. Her friendship with Gennifer had taught her that anatomy and gender identity weren't always the same thing. But until he told her otherwise, he was a he. EJ had seemed pleased to get a sibling this late in the game, but there was bound to be some competition. Human nature. Different sexes would decrease that rivalry.

Marnie looked at her bulging waistline. *At least I always have someone to talk to beside the dogs.* The best thing about Junior was that he couldn't talk back. He kicked again. *Much.*

Addressing her audience of two dogs and Junior, "We're taking a walk around the block. I need to check in with Esther about the neurofeedback study and start the write-up. Then I have a dental appointment before meeting Louise. EJ said she'd take you for a run this evening." Tails wagged. Junior kicked.

***

When Chris arrived at his office, he saw the letter on his desk. He'd left it in plain sight to force himself to deal with it. Willa had gathered the previous four letters from the victim's widow. They were even worse than he remembered. He had to give the author credit for including so many expletives per sentence. The first year the letter came to him as editor, he'd asked a temporary assistant to do some research. *Where did that end up?* It must not have turned up anything. Plus, he remembered feeling less than open to helping someone who addressed him as a F***king A**h*le.

Chris decided it was time to take another look. He started a search and quickly found the article from 2002. *Here it is. Fatal shark attack.*

The article stated that the victim had been fishing at dusk, standing in shallow water beside the jetty at East Beach. Chris knew the spot well. The jetty provided protection from the waves. It was a favored site for fishermen. They could drive almost to the water's edge, cast a line, and secure their rods in the sand while they sipped beer on tailgates. Or wade into the shallow water with rod and reel and gaze out at the passing cargo ships and tankers heading up Galveston Bay to the Port of Houston.

Reading on, he was reminded of the details. Body parts were found on the beach. Police were notified and the medical examiner's office took over from there. The official cause of death was listed as exsanguination secondary to multiple deep tissue wounds consistent with a shark attack. Chris wondered why the attack was unwitnessed. *Weren't there other fishermen in the vicinity? Was it bad weather? Did the actual attack occur past dusk, in the dark?*

The article made a quick pivot to point out the rarity of shark attacks and the even rarer instances of fatalities. Between 1865 and 2003 there had only been five fatal shark attacks on record for the Texas Gulf Coast out of seventy-one unprovoked attacks. *More likely to be struck by lightning is what I heard growing up.* He understood why the story made a pivot. Shark attacks were not a popular subject for a beachfront tourist destination. An internet search revealed that the story had been picked up by several news outlets in Texas and ran once on a national evening news show, probably as a teaser before a station break. Then nothing.

The next step was to review the case file at Galveston Police Department and find out more about the victim and the investigation.

His thoughts were interrupted when Willa came into his office carrying a sheaf of papers and wearing a determined expression. Chris recognized that look and knew he was trapped until he completed whatever tasks Willa was about to lay out for him.

"HR needs you to review and update these job descriptions. I have the bid for the parking lot repair. Have you reviewed the policy on pay transparency?" Willa took a seat opposite Chris.

Remembering that his job was to run the paper, Chris would need to delegate the research on Luther Wood's death. The author of the letter was correct. It was time to put the matter to rest.

"Let's put these administrative tasks on hold briefly. I'm going to bring EJ and Ben up to speed on the Wood's matter and have them do some research. I promise to sit with you at eleven."

Willa nodded her head. She wanted to make sure that they got the tasks done before lunch. "I'll send the interns in."

As EJ and Ben entered Chris's office, he admired their professional attitude. Neatly dressed in island business casual, their open expressions invited strangers to talk to them. The best tool a reporter could have. EJ looked like a younger, slightly shorter, version of her mom, attractive and fit. Ben was a handsome blend of his Pakistani mom, Iliana Sudhan, and his Swedish dad, Bob Jaansen, head nurse in the ER. *Cute couple. I wonder if HR allows me to think that.*

"Hi. I hope you're eager to start your first big assignment. We've decided to investigate an allegation. Could turn out to be a cold case that needs fresh eyes." Chris handed copies of the letters over to the interns.

Skimming the letters, EJ and Ben nodded.

EJ said, "Definitely a cold case. Sounds fascinating."

"It's exciting to do some real investigative reporting," Ben added.

Chris said, "Let's do some introductory pieces describing the crime scene in Galveston in 2003. Then let's do an in-depth review of the police reports of Luther Wood's death. I'll let you decide how you want to break down the tasks."

"Do you remember the case?" Ben asked. He paused from his notetaking to see the expression on Chris's face.

"Only vaguely. I wasn't in Galveston then. My dad wanted me to get some experience at a bigger paper, so I was in Chicago. When I returned, everyone was trying to ignore the Durst case, as well apparently, as Wood's death."

EJ looked up from the letter. "I don't get the reference to this Durst guy."

"Robert Durst is an odd duck and heir to a New York real estate fortune. He was hiding out in Galveston while under investigation for the murder of his wife. While here, he killed and dismembered a neighbor."

"Ugh. Dismembered? When was this?" EJ asked.

"Yeah. Body parts were found in garbage bags, washed up on the beach. Thus, the reference in the letter to a copycat murder. It was late 2001." Chris shook his head in disgust. "Despite admitting to the dismemberment, Durst was acquitted of the murder. The Durst family lawyers made the Galveston Police Department, judge and jury look like chumps."

"You're in for an education if this kind of case floats your boat. Galveston has a long history involving colorful characters and unsolved crimes," Willa said as she entered the office.

Chris nodded in agreement.

EJ raised her eyebrows. "I'm already intrigued."

Ben said, "I was three when this happened. My parents should remember all this. I'll see what I can get out of them."

Chris said, "Great, let me know your progress." When the interns left, he said to Willa. "I'm ready to do the admin work. Gotta keep the paper running."

Chapter 3

Wednesday, January 22, 2020

Louise was happy to see Marnie in the clinic picnic area with sack lunches from the Mariposa Café. Having made it into her last trimester, Marnie had lost some of the stress lines around her eyes.

"You look good," Louise said.

"Thank you," Marnie replied. "I feel like a blimp, but everything is checking out."

"That's reassuring," Louise said as she divided the food up.

Marnie smiled. "Going in for weekly blood pressure and urine checks. I feel like a frequent flier."

"I'm glad Linda's monitoring you closely for pre-eclampsia."

"Different subject. How's clinic life going?" Marnie asked.

"I like it. I like working daytime hours and having most weekends off. Unfortunately, there doesn't ever seem to be an end to the paperwork and computer tasks."

"Speaking of paperwork," Marnie said, "Chris

told me that the newspaper gets a yearly letter from the family of a victim of a fatal shark attack. They ask that the death be reinvestigated. It's been going on for a while, and the latest letter is from the victim's son. He doubts the shark attack story and suspects foul play, maybe even a police cover-up. EJ and Ben are working on the background for the story, if there is a story there."

"When was this?" Louise asked.

"I think Chris said 2002."

"The son may well be right. There were rumors about a Galveston Mafia protection racket back then."

"Galveston Mafia?" Marnie asked.

"Yep! Welcome back to the island." Louise laughed as she gathered her things. "I better get back to the clinic. Thanks for lunch. Let's do this again soon."

"Love to."

* * *

Louise Finnerty carried her laptop and water bottle to her office in the late afternoon. She had seen her last patient. Now she needed to finish her notes, answer messages, renew medications, and check tomorrow's patient list. She kicked her shoes off and turned on some music.

She had been working at the Galveston Island Community Clinic for six months. After fifteen years practicing emergency medicine, she had transitioned into primary care. The learning curve was steep, but she was beginning to hit her stride. A preparatory summer course for doctors entering primary care from other specialties had been a godsend. With help from the clinic staff, she was learning a new, and diabolically complicated, electronic medical record.

What a relief to finish the day before reaching the point of exhaustion. Yes, the day! I don't know when I'll stop being grateful for not having to work nights.

The tradeoff was that she was never done. In the ER, she started and finished her shift with a clean slate. The continuity of care that her clinic patients appreciated turned out to be continuous. *Who knew?* She had to laugh at herself.

She looked around her office. Her metallic desk was ancient. She didn't have a window. The walls were the color of jaundice. *But it's mine!* She had no such private refuge in the ER. She looked across the hall to Connie's office. Connie Garcia had recruited Louise to the clinic. She had been Louise's partner in the ER until the birth of her twins. Then, she transitioned to primary care and had been encouraging Louise to do the same for the last few years.

"Dr. Finnerty, are you still here?" Katia, Louise's medical assistant, called from around the corner. "I'm heading out, gotta pick up my kids."

Louise heard the door close behind Katia before she could answer. She knew it was time to relieve her mom as well. She worked her way through her tasks and was about to shut off her computer when an alert flashed about a critical lab value. A moment later a technician from the lab called. Louise saw the lab value appear on her screen as the technician confirmed the result.

"What the…", she murmured when she hung up the phone. "How did that happen? Bruce MacFarland's blood sugar is forty?"

She texted her mother to explain that she would be

later than expected. Nancy wouldn't be surprised. It wasn't the first time. She opened Mr. MacFarland's medical record, found his number and dialed. Yvonne MacFarland, Bruce's wife, answered.

"Hello, Mrs. MacFarland, it's Dr. Finnerty at the clinic."

"Oh, hello, Doctor. I was about to call the after-hours number. I'm so glad you called me. Bruce had a hard day. We got his blood drawn this afternoon. Remember you ordered it yesterday after we chatted? It really must have taken it out of him. When we got home, he said he needed a nap. I just checked on him and he had a hard time waking up."

"That makes sense with the lab result I just got. His blood sugar is forty. He needs some sugar," Louise explained.

"Should I bring him to the ER? I hate to think about how long we would have to wait. What should we do?" Yvonne was clearly shaken.

"I hear you about the ER. Let's start with a glass of orange juice. Stir two teaspoons of sugar into it and let him drink it. But wait, is he awake enough to swallow?"

"Oh, yes. He's hollering for me right now."

Indeed, Louise could hear Bruce's shouts in the background. *That poor woman.* Louise knew that the retired police detective was a handful, medically and emotionally.

"I'll stay on the line while you give him that drink." She reviewed his previous lab and medications. He had multiple medical problems, including type 2 diabetes, a recent pulmonary embolism, congestive heart failure and worsening dementia. Type 2 diabetes was his only stable condition when Louise assumed his care five months ago. He took a pill every morning and then cheated on his diet all day. He never had low blood sugar. It was always on the high side.

When Mrs. MacFarland came back on the line, she sounded calmer. "He's already doing better, Dr. Finnerty. He told me he wouldn't go to the GD ER anyway."

Louise outlined a plan with her that involved frequent blood sugar checks at home throughout the evening and holding his morning diabetes pill. Against her better judgment, and advice she had received from her colleagues at the clinic, she gave Mrs. MacFarland her cell phone number.

"I'll call you in a few hours and we can take it from there," she said. "Tomorrow, we'll get to the bottom of this." Louise hoped she sounded more confident than she felt. Bruce MacFarland had been a medical enigma since she met him.

With the crisis averted, Louise packed up her computer, texted her husband that she was picking up the kids, and made for the door.

***

Chris headed to the Daily's parking lot at the end of his day. He was accompanied by a few reporters and a new hire, Charlotte, from advertising. It was Marnie's book club evening and maybe a last opportunity to go to happy hour with his coworkers. At least for a while.

"I'll meet you at Hugo's. If you get there first, grab a table in the corner," Chris said.

"Mind if I catch a ride with you?" Charlotte asked.

"My car's in the shop so I took a ride share to work today,"

"Sure. Hop in." Chris was glad to have an opportunity to get to know Charlotte. She had been working in advertising for a statewide magazine in Austin before relocating to Galveston. Hiring her felt like a big win to Chris. She had experience that could boost needed revenue at the paper. He was sure she took a pay cut when she accepted the job. "How have your first couple of weeks at The Daily been?"

"It's been great, but quite a steep learning curve for me. I feel as if everything happens super-fast at a daily paper compared to a monthly glossy." After a pause she straightened her shoulders and continued. "I'm getting there. It's been an education getting familiar with your regular advertising clients."

"Everything from bait and tackle shops to the cruise lines, right?" Chris said, catching a glance at Charlotte in profile. She smiled at his remark. He realized she usually appeared on guard. *She should smile more often.* She wore her light brown hair in a low ponytail. Her jewelry was limited to small stud earrings. *No nonsense.*

Chris continued, "I spent some time in advertising, and just about every other department during summer vacations. Mainly as a gofer. I'm dating myself, but we were still trying to figure out how to use the internet when I started. People wondered if it would catch on."

"Well, it's here to stay. I have some thoughts on how to improve our digital sales by providing clients with ad formats for every season and holiday. Maybe sell some annual packages that way."

Chris turned on to Broadway and headed downtown. "Good idea. Some of our clients withhold advertising if they don't like a particular editorial. It makes sense to have them pay up in advance. We've got to maintain revenue one way or another if we want to cover local politics. Our readers depend upon us, but it costs more and more." Chris thought about his payroll. He wanted to do everything he could to avoid layoffs.

"That's what attracted me to The Daily," Charlotte said. "When I was at the magazine, we did a story on small town papers. These papers close at a rate of two per week in this country and create news deserts. People resort to bots and social media for local news, if they bother at all. More misinformation than actual news. I wanted to see if I could make a difference for at least one paper."

"Well, we're glad you decided to give The Daily a shot. Is that the main reason you decided to move here? Galveston is an interesting place but doesn't have the cool factor that Austin has."

"I was born and raised here. I left after high school and was sure I'd never come back." Charlotte's brow furrowed. "But you never know what life's going to throw you, right?"

"I couldn't agree more," Chris said thinking about his midlife romance and upcoming fatherhood. He wondered what had been thrown at Charlotte.

The streetlights were on when they arrived downtown. Chris stopped at a red light on Mechanic Street in front of the previous home of The Daily. It was a magnificent nineteenth century brick building that had housed the paper for eighty years. The floor-to-ceiling windows were topped with crescents of stained glass. Quite a contrast to the brutalist style of the current HQ.

"Did you know the Daily was the first paper in the United States to have its own building? And the first to have a telephone line?" he asked. Charlotte shook her head. "Sorry to be such a tour guide," Chris went on. "You grew up here after all."

"Yes, but I was more interested in hanging out with friends and scrolling through Facebook than learning about local history. I feel like I have a new city to explore. I even signed up for a ghost tour at the Third Coast Hotel."

Chris laughed. "Good for you. Those tours have been successful. A friend of mine from high school came up with the idea."

"Would that be Anita? I'm blanking on her last name. We've already met. She's interested in running more ads and has some good ideas for digital content."

"Martin. Yeah. That sounds like Anita. She's a go-getter. Breathed new life into that place." Chris blushed remembering his short but torrid relationship with Anita after their senior year of high school. *Definitely a go-getter. Way too much of a woman for me at eighteen.*

Glancing back at the old building, Chris said, "My grandfather told me that a town was as strong as its newspapers and banks. Back in his time newspapers were competing against each other. Now we're competing with market forces just to keep publishing."

"You've got a good team. They're motivated. I can tell they respect the mission of The Daily," Charlotte said as Chris pulled into a parking spot in front of Hugo's. "It's a breath of fresh air after the magazine where we were cogs in a corporate machine. Kind of soul crushing. I wanted to work someplace where things mattered. I'm going to like it here." She grinned.

"I sure hope so," Chris said.

***

Didier arrived home with the pizza a few minutes before Louise and the kids. He had the refrigerator open and was rummaging in the lower drawers. Chico, the family mutt, was happily milling around as all four crowded into the kitchen.

"Looking for something green to complement our entrée," he said. "We have broccoli and snap peas."

"Perfect," Louise said.

Louise passed Didier a beer and poured herself a glass of wine.

They asked the children about their days at school and, as usual, learned very little. Noah had put them on a need-to-know basis with the beginning of third grade. Cora, at seven, was starting to follow his lead, but usually disclosed more. That night's topic was Cora's upcoming turn to take the class guinea pig home for the weekend. Louise extracted a promise from Cora to keep her door closed and Chester's cage on her desk to make sure Chico didn't try to make friends.

When the kids headed off to watch TV, Didier and Louise took their drinks out on the veranda. It was warm enough to sit outside on that midwinter evening. The salt marsh that spread out beneath them was catching the last glimmer of the sunset. They chatted about their days.

"How did things go at Feathers today?" Louise asked, referring to his birding store and travel company.

"Not bad. Sales are staying up even after the holidays. How were things at the clinic?"

"I saw Bruce MacFarland today. It's been two steps forward and three steps back since I became his physician."

Didier noted her discomfort. He knew that Louise couldn't talk in detail about a patient without breaking confidentiality.

"Yeah, last time Yvonne MacFarland came into the shop, she said that you've been great. She's very thankful for your care."

"That makes me feel a little better. I can't figure out why he keeps having so many problems. Or maybe that's what primary care is like. People get older and sicker. At least it's not like the ER where my patients died in front of my eyes." Louise shook her head.

"I'm thinking about having my new assistant, Foster, do some work around the MacFarland's yard to reciprocate for all the volunteer work Yvonne does for our Island Bird Society. Apparently, Bruce can't do much these days."

"I'm sure Yvonne would appreciate the help." Louise took a sip of her wine. "I saw Marnie for lunch. She seemed chipper today. Much less anxious. Tomorrow I'm eating with EJ. She wants to pick my brain about some Galveston history for an assignment she has at the paper. Her intensity reminds me of Marnie."

"Uh oh," said Didier. "The apple doesn't fall far from the tree."

***

Settled into her bar seat, EJ looked at Ben with his friends in the corner, laughing and talking. After their first real day of investigative research, Ben had insisted that she join him and meet some of his high school friends. The last three years Ben had been at Rice University in Houston. Like her, he was a senior. He maintained a good relationship with his friends from home—who included several attractive women.

EJ was at the bar waiting for service. *I'm supposed to grab a beer and join the group, but I don't feel that I belong here. Too many changes in my life recently. I wonder if I was always an old soul or just since my dad's death.*

She settled onto the bar stool.

"Still happy hour, two for one," the bartender said.

"That should be plenty for me." EJ smiled. She was a careful drinker. She hated—really hated— hangovers. *A Christian drunk.* Her mom often joked that it was one of EJ's great-grandfather's favorite sayings.

Looking around the room at the laughing crowd, EJ shook her head. *Maybe I should have stayed to finish my last semester in New Haven, but I was so tired of the cold and gray. And I was out-of-step with my peers there. Everyone was waiting to hear about law or medical school or financial internships in NY or the Bay Area. I was thinking about the fragility of life.*

"A penny for your thoughts. Very serious thoughts from your expression."

EJ looked up from her bar stool to see an

27

attractive man, probably around thirty, smiling at her. She liked how his white untucked shirt flattered his light brown skin.

Always serious, that's me," she said. *Did she want to continue the conversation?* "Do you have some good news to cheer me up?"

"It's not supposed to rain tomorrow?"

Wiping sweat from her brow, EJ laughed. "At least outside. I have a hard time getting used to sweating this much in January."

"Where are you from?" he asked.

"I was born here but raised in Colorado. No sweat there, summer or winter. I spent the last three and a half years in New Haven." *Why am I telling this guy all this?* "Where are you from?"

"Actually, I was born in Galveston but moved around a bit. Mostly from the Dallas area." He extended his hand as he grabbed the recently vacated bar seat next to EJ. "Hi, I'm Taylor. What brings you to Galveston?"

"Hi, I'm Ellie Jean, better known as EJ." EJ felt herself relax and smiled. "An internship with the Bay City Daily. And family—my mom's partner, Chris, runs the Daily. What brings you here?"

Taylor liked her smile. "My job. I work in real estate and my firm opened a branch in Galveston. Second home sales on Galveston Island are picking up again. No hurricanes for a few years and the buyers are coming back." He took a sip from his drink. "Reporter, huh? Is it as exciting as the movies portray it or mostly just looking at computer screens?"

Past images of violence from the Bay City Daily flashed through her mind. "Mostly the latter."

"Your newspaper had a few national stories recently, didn't it? The murders in 2018? Something about the EPA?

EJ had always wondered how much of the stories filtered to the public. "Yeah, I said 'mostly' looking at computer screens. Sometimes there is more excitement that we need."

Taylor flashed her an open smile. "Can I buy you a drink?"

EJ thought for a minute. It would be her three-drink-limit. Luckily, she could walk home from here. But if she stayed, Marnie might be asleep when she got home. She loved her mom, but the last stage of this late-in-life pregnancy was making her mom poor company. And she admitted that Taylor was the first man in Galveston who aroused her interest. Maybe because he was a little older or maybe because he looked like he could buy her a drink without expecting a quick hook-up.

"All right," she said. "I'll have a Dirty Dog Lager."

After the beers came, she asked, "Has Galveston changed a lot since you were a kid? I was born here but left when I was two, so I have no memory of it from then. My family did come here to visit over the years."

"My mom and I left when I was ten." Taylor hesitated. "Soon after my dad died."

EJ nearly choked on her beer. *Maybe it was pathos that had attracted her to Taylor.*

"Sorry, not much of a good opening gambit for bar conversation. It just sort of slipped out," he said.

"I'm sorry for your loss," EJ said.

"Thanks, it was a long time ago but being back

here makes me think about him." Taylor paused and then said, "What were you doing in New Haven?"

"Finishing my last semester at Yale. But it turned out that I could take this internship and complete my senior paper here in Galveston. The thought of beaches and sunshine versus a cold dreary winter in the Northeast won out. Also, Mom and her new partner live here now and are expecting their first child next month." *Now I'm the one oversharing.*

Taylor raised his eyebrows. "That's got to be a change for you. Do you have any other siblings?"

EJ laughed. "No, this is a big change for all of us. I think it's been harder on my mom than she thought. And I gathered, not really planned. I like her new partner, though. I think things will work out. Just right now, home can be a bit dicey." *I'm not going to bring up my dad's death. Only so much sharing over a drink in a bar.*

Looking for another topic of conversation, Taylor asked, "Those murders here a few years ago—they were somehow related to a tropical disease, right?"

EJ nodded. "Right. Dengue fever. A tropical disease aka break bone fever. With global warming it's becoming more of a problem in the US. Now it seems there's a new virus coming from China. Have you heard about it?" Taylor looked confused. "I wonder if it'll be like the SARS virus from fifteen years ago. My mom's a doctor. She said that if that had become more transmissible, it would have been a global epidemic."

"Wow, we've gone from deaths to family drama, to global epidemics. We have a knack for light conversations," Taylor said. "Seen any good movies lately?"

"This will surprise you, but I really liked "Little Women.""

"I think my favorite was "1917"."

"They certainly avoided any women in that one."

Taylor smiled, "Even I noticed that, but war movies— what can you do?"

"I think there is a lot happening with women in war zones. Running across battlefields is easier cinema."

EJ saw Ben and his friends looking at her from the corner and realized that it was time to go.

"I came over with some friends and it looks like they're getting ready to leave. Let me introduce you and then I think I'll leave with them."

"Can we exchange numbers?" Taylor asked.

"Sure," EJ said.

EJ led Taylor over to her friends and made introductions. "This is Ben—he's the other intern at the paper and also a family friend." EJ paused as she looked at the rest of the group. "For a reporter I sometimes suck at remembering names. Can you take over, Ben?"

Ben shook hands with Taylor and then, smiling, introduced his four friends.

"See you around," EJ said to Taylor as she headed to the door.

Taylor nodded and smiled.

Chapter 4

Thursday, January 23, 2020

Chris told Ben and EJ to start their investigative report by writing an article to set the scene of Galveston in 2003. They divided the assignment. EJ would write about the crime scene and Ben would tackle the local business and political situations.

Needing some inspiration, EJ arranged to meet Louise for lunch outside the courthouse. The old courthouse. There was a scenic plaza in front of the building with palm trees planted in two concentric circles. A plaque announced that the courthouse was built in 1966. *There must have been a building boom in the sixties. The architecture of this building is as uninspiring as the Daily HQ.* EJ's preliminary research revealed this building to be the sixth of seven Galveston County courthouses. The newest incarnation was the Galveston County Justice Center on Broadway. It took over most of this courthouse's functions in 2006. But this courthouse saw action during the time frame of interest to EJ.

EJ looked up when she heard a familiar voice,

"Hi, EJ, sorry I'm late," said Louise as she took a seat on the bench, somewhat winded by her power walk from the clinic. She reached into the sack she carried and pulled out two turkey subs.

EJ brightened at the prospect of the sandwich. Also, because she was happy to see Louise. Her relationship with her mom's best friend had always been special. Without the overlay of mother-daughter baggage, the two had an easy time connecting.

"How are the kids?" EJ asked. She had gotten close to Cora and Noah when she was their camp counselor the summer before.

Louise filled her in between bites. "The kids are good when they're not threatening to kill each other. This war of words just started." Louise shook her head. "At least I'm around more to moderate. This clinic job has made home life a lot more manageable. What about you and the crew over on 18th Street?"

"I'm good. Still getting my bearings. I can tell you I don't plan to have any children myself after being around my pregnant mom. She's been unbearable."

Louise laughed. "I'll remind you about this conversation someday. You need to cut your mom some slack. She was fine when she was pregnant with you, but since then her OB history has been a nightmare."

EJ looked irritated. *Mom should have thought of that before she had a "surprise" pregnancy.*

Sensing EJ's mood, Louise changed the subject. "Why are we eating in front of the old courthouse? Is it about the confederate statue? Can you believe it's still standing?"

They both took bites of their sandwiches and gazed up at the statue of a weary confederate soldier carrying a rolled-up flag. It dominated the plaza.

"Man, the symbolism is laid on thick. They keep arguing about taking it down in city council meetings, but here it is," Louise said. "But hey, the demographics are changing. I'm not giving up. That statue will come down."

Now that EJ was in her twenties, she had a hard time containing her disgust for the vestiges of the Lost Cause and racism that littered the South. There was so much she was unaware of during her trips to the island as a child.

"Soon, I hope." EJ took a bite of her sandwich. "I'm not here about the statue, although I wouldn't mind taking a crack at that story. I have a new assignment at The Daily."

"Your mom and I were just talking about your investigation."

"All in the family." EJ smiled. "I'm looking into the crime scene in Galveston in the early 2000s. I have lots of stats but wondered what it felt like to the locals."

"Well, I finished med school here in 2001 and was in Houston for residency before moving back with Didier in '05. I can tell you that the drug cartels were very active up and down the Gulf Coast. We treated plenty of gunshot wounds in the ER. I saw more grieving parents than I care to remember. Families were caught in the crossfire of warring gangs and lived in terror. There was this one little girl, killed in a drive-by shooting." Louise hesitated. "Not sure I want to remember…"

"That must have been hard." EJ paused before

pressing forward. A single pigeon was now joined by three more.

"I'm trying to figure out the relationship between the cartels and this so-called island Mafia. Can you shed any light?"

"Galveston's Mafia has been an object of shame, ridicule and, believe it or not, pride depending on who you ask," said Louise, looking at her watch. "Chris loves to talk about all the ins and outs. Ask him to tell you about Little Vic Maceo. He loves that story."

They dumped their remaining crumbs for the birds and packed up their trash. EJ frowned trying to unpack Louise's contradictory description of Galveston's underbelly.

"Thanks for the sandwich, Louise. And the company. Do you mind if I run some ideas by you when I get more organized about this story? You said you had some clinic patients from the police department. Anyone from that era?"

"I have quite a few PD patients. And their family members. But I'm not sure it would be ethical to ask them to contribute. You know, coming from their doctor. I'll think about it. Maybe somebody we know outside of the clinic."

"Sure, I get it," EJ said. "Thanks for listening."

"Be nice to your mom! She's a handful pregnant or not."

"Ha-ha. You got that right. I will. Promise." EJ came in for a quick hug.

She watched Louise head off in her purposeful way in the direction of her clinic. EJ wanted to get back to the paper and dig into the archives. The visit to the old courthouse and lunch with Louise had given her some ideas.

***

Didier LaSalle poked his head out of his office in the back room of Feathers. He gave his neck a stretch as he took in the room. A few customers were browsing in the book area and his assistant, Foster, was tidying the hats. Didier looked on approvingly when Foster moved from hats to rearranging the bird feeders.

It wasn't long ago that all those tasks fell to Didier as owner and sole employee at Feathers, his birding store located on Galveston's Seawall Boulevard. Over the past five years business had been so good that he hired several students from Texas A&M– Galveston, to help at the store. Most were pursuing degrees in marine biology. Foster was majoring in tourism and community development. Didier made a mental note to keep track of Foster. His career choice would sync well with Feathers' trajectory.

One reason for Feathers' success was Didier's year-round tours for birders. The Texas Gulf Coast had long been recognized as a 'Best Birding' site in the US, followed by California and Arizona. Didier continued to enjoy leading tour groups when he could. His international tours were concentrated in Mexico. Business was so good that he contracted two local guides to help with those tours. Didier had too many duties at home with two school-age kids and a working wife. He was about to go back to his desk when he saw Yvonne MacFarland come into the store.

"Hello Didier, do you have a moment?" she asked as she approached the back of the store.

"Hi Yvonne. Good to see you again. How are you? Last time you were here you had a full plate. Thanks again for all your help with the volunteers at the Christmas Bird Count. How many counters did you have this year?"

"You're so welcome. Honestly, I couldn't say. I'm better at keeping track of my bird sightings," Yvonne said. Her southern accent was soft, her voice high pitched.

As always, Yvonne was turned out well. She wore pressed jeans and a fitted vest over her blouse. Despite the effort, she appeared tired.

"Your wife, bless her heart, took Bruce on when Dr. Boyd retired. And it's been one thing after another. But she keeps on solving his problems. We're so blessed to have her taking care of him."

In the past, the retired detective had attended many of the Galveston birding events with his wife. Didier thought that Bruce enjoyed talking about his old cases more than the bird sightings.

He smiled.

Yvonne continued, "You know, sometimes I just need to get out of the house." She paused. "Our freestanding feeder needs work. It has a little gazebo on the top and I think it's become top-heavy and started to tilt. Bruce used to take care of it…" she trailed off. "I thought I should get something smaller and easier to manage."

"Of course. We have a lot to choose from. But maybe Foster can fix the one you have. It would be on me. Consider it repayment for all your volunteer hours."

Didier knew that Foster was earning some extra money doing handyman work and gardening for the MacFarlands and a few other birders.

"Hi there, Mrs. MacFarland. I didn't see you come in." Foster approached from the feeders. "Did I hear my name?"

Didier noted the young man's polite but easy affect. He was good with the clients. He knew when to let them roam the store in peace and didn't try to upsell the products. Yet, he managed to sell more of the big-ticket items like binoculars and camera equipment than any of his other employees.

Didier left the two of them to work out a plan for the tilting feeder. Yvonne waved to him as she left with two new hummingbird feeders in hand.

***

Louise smiled as she walked the ten blocks from the old courthouse to her clinic. EJ appeared invested in her new assignment and seemed to be getting her footing at the paper. Louise caught a glimpse of Marnie's tenacity in EJ. *I hope she has the right amount of that DNA.* Marnie's determination had resulted in some major drama in the past two years. *Getting involved in two murder investigations in two years has been plenty for me.*

As she approached the clinic, her thoughts turned to her afternoon schedule. When she glanced at it before lunch, it looked reasonable. A few well woman exams, two diabetes checkups, one new patient and a follow up with Bruce MacFarland.

The Galveston Island Community Clinic came

into view when she turned the corner at Sealy and 19th Street. The single-story building had been a recreational boat sales and service establishment in a previous life. A volunteer organization bought it and renovated it into a free clinic forty years earlier. Twenty years later, the free clinic gained the status of Federally Qualified Healthcare Center. Money to run the facility and pay the staff came from government programs, private charities and whatever the patients could afford. Louise couldn't imagine all the hurdles and paperwork it took to get and keep its status and maintain funding. She was glad to be a worker bee physician and not an administrator.

To keep afloat, the clinic leadership offered competitive contracts to several Galveston organizations. It provided care to the Galveston Police Department and the Galveston Independent School District. The clinic staff cared for a steady roster of cops and teachers.

Louise had interacted with GPD officers daily when she practiced emergency medicine. Now some of them were her patients. Their trust in her as a doctor had made her transition easier. Louise also picked up Dr. Boyd's patients after his retirement. They had aged along with him, collecting diseases and diagnoses as they grew older. That's how Bruce MacFarland had come under her care. Louise dove into her afternoon session. She almost remained on schedule.

"We have thirty minutes with Mr. MacFarland today," Louise said to her assistant, Katia. "We're going to need it."

"Yeah, I read your notes and saw that you wanted to do a 'thorough review' of his medications," Katia quoted. "He takes twelve different meds and lots of vitamins."

"I've been wondering if he's been overmedicating or not taking them correctly. Last week his blood sugar bottomed out. The week before his coagulation numbers went haywire. Is his wife in there with him?"

"Yes, she is. She doesn't look so great herself. I asked her if she wanted to make an appointment for her yearly. She keeps putting it off," Katia said. "I think he's wearing her out. I'll get Dr. Garcia's MA to give her a call."

Louise appreciated the staff's concern for the clinic's patients. So different from the 'treat 'em and street 'em' model in the ER. She opened her spiral notebook and reviewed the notes she made after going through MacFarland's record. Old school, she knew, but better than scrolling and staring at a computer screen when she was in the room with the patient.

"Hi Mr. and Mrs. MacFarland," she said as she entered the exam room. Her smile faded as she appraised the couple.

"You can call me Bruce, honey," Mr. MacFarland said. His sad attempt at a grin softened Louise's reaction to the 'Honey.' His fleshy face was blotchy and bloated. There were bruises mottling the portions of his pale legs visible below stained golf shorts. His ankles were swollen and strained the house shoes he had chosen to wear to the clinic. *Probably the only footwear he could still get his feet into.*

Mrs. MacFarland shook her head when Louise looked her way. Louise wasn't sure if she was silently apologizing for her husband's choice of words or his appearance. She looked exhausted.

"Let's get to work. You're my last patient this afternoon and we don't have to rush. I want to go through our list of your medications and compare it to what you're taking."

"I have them all right here. And you can call me Yvonne, Doctor," she winked at Louise as she emphasized her title. She produced two large Ziploc bags from her gigantic purse and started to lay out the pill bottles.

Louise quickly separated the prescription meds from the numerous supplements and vitamins in the lineup. She found his cardiac medications and put them to one side. There were three different bottles of his anticoagulant, warfarin, each at a different dosage. He had one bottle of an oral hypoglycemic medication that he took to treat his diabetes. It was one of the older medications and could cause low blood sugar at inappropriate dosages. The newer medications for diabetes were much safer. Louise had been at the clinic long enough to know that insurance often didn't cover the newer medications. Plus, many of her older patients didn't want to make any changes. Louise reviewed them all, removed duplicates and meds that should have been discontinued. Katia busied herself reconciling his medications on the medical record.

"I don't know how this got so mixed up," Katia said under her breath. Louise did. The information in the electronic medical record looked nice and neat. But if it wasn't kept up to date, it was worthless.

"Katia, please make a list of all these for me," Louise indicated the multiple containers of supplements.

The rest of the visit proceeded with more

questions and answers about Bruce's conditions and current symptoms. Louise reviewed recent consultation notes from his specialists and attempted to incorporate recommendations into Bruce's regimen. She reduced his diabetic medication dosage.

"We don't want to see any more of those low blood sugars," she explained. "Please try to stick to a healthy diet. Come back and see me in two weeks. Let's recheck your labs on Saturday." She wanted to encourage him to get some exercise but thought that would be futile. The four of them had been at it for an hour.

Leaving the exam room, Yvonne took Bruce's elbow when he wobbled. As he shuffled down the hall, he regained his balance and shook her off. Louise watched the interaction as she unplugged her laptop from the charger and slipped off her white coat. She headed back to her office to finish her notes and deal with patient refill requests. She heard the clinic staff heading out the door.

"See you tomorrow, Dr. Finnerty," Katia called from the end of the hallway. "I'll have that list of Mr. Mac's supplements for you in the morning."

"See you then," Louise answered, eyes glued to her computer.

Last one here again. She was getting quicker, but still got bogged down in the electronic medical record. *God damned EMR!* Old Dr. Boyd had made a minimal effort to learn the system. Connie Garcia says it was the EMR that forced him into retirement. It was real detective work to try to find out what was going on with the patients Louise had inherited. Louise snorted. *Many of whom were detectives themselves.* Thirty minutes later, at 6 pm, Louise packed up and left. The security guard looked up from his phone and wished her a pleasant evening.

"Same to you, Roger. Have a good one."

Louise headed to her parents' house. The kids were spending their after-school hours with her mom and dad. It was either that or stay for aftercare at the elementary school. Her mom, Nancy, offered to have them and the kids jumped at the option. They got a healthy snack and worked on their homework until Louise picked them up.

She pulled into the driveway of her parents' newly renovated home. The Finnerty vacation beach house had become their year-round home several years before. The house was on the skinniest neck of the island called Pirates Beach, a reference to the island's history as a haven for pirates and privateers in the eighteenth century. It sat on beachfront property that continued to grow in value despite the frequent storms. Like Louise's house, it was built on sturdy stilts to withstand storm surges. A deck lining the entire back of the house provided a magnificent view of the Gulf of Mexico.

Nancy had retired from her job as a high school principal. Her husband, Claude, was semi-retired. He couldn't give up the classroom and continued to teach math at the community college on the mainland. Louise's children were their only grandkids. Their devotion was a major source of support for Louise and Didier as they juggled their home and work lives.

Louise went in the unlocked front door and found the kids on either side of Claude on the couch watching TV. Cora had an enormous bag of Cheetos on her lap that Noah made a grab for. All three were laughing at an episode of The Simpsons. *So much for the healthy snack.*

"They actually did do some homework," Nancy said with a chuckle when she joined them.

Louise liked to see her kids sharing a laugh with her dad. He'd mellowed since she was their age. She decided to plunk herself down with them till the show finished.

"Okay, you two. Time to go!" They gathered their backpacks, water bottles and sweatshirts that were scattered around the room. Louise thanked her parents for the millionth time and went over the schedule for the rest of the week.

"Hasta manana!" called Cora from the driveway.

***

Chris was getting ready to call it a day. The paper had been put to bed. He paused to look at the historical photographs on the wall. The black and white pictures showed groups of serious white males huddled over the news desk. Starting with the twentieth century there was an occasional woman in the photos. Their expressions were more severe than the men's. By the 1990s, the demographics were changing. There were several women and a few people of color in photos of the newsroom. Also a few piercings and tattoos. *We're beginning to reflect our community.*

Straightening his desk, he glanced at the photo of his new family. He, EJ and Marnie were celebrating the new year together at Garrett's Trattoria. *I've always wanted a family, but I didn't understand how fully it would change my life. And that's starting with a twenty-*

one-year-old 'step' daughter. This baby is going to be completely different. He switched off his computer. *I wish Marnie seemed more settled and less sad. She's not the driven woman I met eighteen months ago trying to uncover the story behind her friend's death. I'm not used to putting limits on my time at the paper. Am I capable of being there for all of them?*

He shook his head, stood and left his office. On his way out, he heard typing from the interns' cubicle. He peaked in and saw EJ at work.

"Trying to impress the boss, EJ? It's late," he said, glancing at his watch.

EJ pushed her chair back and smiled. "I lost track of time. I've been getting up to speed on the Galveston Mafia for background. I must have gone down a rabbit hole. It sounds like the Maceo brothers ran a tight operation and limited it to the island. What's interesting is that they were so well tolerated even when they broke all kinds of laws related to prohibition, gambling, prostitution and let's see…murder?" She looked up. She had several open books on her desk and an article from Texas Monthly on her screen.

Chris nodded in agreement. "You've got it right. Our city elders were happy to look the other way as their businesses helped Galveston's economy and supplied 'entertainment' that was hidden in plain sight. As for murder, there were a lot of unsolved homicides back in the thirties and forties. But the victims were other gangsters, and the investigations were never forthcoming. The Maceos were careful to steer clear of the upright citizens of Galveston during their vendettas."

"Interesting," EJ said, flipping through a book of

Galveston history. "Apparently, they even contributed to local charities."

"Right. Model mobsters."

"So how did things play out for them? It's not like Galveston has an active Mafia family nowadays."

Chris pulled up a chair from a neighboring cubicle, warming to the topic. "I wonder about that myself. But here's what I know. In the fifties the authorities finally got serious about getting rid of gambling and prostitution on the island. The senior Maceo bosses died and that wing of the family either went legit or used their experience in running illegal casinos and adult entertainment to set up shop in Las Vegas. Our friend Garrett's *distant* cousins, the Pappalardos, stayed on and some got into the drug trade. It wasn't long before the Mexican cartels moved in and took over. People say the Pappalardos ran protection rackets for the cartels. Law enforcement was so used to doing business with the island Mafia, that it made sense for them to assist the cartels and participate in their criminal businesses where they could. But as the following generations of Pappalardos came of age, they cleaned up their act."

"The Pappalardo family is currently law-abiding?" EJ asked, giving her neck a stretch.

"Seems to be. Sal Pappalardo was a recent county sheriff. By all accounts he ran a clean department. His son, Richard, owns several hotels and sits on the arts council. I have an old friend from high school, Anita Martin nee Pappalardo, who works as a manager at the Third Coast Hotel."

"Do you think Anita would be willing to talk to

me about her relatives?"

"Let me give that some thought. I imagine it might still be a touchy subject."

"Louise said to ask you about Little Vic Maceo."

"What a story." Chris smiled and shook his head. "Back in the nineties, Little Vic was one of the last remaining Maceos from the previous generation. He had a dispute with an accountant about a real estate deal and came to his office with an ancient pistol. He shot him and nearly killed him. The accountant ended up with a shattered arm. When Little Vic was arrested, he told the officer, 'You don't handcuff a gentleman in this town!' And the best, or worst part of the story, is that within minutes of the shooting people were joking about it."

"Joking?"

"As if they were kind of proud that it couldn't have happened anywhere but Galveston. People kind of revel in the seamy history of the island Mafia."

"Kind of like bragging you have horse thieves in your family tree, I guess," EJ said as she gathered her things and slipped her laptop into her backpack.

"Yeah. But it can be a slippery slope. We must make sure we avoid anything that the Maceo descendants could construe as slander. Especially the ones in the hospitality business. The last thing the paper needs is a defamation suit. The legal fees for that kind of case are the reason several small-town papers I know of have had to close shop."

"I'll be careful," EJ said.

As they walked out, Chris brightened, "That doesn't mean I can't share some island lore with you. Back in the day, Galveston's red-light district was the only one in the county supported by local officials *and* the Catholic church. And then there are the rumors of Mafia money buried around the island. ..."

Chapter 5

Saturday morning, January 25, 2020

Taylor drove by the small house where he grew up. They had lived within walking distance of Ball High School. His dad had loved teaching there. He loved teaching in general. As one of only three faculty members of color, he had offered a different perspective on American history—his favorite course to teach. The students, White, Black, and Brown, had responded to his genuine interest in their well-being. He spent long hours after school helping them with difficult home situations as well as plans for life after high school. They had voted him favorite teacher year after year.

Taylor's mom had struggled with his dad's time commitment to the school. Her own family had distanced itself from her when she married a Black man. She could not ignore the subtle, and not so subtle, racism that permeated this old southern city. *She was always a bit fragile. And paranoid. But dad's death would have pushed many people over the edge.*

Taylor was never sure where the money had come from to help them move to Dallas. Feeling isolated, his mother had chosen to move close to Luther's family to raise her biracial son. *Lucky for me*. His paternal grandparents had been his anchor growing up. Eventually his mom's paranoia worsened, and she was diagnosed with schizophrenia. With medication, she was able to maintain a home for them. Luckily, she had qualified for disability, and with his dad's pension, they were able to keep their heads above water. Taylor had loved his mom but if he hadn't had his extended family for support, it would have been a difficult upbringing. He had excelled in sports and academics during high school and earned a scholarship to UT-Austin.

Texas was experiencing a booming real estate market when he graduated. Because of his quick smile and easy manner, Texas Realty, a large company with multiple subsidiaries, recruited him to work in Dallas, an area experiencing an influx of new and diverse buyers. After a few successful years, his company offered him a stint at their new office in Galveston, Sand Dollar Estates. After the death of his mother from breast cancer, he jumped at the chance to go to the warmer climes of Galveston. *Just like EJ, beach and sunshine*. It also offered him a chance to find out what really happened to his dad in 2002.

He hadn't toured his hometown in a long time. Galveston real estate had seen the typical boom and bust during the last fifteen years. He'd missed the last big hurricane to hit Galveston, Ike in 2007. The island dodged a bullet in 2017 when Hurricane Harvey swept up to Houston and points east. Following the voice of his GPS app, Taylor left his old neighborhood and drove toward the seawall.

This was the area which his company had designated as properties of interest. Many of the older homes were ready for makeovers. The Galveston Seawall, built after the Great Storm of 1900, along with the elevation of the city's ground level had performed well along this stretch of beach.

Fortunately for Taylor, it was also the neighborhood where the detective who had investigated his dad's murder lived. He couldn't imagine a better cover story than being a real estate agent. Truth was easier than fiction. Taylor had done an extensive internet search on Bruce MacFarland. He had been a lead detective on many cases for twenty years until his retirement in 2014. Taylor was curious as to how the visit would go.

The MacFarlands' house was a low slung, brick ranch style that sat two blocks back from the Galveston Seawall. The off-white bricks were dingy, and the pale-yellow trim was peeling. It must have been built in the sixties and withstood multiple storms. Taylor knocked on the door. A woman in her mid-sixties answered it.

"Hi, my name is Taylor Wood and I'm a local real estate agent making some cold calls in this neighborhood. My company is very interested in acquiring some homes in this area and I was wondering if you were thinking about selling?"

Yvonne MacFarland seemed surprised. "I'm sorry, we haven't really discussed it. My husband has been very sick recently and that has absorbed all our energy."

Seeing an opportunity, Taylor said, "Many of our clients find these large homes difficult and expensive to maintain over time. They're thrilled to see how much their homes have appreciated recently. Should I come in and have a quick look? I'm very good at estimating current prices and I can leave you some information about our company. Feel free to check me and my company out before I come in."

Taylor handed Yvonne a card.

"My husband is taking a nap, but I guess it wouldn't hurt for you to come in. Let me just give the company a quick call. I know that scammers prey on old people."

As Taylor waited on the front stoop, he looked at the front garden. It was weedy and overgrown but had great potential. Both the bird feeder and bird bath were crowded with birds.

"Thank you for waiting," Yvonne said. "Come on in. Your employer gave you glowing reviews. I could use some company for a bit and would like to get a thumbnail estimate on the house."

As he walked through the house, Taylor noted the old-world Italian charm—very popular in the 1960s when Galveston was rumored to be home to a branch of the Sicilian Mafia. Many of MacFarland's cases, which were available under public access laws, referred to mob activity.

"Let's sit in the living room. It's close to the bedroom where Bruce is napping. I want to hear him when he wakes up. Can I get you a cup of coffee?"

"I'd love one, black," Taylor said. "Do you mind if I use your bathroom while you're in the kitchen?"

"Oh no. It's just across the hall."

Taylor noted that the tile was pale green and

seemed to be original. He guessed late 60s. It was so old that it was almost back in vogue. It had stood up well to decades of use. He noticed multiple pill bottles scattered around the sink. *MacFarland's sick indeed.*

There was a knock on the bathroom door.

"Just a minute," Taylor said.

As Taylor came out to the bathroom, he looked at a young man with a long blonde ponytail wearing cargo pants with bulging pockets. "Oh, sorry man. I didn't know anyone else was here besides the MacFarlands."

Taylor extended his hand, "I'm Taylor Wood."

The young man seemed to hesitate for a second and then, taking Taylor's hand, said, "I'm Foster. I was just helping with some of the maintenance of the bird feeders in the backyard. I've been helping Yvonne out recently."

"I'm sure she appreciates it. It seems that her husband has been sick."

"Yes, for some time. Mr. MacFarland is getting more confused lately and I fill in whenever Yvonne needs help. Are you a friend of the family?"

"No," Taylor said with a smile as he handed Foster a business card. "I'm canvassing the area for homes that might come on the market soon. Mrs. MacFarland invited me in to give a quick estimate of the value of their home."

Yvonne saw them chatting in the hall. "Oh, you've met. I meant to tell Mr. Wood that we were getting some help to spruce the place up."

"I'll just use the bathroom for a minute and go back out and finish the chores. I'll be back tomorrow to tackle the front yard," Foster said.

"Thank you, "Yvonne said. "You've been a lifesaver."

Back in the living room Taylor tried to get comfortable on the retro-modern furniture covered in plastic. "How long have you lived here?"

"We bought it in the early 2000s. Bruce came into an inheritance from a relative, and we were thrilled to get the home of our dreams. I think the furnishings have held up well, don't you? They came with the house. They're almost antiques now and back in vogue."

Taylor almost choked on his coffee. Unused living room furniture covered in plastic was guaranteed to hold up well. It remained as ugly fifty years later as when it was first made.

"Beautifully," Taylor smiled.

"We've enjoyed this place and our walks on the beach and watching the birds. But the sea air does cause things to age and maybe we've gotten a little behind on maintenance," Yvonne said wistfully. "What do you think it is worth?"

Having researched the house online, Taylor said, "With its location and size, you're in the one point five to two million range."

Yvonne gasped. "That certainly could solve a lot of problems."

They both heard Bruce stir in the other room.

"Why don't I leave you a brochure and some contact information? You can talk it over with Mr. MacFarland. I'll call early next week and see what questions I can answer for you."

"All right," Yvonne said as she ushered Taylor to the door. "Bruce can be grumpy when he wakes up. It's best if I don't have anyone here then."

"Yvonne, where the hell are you?" came a shout from the bedroom.

Taylor nodded and eased out. He felt sorry for Mrs. MacFarland. He did wonder about the convenient inheritance from an unidentified relative that occurred soon after his dad died.

***

Saturday afternoon, Louise was checking her computer before going to Noah's soccer game. She wanted to make sure that Bruce MacFarland's labs were improving. *Who said no weekend duty?* Back in normal ranges. *That's a relief.* She had read that, to follow all medical guidelines, doctors needed a twenty-seven-hour workday. She believed it. *Back to being a mom.*

She gathered up the soccer game treats and drinks—it was her day to bring snacks. "Let's go guys! We're going to be late."

Chapter 6

Monday, January 27, 2020

"Hello?" Louise answered her phone, puzzled by the number she didn't recognize.

"Oh, Dr. Finnerty, this is Yvonne MacFarland. Did I catch you at a bad time? I really hate to ask you this but…"

"No, It's fine, Yvonne. What's going on?"

"It's Bruce. He's in the hospital. He started to vomit and then there was so much blood. He passed out, so I called 911."

"Oh, no! Is he in the ER?" Louise asked. *What the hell is going on? Didn't I see him Friday?*

"He was. Now he's in a hospital room where they can monitor him. Not the ICU exactly, but lots of machines and lots of doctors. He's getting a transfusion right now. He has one doctor who seems to be overseeing his case. Dr. Chin, I think."

"Yes. That would be Larry Chin. He's a hospitalist. A good one."

"But Dr. Finnerty, the reason I called you at home is that nobody can understand how this happened. His lab work is all out of whack again. I explained that everything looked satisfactory on Saturday. Dr. Chin said he needs to get his records from the clinic and that won't happen tonight. Is it asking too much for you to come by and look at Bruce and talk to Dr. Chin about what's been going on?"

Louise looked at her watch, 7 p.m. Didier could handle the kids. She could go to the hospital and be back by nine. "Yes, I can come to help figure this out."

She explained the situation to Didier. He nodded, "Bruce MacFarland? In the hospital? Poor Yvonne."

Knowing that her current job did not include after-hours visits to the hospital, she told herself that this was a reasonable exception. *I did give Yvonne my phone number. Big mistake?*

Louise was out the door and into her car. An onshore breeze was making the sago palms rattle as their stiff fronds danced. The rain that had threatened all day began. She hoped the fifteen-minute drive across the dark island would help her get her bearings on Bruce's case. Louise's phone rang again. It was Marnie. "Hey, what are you up to this evening?" Her voice sounded a bit shaky.

Louise explained she was making an unplanned visit to the hospital and gave Marnie a thumbnail of the case.

"Aren't you supposed to turn your clinic patients over to the hospitalists? Do I sense you're having trouble with boundaries?"

"You're right about the hospitalists. You may be right about the boundaries, too," Louise answered.

"Well, believe it or not, that works out for me tonight," Marnie's voice brightened a bit. "I'm a patient at the hospital."

"What? Why?"

Marnie explained that she had seen her OB earlier in the day for what she thought was an uncomplicated UTI. "But when I got to Linda's office I had a fever and started to vomit. She explained that I needed IV antibiotics and that was going to require a twenty-four hour stay in the hospital until I could keep food and medications down."

"Oh no. What room are you in? I'll come by after I see what's going on with my patient."

"I'm on the OB ward. Third floor, room 3030. Come by when you can. I don't expect to get any sleep anyway. Plus, I'm kind of scared. Chris is even worse," Marnie said with a weak chuckle.

"See you soon." Louise ended the call. She listened to the rain pounding on her car abruptly stop as she pulled into the hospital garage.

Louise took the elevator to the third floor. She knew the territory well. It was a telemetry unit. A place to admit fragile patients, one step down from the ICU. She had visited this unit many times as an ER doctor, called to manage after-hours cardiac arrests. It was strange to be back as a consultant, or whatever her role would be tonight. Louise had maintained her hospital privileges in case her clinic job turned out to be a bust. It permitted her access to Bruce's case.

She explained the nature of her visit to the nurses at the central nursing station. Louise knew some of the staff even though the turnover had been enormous.

"I'm taking care of him tonight, Dr. Finnerty," said Tammy, one of the RNs that Louise recognized. "I sure hope you can shed some light. He's in 3124."

"I'll do my best. Let me go in and talk to his wife. Have you seen Dr. Chin around? He's on the case, right?"

"Yes. He's admitting a new patient from the ER. I'll let him know you're here when he comes back up."

Louise headed down the crowded hallway to 3124. She zigged and zagged around a few laundry carts, an empty meal trolley and several IV poles. She saw Yvonne first, sitting on the edge of her seat. She was holding a tissue and kneading it with her hands. Louise glanced at Bruce. If she thought he looked poorly in the clinic, he now looked like death warmed over.

"Oh, you're here," Yvonne said as she jumped up. "Thank you so much for coming. Nobody knows what's going on. I feel so helpless."

Louise came over to her and gave her hand a squeeze as she assessed Bruce. His monitor showed a blood pressure of 90/60, pulse of 110 and an oxygen saturation of 92%. *Stable, but not great. All compatible with a recent gastrointestinal bleed.* He had a central line and a peripheral IV. A unit of blood was being infused along with platelets and fresh frozen plasma. *A full court press to manage hemorrhage without going to the OR.* Oxygen was being provided by a cannula to his nose.

When Louise touched his arm, Bruce opened his eyes and looked at her. He looked over at his wife, confused.

"It's Dr. Finnerty, from the clinic, hon," Yvonne prompted.

"Hi Mr. MacFarland. I'm sorry we're meeting again so soon," said Louise.

He blinked and closed his eyes again. He

mumbled a few words that neither woman could understand.

"I've never seen him this bad before. He doesn't know what's going on. He must be so scared." Tears filled Yvonne's eyes.

Tammy was at the door. "Dr. Finnerty, Dr. Chin is out here at the station. Can you talk to him now before he gets called to the ER again?"

"Thanks. Hang in there, Yvonne. I'll be right back," said Louise.

Louise pulled up a chair at the nurses' station next to Dr. Chin. "Looks like you're having a busy night, Larry."

Eyes glued to the computer, he shrugged. "Yeah, I'm getting pounded with admissions. But if you can shed some light on Mr. MacFarland's case, that would certainly help me get through the night. Him too."

Louise gave him an overview, starting from when she picked up Bruce as a patient five months earlier. "I'll admit, I just can't get a bead on his case. It's been a roller coaster with his labs and his symptoms. But overall, it's been a downhill course."

It was clear from the admitting lab that Bruce's blood clotting numbers were way off. That must have been the cause of his internal bleeding.

"GI thinks he has an ulcer. He's not stable enough to get scoped tonight. We'll try to get his clotting under control with Vitamin K. He's getting transfused since his hemoglobin was in the toilet. I think he's on his third unit right now."

"He had complete labs done two days ago. His clotting numbers looked good. He looked like hell, but his lab looked fine. For once."

"His wife said he's on warfarin because of a previous pulmonary embolism. Is that accurate?"

"Yes," Louise said. "His previous doctor had him on it long term."

"Then there's his blood sugar. Thirty-five on admission. He was obtunded, which didn't help with all the vomiting. May have aspirated based on his chest x-ray."

"No way!" Louise exclaimed. "We just dealt with that. I went through all his meds and cut back on his diabetic medication dose. His wife was checking fingerstick glucoses and they've been fine."

Dr. Chin's cell phone rang. While he took the call, Louise continued to peruse Bruce's medical record.

"This is not making sense, Larry. This is a dramatic change in Mr. MacFarland's lab and condition."

"I'm used to things not making sense in this job. Let's work on getting him stabilized tonight. Then we can do some more detective work. I'll get input from hematology and endocrinology."

Louise slumped in her chair.

"Hey, point taken. I get it. This was a sudden change. Don't beat yourself up, Louise. There are things we can fix and…" Just then, he received a STAT call related to a patient on another floor. Louise watched him half run to the stairwell next to the bank of elevators.

I'm not sure I'm shedding any light on this situation. Louise watched as Dr. Chin disappeared. She noticed the elevator doors open. A man she thought she recognized walked up to the nurses' station and asked for Bruce MacFarland's room number. His tone was brusque.

After completing a note in Bruce's medical record to summarize his conditions, medications, and outpatient course for Dr. Chin and the future consultants on his case, Louise returned to room 3124.

Yvonne looked up at her as she entered. "Dr. Finnerty, did you have any luck out there?"

Before she could answer, the visitor at the bedside looked from the monitor to Louise. "He no doubt had a massive gastrointestinal hemorrhage. Yvonne says you're his new doctor. This should never have happened."

Louise was taken aback.

"Dr. Finnerty, this is our good friend, Jim Melvin. Dr. Melvin. He's one of Bruce's best buddies. They worked together on many cases over the years."

The name jogged Louise's memory. James Melvin looked younger than his almost seventy years with an upright six-foot posture and a lithe build. He had been the Galveston County Medical Examiner for ages before retiring a few years ago. She recalled him as a showboat in press conferences. Louise remembered the complaints from classmates who did pathology residencies under him. He had the reputation of being a demanding and demeaning attending. The rumor was that he thought he was God's gift to women.

Louise decided to ignore Dr. Melvin's remark and turned her attention to Yvonne.

"I went over everything with Dr. Chin. He agrees that there has been a dramatic change in your husband's condition that precipitated this episode. I know we just reviewed his medications, but I think we need to look at them again. My best guess is that he's over-medicated. Again."

Yvonne winced. "But we've been following your orders to a tee. I just don't know…"

"Yvonne, you're exhausted. Let me take you home," said Dr. Melvin. "It's going to be a long haul for Bruce, and you need to keep your strength up. I'll pick you up in the morning and bring you back to the hospital."

"That's a good idea, Yvonne. And please bring all his medications. All of them, even his supplements," Louise said. She patted Yvonne's shoulder and left the room without another word to Dr. Melvin. She wanted to see if Bruce's recent lab had been reported.

A few minutes later, Yvonne passed the station and gave her a little wave. Dr. Melvin walked past her without a glance. After looking at his recent labs, Louise realized there wasn't much more she could do to help. She texted Marnie and said she was heading to her room.

Louise thought that Marnie looked wan but Chris, sitting with his head down, looked as if he had been put through the ringer. "Hi Marnie and Chris. How are things?"

Marnie looked at Louise and gave a big smile. "Overall things are going well. Junior's still kicking up a storm. Per usual, he was quiet during the day but the minute I lay down he started to boogie. How's your patient?"

"His quick deterioration makes no sense. I'm going to be working with Dr Chin, his hospitalist, to review everything. I wonder if his meds are screwed up again." She pulled up a chair closer to Marnie's bed. "What's the plan for you?"

"I should be out of here tomorrow morning. I'm

keeping my meds and food down. My fever is gone, and I feel much better."

Chris looked up. "Let's not rush this Marnie. Let's make sure that's what the doctor thinks is best."

Marnie gave Chris's hand a squeeze. "I'm going to follow the doctor's orders but I'm sure she'll let me go. Hospitals are the most infectious place you can be. Have you noticed that a lot of the staff are already wearing face masks? I think the 'flu' from China has everyone on edge."

"It does sound ominous," Louise said. "That's all this country's piecemeal health care system needs—a pandemic."

"Chris, I want you to head home. I need you rested when I get there. You too, Louise," Marnie said as she patted her stomach. "I'm going to try to sleep as much as I can."

Louise took her clue. "Let's go, Chris. Marnie's orders."

Louise gave Marnie a hug and went to the door. Chris quickly followed.

***

Marnie looked at her phone again, hoping she had slept more than thirty minutes. *Nope, damn, it's only 2:45. Will this night never end?* Chris and Louise had left hours ago. *Here's hoping I'm discharged in the morning after another dose of antibiotics. At least Junior doesn't seem to be disturbed.* She was not having contractions, and a quick bedside ultrasound had confirmed that he was fine.

The pain in her neck had not been relieved with

Tylenol or repositioning. It was a constant reminder of the injury she suffered the previous summer when a psychopath had attacked her on a hiking trail and knocked her into a roaring creek. *Better not to think about that right now.*

Marnie knew the best remedy for her pain was to get up, take a short walk, and do a few stretches. She didn't want to disturb the nurses. They had their hands full. She stood up shakily and took a moment to steady herself. With her IV pole in hand, she slipped out of her room and walked toward the elevators that separated the two sides of the third floor.

On the opposite side of the elevator bank, the signage indicated the entrance to the telemetry unit. It looked like a mirror image of the obstetric unit only with more monitors at the nurses' station. Her neck was starting to loosen up. She reversed course to return to her room, swiveling the IV pole.

"Whoa!" cried Marnie as she regained her balance. A man dressed in hospital scrubs steadied her. His basket of phlebotomy supplies had caught her IV pole and pulled her off balance.

He grabbed her arm to offer support. His gaze lingered on her wrist band.

"Are you okay, miss? So sorry," he said.

Marnie caught a glimpse of his green eyes. He was wearing a surgical mask and hat. A flimsy, paper lab coat hung loosely. "No harm done," Marnie said. "I shouldn't have been out of bed anyway."

"Can I help you back to your room?"

"No thanks. I've got it from here."

She watched him disappear down the hall, then

walked carefully back to her room and lumbered into her bed. The short walk had helped her pain but resulted in a wave of exhaustion. She soon drifted off to sleep. When she awoke to the clatter of the morning routine in the hospital, she wondered if her stroll had been real or a dream. Her fuzziness disturbed her. *Just like an old person with UTI confusion.*

***

The third-floor telemetry unit was finally quiet at 3:00 a.m. Two weary nurses were at the station surrounded by monitors for the twenty patients on the ward. The lights had been dimmed. A phlebotomist walked down the hallway, carrying a basket of the equipment he needed to draw blood.

He entered room 3124 and pulled the privacy curtain that hung from a rail above Bruce MacFarland's bed. He appeared to be asleep. In a practiced maneuver, he detached the leads from Bruce's chest and attached them to the stickers in place on his own chest. It took him less than fifteen seconds. The monitor gave off an alarm. A nurse approached to assess the situation. She drew back the curtain. When she looked at the monitor, she saw a normal rhythm.

"Sorry," said the lab tech, hunching over his patient and keeping his back to the nurse. "I think I jostled his leads when I pulled back his blanket to get to his arm. His pulse oximeter fell off too. I'll put it back on."

"No problem. These alarms go off all shift." She turned and walked back to her desk.

The tech put the pulse oximeter on his own left little finger. The beeping stopped as it registered a very satisfactory oxygen level. He waited for the blood pressure cuff on Bruce's arm to cycle. 95/70. He had five minutes until it would inflate for another reading. First, he removed the cap on the IV and injected five milligrams of morphine to assure that he didn't wake up. To simulate a blood draw, he punctured Bruce's inner elbow with a needle and covered it with a gauze pad and tape. Working quickly, he took a fifty-cc syringe from his basket, pulled back the plunger and injected air into the central IV line. He repeated the procedure with an additional fifty cc injection of air. He raised the head of the bed. At the last minute before leaving the bedside, he replaced the monitor leads, IV caps, and pulse oximeter. He gathered his equipment and walked briskly to the elevators and stairwell. He kept his gaze focused on the floor.

Intent on avoiding another run-in with a wandering patient, he made it down the stairs. He was at the first-floor landing when he heard the overhead announce, "Code Blue, 3124. Code Blue 3124." Dr. Larry Chin pushed past him, taking the stairs two at a time.

Chapter 7

Tuesday, January 28, 2020

The phone woke Louise at 5 a.m. She recognized the hospital prefix and was instantly wide awake.

"Louise, it's Larry Chin. I hate to wake you, but I thought you should hear it from me. Bruce MacFarland coded. He didn't make it."

"Oh, Jesus. What happened?"

"I wish I knew. He was stable when I was up on telemetry at about two. His labs were starting to look better. Then a code blue at a little after three. Basically, he was in asystole. No response to CPR and protocol drugs."

Louise knew this was a grim situation having confronted it many times in the ER.

"There's more you need to know," Larry continued. "Things didn't look right in his room. The police have been notified."

"I can't believe this. Is his wife there?"

"She's on her way in. I need to see if she's arrived and talk to her."

"I'm on my way."

Louise dressed quickly and quietly. Despite her efforts, Didier woke up.

"I must go back to the hospital. Bruce MacFarland died overnight. I need to be there for Yvonne. This is all such a mess, and I…" she whispered. Her voice quavered.

"Go ahead. I've got the kids covered. And stop blaming yourself. Bruce was a very sick old man. You can't save everyone."

She nodded and gave him a feeble smile as she tiptoed out of the room. She appreciated his support but wasn't ready to forgive herself for Bruce's death.

When she arrived at the hospital, she saw several police cars parked outside the main entrance. She made her way to the third floor. Before she could get to room 3124, she was met by Detective Iliana Sudhan.

"Good morning, Louise," Iliana said softly. "Let's talk over here for a minute." Sudhan directed her to a room usually saved for patient-family conferences.

"I should really talk to Mrs. MacFarland," Louise said.

"Of course, in just a few minutes. She's with the hospital chaplain right now talking about arrangements."

The small conference room was already overcrowded with two uniformed officers, the hospital CEO, and the head of risk management. Louise felt her stomach drop as they all looked at her.

Sudhan spoke first. "We've interviewed Dr. Chin. We're going to create a timeline to account for every person, staff, and visitors, who interacted with Mr. MacFarland overnight. We're investigating the circumstances of Mr. MacFarland's death as suspicious.

The night nurse who responded to his flatline said that his IV had been tampered with. She's sure of it. She always caps the central line with the red cap and the IV in the arm with the blue cap. They were switched."

"What? When?" asked Louise.

"We'll be taking statements all day to try to answer those questions. We've already sent blood to the crime lab for toxicology. There will be a post-mortem exam later today."

The hospital CEO spoke up. His tone was grave. "Dr. Finnerty, as you can imagine, this is a major PR issue for the hospital. We thank you in advance for your cooperation and understanding about the confidentiality issues, both for the hospital and the MacFarland family."

"Certainly," Louise answered, regaining some of her composure. *Was this a medical screw up, murder or both?* Events were changing so fast; she couldn't keep up. "I'll make myself available all day. May I talk to Yvonne now?"

"Sure, go ahead," Sudhan said. "When you're done, one of the officers will bring you downstairs to the conference room we've been assigned. Dr. Chin is down there now with the staff from evening and night shifts who interacted with MacFarland. Everyone will need to give a statement."

Louise called the clinic and asked the nurse manager to reschedule her patients. She apologized and said she would explain as soon as she could. Looks like a long day.

***

Home from the hospital, Marnie sat in her sunny study with her pups at her feet. *Glad to be home. Glad to feel better.* Junior seemed to be doing somersaults. Marnie smiled. *Glad he's feeling better also.*

She had pushed Chris to go to the office for the afternoon. After the scare and hospitalization, he needed to check in. She could use a few hours alone.

"I need to start getting organized," she said to herself. "This baby may come sooner than I thought."

She pulled out some note paper and started making a list. *I still like pen and paper for this—love to cross things off.*

-Get the latest data from the study in Aurora. Make sure things are on autopilot for a bit.

-Sign up for childbirth classes—Chris needs this.

-Finish the nursery.

Marnie put the paper down and switched to her laptop. She pulled up the class description of the hospital's Childbirth 101.

"This course is intended to prepare new parents for the adventure that awaits them. We will cover coping with labor and birth, anesthesia options, cesarean sections, postpartum care, breastfeeding, and newborn care."

"Oh, brother!" she muttered to herself. It had been twenty-one years since EJ was born. *I wonder if the 'adventure' has changed much.* She hoped there would be some other mothers in her age group. She wanted Chris to see that she wasn't the only woman over forty in the United States about to give birth.

"I just want to make sure I don't hemorrhage after this delivery like I did with EJ," Marnie continued muttering to herself. She still hadn't told Chris about that. She was afraid it might send him over the edge.

She signed up for the class, made a big line through the item on the list, and decided it was time to take a little stroll around the house and yard. She was supposed to get up and walk every hour or so during the day. *No blood clots for me.*

As Marnie settled back down to tackle her list, EJ arrived.

"Hi Mom," EJ called out as she came in the back door.

"I'm in my study. Join me."

EJ bent over and gave Marnie a kiss. "I'm so glad you're home again," EJ said. "How are you feeling?"

"I feel good. I started feeling better about this pregnancy when I saw Junior on the ultrasound at the hospital. He weighs about three pounds. It's amazing how much detail you can see on ultrasounds now. He was smiling."

EJ settled into a chair near Marnie and handed her a fruit spritzer. "We must quit calling him Junior. It makes my skin crawl every time. What are the current thoughts on a name?"

"Tobias? Preston?"

EJ faked a gag.

"What do you think about Jon—that's the name Chris and I are planning on.

"I like that."

Changing the subject, Marnie asked, "What are you doing at home at three in the afternoon?"

"I was at the paper late last night since you and Chris were gone—don't fret. Chris asked me to leave early and check on you and work from home if I need to. Or to take care of these lazy mutts." She smiled as she glanced at the two spoiled labradoodles sprawled on 'their' couch.

"What were you doing at the paper so late?"

"I was doing some serious archival digging into the death of Luther Wood. Ben found out that the investigating detective was Bruce MacFarland."

"That name sounds familiar," Marnie said.

"Huh," EJ said. "Small city. Anyway, the death does appear to have been swept under the rug. Which leads me to my next topic. I met a guy at the bar when I went out with Ben and his friends. He said his name was Taylor Wood. I think he might be the person who wrote the letter that got this investigation going."

"Seems like an unlikely coincidence," Marnie said. "Do you think he was stalking you?"

EJ looked uncertain. "I really don't think so. The problem is that I kind of liked him. I thought I might invite him to dinner this weekend and get your take."

Marnie was flattered that EJ wanted her opinion. "I'd feel much better about you dating him after I meet him. I'll get Rosa to help me cook dinner and join us."

"That reminds me. I keep meaning to ask why Rosa never had a family of her own."

"It's a long story but the short version is that her fiancé was killed when she was seventeen. He joined the army to gain citizenship and was sent to Korea in 1977. They had planned to marry once he returned, and Rosa would get citizenship through him. He died in a helicopter accident near the DMZ. She was devastated, quit school, and went to work for the Hills. That's why she never received her high school diploma. She's known Chris since he was born."

"People's stories that we never know." EJ sighed.

"Yep. She told me that as she recovered from that trauma, her sister started her family and then her parents needed help."

"She must have gained citizenship along the way?"

"Her family was granted amnesty by President Reagan's bill in 1986."

"Wow, life can be complicated." After a minute, EJ said, "I'm going to go change and take these pups on a run. See you in a bit." She gave her mom another hug and headed to her apartment.

Marnie returned to her list. She decided that she wanted to paint the nursery a pale yellow. She and Chris had picked out baby furniture a few days ago. She was going to add a good rocking chair and a double bed so that she could comfortably lie down when nursing. She would attach a bassinet to the bed for safe sleeping. It was a luxury to have such a big room for the baby. And money to buy what she wanted.

EJ's 'nursery' had been a walk-in closet. She remembered the small apartment she and Adam, her first husband, had when EJ was born. They were still doing their residencies. *What would Adam think of this turn of events?* She continued to feel his approving presence. He would have wanted EJ and her to succeed in this rushing river called life.

Her phone rang, interrupting her reverie. It was Louise.

"Hi Marnie. How are you feeling?"

"Good. Glad to be home. How's your patient?"

"That's why I'm calling. He died last night after I left. It's complicated."

"Oh Louise, I'm sorry."

"I've been at the hospital all day dealing with the aftermath. I need to run this case by another doctor who wasn't involved in his care. See what I missed. Do you feel up to it?"

"Yes, sure. Aftermath? You said he was sick. What else is going on?" Marnie asked.

"I'll explain when I see you. The police are involved."

"Come on over. We can talk now and maybe you could stay for dinner. Rosa made some chicken enchiladas—she assured me that there would not be too much heat for me and the baby."

Louise laughed. "I remember when you ate chili rellenos with hot sauce before EJ was born. Glad you're watching the heat until your due date. I'll let Didier know that he's on kid duty again tonight. See you in a few."

***

"Can I get you a glass of white wine?" Marnie asked.

"Please."

Marnie brought her seltzer and Louise's wine to the enclosed sun porch.

"This is a lovely old house," Louise said.

"It really is. I'm glad that I came after the restoration was completed. There's at least one sunny place to sit all day long. Chris tells me that, in the summer when the sun is overhead, there is also always a shady spot to sit."

"Do you miss Colorado?"

Marnie paused. "I think sometimes I miss my solitude. And my Colorado house is where I've spent half my life, so yeah. I miss it. We've agreed to spend the better part of the summer there and that will help a lot."

"Snowbirds," Louise said.

Marnie smiled. "Yep. But let's talk about your patient before Chris and EJ get here."

"I was sworn to confidentiality, but soon the news will come out that Bruce MacFarland died in the hospital last night. Chris probably knows already. Bruce was a retired detective. Well known in the community. He and his wife are regulars at Feathers and Didier knows them through the birding community."

"Oh wow. That's kind of weird. EJ just mentioned his name. She said he was lead detective on the Wood's investigation—the project she and Ben are working on for the paper."

Louise looked surprised. "That's an odd coincidence but the time frame fits with what he was doing at that point in his career. I've been following him for his multiple health problems for the last five months. It seemed that just when we would get him stable, something would change. In the last week I reviewed all his meds and was taking a closer look at his supplements. Four days ago, his labs were normal. Then after one weekend at home, he had a massive GI bleed and admission to the telemetry ward at the hospital. His labs were totally out of whack on admission. Both his labs and vital signs were improving before I stopped by to see you last night. Later, he coded and died."

"Wow, that does seem suspicious."

"Neither Dr. Chin, the hospitalist, nor I can explain MacFarland's quick deterioration from a medical standpoint," Louise paused. "There's more. His nurse thought his IV had been tampered with."

"Interesting," Marnie said. "What's going to happen next?"

"So…this will surprise you, but I want to see what we can find out. Sudhan is on the case, thank God. There will be an autopsy to determine the cause of death. If he was murdered, I want to know who, how, and why."

Marnie laughed. "It is a role reversal for us. The last two times we investigated a murder, I was the one who needed to know those answers. How can I help? I'm limited in my mobility."

"That's fine. I want you to do some on-line investigation."

"Let's talk about it with Chris and EJ. Chris is nervous about my activity and, while he can't control me, I don't want to make our relationship difficult right now."

***

As Chris, Marnie, Louise, and EJ gathered for dinner, Rosa placed the platters on the table and excused herself. She had made a plate to take home and wanted to get there before her sister was scheduled to call.

"Thank you so much, Rosa," Chris said.

Rosa beamed. "It is fun to cook for such an appreciative audience. See you tomorrow." She went out the kitchen door.

"Let's eat." Marnie grinned. "I'm starved. Louise

has had her cocktail and the rest of you can drink your beer with your enchiladas."

"How's your research going?" Louise asked EJ.

"I'm learning a lot about the crime scene in Galveston around the time of Mr. Wood's death. Lots of violent crime related to the drug cartels. And suspicion of police protection rackets. Maybe a smattering of Galveston Mafia to go with it all?" EJ glanced at Chris.

Marnie caught the interaction. "You finally got someone to listen to your stories about the island's more colorful characters," she said to Chris with a smile.

"All in the line of helping EJ gather background." He returned her grin.

"My next step is to access police and court records from that time—the ones accessible to the public." EJ added.

"How is it working with Ben?" Marnie asked.

"He's great. He's been working on the business and political scene, digging through the archives. He's also been pumping his mom for information about all the above, but she's been closed mouth. She was just a newbie on the force then."

Oh," Marnie said. "That reminds me. We're scheduled to have dinner at Sudhan's this weekend. With everything that's been going on, I forgot to tell you and Chris. Maybe we could meet Taylor next weekend?"

"Who's Taylor?" Louise asked.

"He's a guy I met the other night. I'm thinking he might be part of the Wood family but operating under the radar. I liked him. I wanted to get mom's take on him."

"First I'm hearing about this," Chris said, eyebrows raised.

"I was going to tell you tonight. I just met him once and we've exchanged texts a few times. The letter was signed by T. Wood and his name is Taylor Wood. Seemed a little coincidental."

"I'll say," said Chris. He put his fork down, looked at Marnie, and then at EJ. "I would proceed very carefully, EJ. If it is the same guy who wrote the letter, he has an ax to grind, and I don't want you..." Chris stopped mid-sentence when he noticed Marnie staring at him, no longer smiling, and shaking her head.

Sensing that it was a good time to change the subject, Louise said, "Well, Didier and I were hoping to throw a Mardi Gras potluck. Maybe we could have a bigger party and include Taylor and the Sudhan/Janssens. Feel like a baby shower?"

"Oh, please no. A party sounds fine though." Turning to Chris, Marnie said, "Louise wants me to help investigate the unexpected death of her patient, Bruce MacFarland. Cool with you?"

"Wait, the retired detective who investigated Luther Wood's death?" EJ asked.

"Yep. What do you think, Chris?"

"I caught wind of MacFarland's case this afternoon at our editorial meeting. It'll make tomorrow's edition," Chris said. "As long as you're following doctor's orders. How much trouble can you get into at home?"

Maybe more than we think. "Great," Marnie said. "EJ will be glad that it keeps me out of her investigation."

"Might be helpful to me as well," EJ said.

Chris said. "Let's eat."

Chapter 8

Tuesday, January 28, 2020

Iliana Sudhan was transcribing interview notes on her laptop when Detective Jose Torres entered the hospital conference room at 5 p.m.

"I brought you a coffee, boss," he said, handing her a cup of hospital brew.

"Thanks," she said, taking a sip. She pushed back from the table and stretched her shoulders. After his recent promotion to detective, Torres had become the best junior partner that she'd ever had. "It's been a long day."

"Looks like you got most of the statements taken. Any promising leads?"

"Not really. One loose end is still dangling. The staff and doctors who were in contact with MacFarland had timelines that checked out. Weren't you working with hospital IT to confirm what we could?"

Torres pulled out his notebook. "Sure was. And it was very helpful. Turns out that every time a nurse or tech has an 'encounter' with a patient," Torres used air quotes and kept talking, "Like giving meds or taking vital signs, they scan the patient's bar code on their wrist band, and it goes into the medical record. We can match those scans with the timelines the staff members gave you. What's the loose end?"

Sudhan shuffled her papers. "Here it is. Nurse Peggy Simpson saw a lab tech go into Mr. MacFarland's room sometime around 3 a.m. She knew the docs were following his lab numbers closely and didn't give it another thought. When I asked her to provide the name of the tech, she said she couldn't. She didn't get a good look at him."

"Let me get back to IT on that," said Torres. "Anyone doing a blood draw has to scan the wrist band." He hopped up and headed to the door.

"Wait up Torres. You can call your guy from the car. We need to pay a visit to Mrs. MacFarland. She wasn't in any condition to talk to me here. I said it would be fine if she went home, and we would come by."

It was a short drive from the hospital on the grounds of the University of Texas Medical Branch to the MacFarland home on Avenue M. Sudhan was glad to have Torres along. She was aware that in the past, his enthusiasm to solve cases occasionally outstripped his common sense. But now, he was settling into a more measured approach. And Sudhan appreciated Torres's easy manner. It helped people open up.

After finishing his call, Torres stepped out of the car and joined her, already halfway up the front walkway.

"Anything helpful from IT?" she asked.

Before he could answer, a woman, who appeared

to be a heavyset and younger Yvonne MacFarland, opened the front door. Sudhan introduced Torres and herself and explained the purpose of their visit.

"I'm Betty, Yvonne's sister. I drove up from Matagorda as soon as I heard. Yvonne said she was expecting you. Please come in."

The detectives followed Betty through the foyer and the living room. The parquet floor and mid-century furniture with plastic evoked the sixties. Pictures of birds, in flight and at rest, adorned the walls. Some of the walls were decorated with murals. Sudhan did not see any sign of family photos. Betty led them to a paneled office where Yvonne sat half reclined on a plaid sofa and ottoman.

Yvonne attempted a smile. "Thank you so much for letting me go home today, Detective Sudhan. I don't think I could have lasted another minute in the hospital after they took Bruce away."

"Again, we're very sorry for your loss, Mrs. MacFarland. This is my partner, Detective Torres."

"My condolences, ma'am. Your husband is a legend at the department," Torres said.

Sudhan gently led Yvonne through the interview, trying to cover everything she remembered from the evening before. Since the events were still so raw, she kept it short.

"I don't think I could have gotten this far if it weren't for Jim Melvin. He's been such a godsend since Bruce started to decline. And now, he has *me* on his hands. I don't know where to begin. The house, the funeral, bills, I just don't know." She closed her eyes. "And the autopsy. I just can't believe someone would want to hurt a helpless old man like Bruce."

"I'm glad you have your sister here with you," said Sudhan. "We'll let you rest. If you don't mind, we need to collect all of Mr. MacFarland's medications and deliver them to the medical examiner's office for review."

"Yes, I understand. They're all in the kitchen. And some of his vitamins are in his bathroom. Betty can show you."

"I'll wait here with Mrs. MacFarland. Torres, why don't you go with Betty?"

Sudhan noticed a folder from an island real estate group amid the jumble on the coffee table. There had been no For Sale sign out front. *Something to follow-up on later.* Torres returned with two evidence bags stuffed with pill bottles.

As soon as Torres pulled out of the MacFarland driveway, Sudhan's phone rang.

"Sudhan, here," she answered, recognizing the caller as a sergeant assigned to the case. "Let me put you on speaker. I'm with Torres."

"The preliminary autopsy results are in," the sergeant said. "Cause of death: Cerebral air embolism based on extensive collection of bubbles found throughout the cerebral vessels. Not sure what any of that means."

"Nor am I. I'll call the medical examiner's office to discuss. Who did the postmortem?"

"Dr. Tina Garcia. Here's the number."

Sudhan looked at Torres as she dialed. "This just got a lot more interesting."

After a brief hold, Sudhan had Dr. Garcia on the line. She dove right in. "Dr. Garcia, I'm glad I caught you. Do you have a minute?"

"Yes, sure. Let me guess. You're calling about Bruce MacFarland, right? I just sent the preliminary report to the police department."

"Air embolism? Can you help me understand?

"It's not too common," Dr. Garcia began. "At least not in the hospital setting. Around here we see it occasionally in scuba divers who ascend too fast. Are you familiar with 'the bends'? Gas bubbles can form and go through the circulation and block a blood vessel. Depending on where that blood vessel is, it can be fatal."

"Right, but in the hospital?"

"That can happen when air is introduced into an IV line. A little bit of air in an IV is no problem. But a large amount of air, especially if it goes into a central line, can cause all kinds of trouble. In this case, a massive stroke. MacFarland did have a central line. Makes sense considering his GI bleed. I'm looking at the description of the scene. Wait—here's something in the photos. The head of the bed was elevated. That's not likely in a patient with low blood pressure after a hemorrhage. If this is foul play, the person responsible for the air injection would know that the best way to get air to the brain would be to elevate the head of the bed."

"Thanks, Dr. Garcia. I'll be on the lookout for the final report."

Sudhan ended the call. "I'm going to need to run this by the hospital staff and doctors. The position of the bed, this business of IV tampering..." She turned her attention to Torres, "And what did you find out from hospital IT?"

"This is where it gets even more interesting. IT says there were no hits in the system from the lab during the time his nurse spoke to the phlebotomy tech."

"That person would have supplies. Including syringes," Sudhan said, glancing from the road to Torres. "We need to track this person down."

Chapter 9

Thursday, January 30, 2020

Louise and Marnie sat in Marnie's car outside the Galveston Community Clinic. Patients had started to arrive and were making their way to the entrance. Iliana pulled up along the passenger side of the car and got out. Louise rolled her window down.

"Over here, Iliana."

"Thanks for agreeing to meet with me this morning, Louise," Iliana said as she approached. "I know you have a full day. I come bearing gifts—fresh kolaches." It took her a minute to register that Marnie was seated in the driver's seat.

"Hop in, Iliana." Louise said. "We decided two heads are better than one on this subject. Plus, I had a flat tire and called Marnie for a ride while Didier dealt with it." Iliana slid into the back seat.

"I appreciate your input on the case. What do you two think about an air embolism killing Bruce MacFarland?"

Marnie began, "From what you told Louise, it

sounds like a well-planned murder scenario."

"Tell me about the central line that Dr. Garcia mentioned. And this business about the head of the bed," Iliana asked.

"The line is easy to explain," Louise began. "Bruce was in critical condition. He had lost a lot of blood and needed a transfusion and IV fluids to maintain his blood pressure and avoid shock. The central line goes from a large vein in the neck to right above the heart. Not at all unusual in a case like this. It provides rapid access and helps monitor cardiovascular status."

Marnie continued, "The positioning of the bed is important. If the killer injected a syringe full of air into Bruce's central line which ends right above his heart, after it filtered through the heart chambers, it would go directly to the highest part of the body, just like the way bubbles float upward. Elevating his head all but assured it would go to his brain and kill him quickly."

"Isn't it possible that a nurse had elevated the head of the bed for comfort?" asked Iliana.

"Unlikely in this case. Bruce's blood pressure was marginal, at best. In that case, we keep the patient horizontal or even slightly head down," Louise said. "And I can testify that Bruce MacFarland was lying flat on his back during the entire time I was present. You'll need to ask his nurses, but I can guarantee you'll get the same answer."

"Thanks. That helps. I wanted a thorough understanding of the situation before I spoke to Mrs. MacFarland again. We have a few new leads to track down. I'll leave you two to get on with your days." Iliana exited the car.

"Interesting," Louise said to Marnie as she opened her door to get out. "Thanks for the ride. I'll call you at lunch."

Wait!" Marnie said. "Aren't you going to share those kolaches with me and Jon?"

"Who?" Louise asked, confused.

"Jon," said Marnie, patting her stomach.

Louise laughed and rolled her eyes. "I wouldn't dream of denying either of you." She removed a few kolaches and slid them through the window to Marnie.

***

While Torres was at the hospital trying to track down the phlebotomy tech, Sudhan headed to the MacFarlands'. She was glad that Betty answered the door. Yvonne was seated in the office again. She was in fresh clothes but looked as if she hadn't slept the previous night. Sudhan let her know that the police had evidence that her husband had been murdered.

Yvonne gasped. "I always knew Bruce would pass before I did. His health was so poor. But I never thought it would be like this." Yvonne paused, eyes swollen with tears. Betty passed her a tissue.

"I'm so sorry. It's a lot to process," Sudhan said. "And I'm sorry to ask you to think hard about whether your husband had any enemies. Had he received any threats?"

"Oh dear, I just don't know. I know he crossed paths with some very shady characters over the years," Yvonne said. "You would know about that. He worked on cases involving gangsters back in the day. Up to his retirement, he was busy busting local drug dealers. But he never told me any of the details. He was old-fashioned that way."

"We already have staff looking back at his case files to see if anyone or anything sticks out."

"Maybe you should talk to Jim Melvin. You know, he and Bruce were thicker than thieves. I heard them reminiscing all the time. They would sit out back and drink beer and talk and talk."

"I'll do that. In the meantime, please take care. Call me if you have any questions or if anything comes to mind. The entire department has made your husband's case priority number one." Sudhan left her card on the coffee table. She saw the real estate folder again. "One more thing Yvonne – were you and Bruce thinking about selling your house?"

"I'll admit, the thought hadn't entered my mind until a nice young man stopped by last week and asked me the same question. Bruce was napping. The young man was so polite. We got to talking. He said he lived in Galveston as a boy and just returned. He works at Sand Dollar Estates Realty. He said they're looking to buy up property in this neighborhood for development. The price he thought we could get was much more than I would have dreamt. But I can't begin to think about that now."

"Could you describe this young man?"

Yvonne opened the folder and pulled out a business card with a photo which she handed to Sudhan. "He was a young Black man— about thirty? Beautiful green eyes. Such a sweet smile. I think he'll do well."

"Thanks again, Mrs. MacFarland. I won't take up any more of your time," Sudhan said, turning her attention to Betty. "Will you be staying with Yvonne for a while?"

"Oh yes, dear, as long as she needs me."

As soon as Sudhan got in the car, she called Torres. "Do me a favor. Call Sand Dollar Estates. Ask them if they have a Taylor Wood on their staff. I think we have a new person of interest. I'll fill you in when we both get back to the station."

Charming real estate agent making a cold call. Jim Melvin, thicker than thieves. Sister here for the long haul. Just what shape were the MacFarlands' finances in? Sudhan's mind was racing. She had to slam on the brakes to avoid a couple on a bicycle built for two as they ran a stop sign on their way to the Pleasure Pier.

*****

Late that afternoon, Louise drove across the causeway that connected Galveston Island to the mainland portion of the county. Dr. Tina Garcia had requested her help on the Bruce MacFarland case. It was a short drive to the nondescript concrete box of a building that sat on a corner of the Mainland Medical Center campus in La Marque. Scruffy grass separated it from the hospital proper. It looked like an afterthought.

After passing through the front entrance and explaining the purpose of her visit to the security guard, Louise was met by Dr. Garcia. She led Louise through the double doors and into the restricted area of the facility. Tina Garcia was the sister of Louise's partner, Connie Garcia. "Thanks for coming, Louise. I hope you didn't hit traffic on the causeway."

"Nope, clear sailing. Your sister is holding down the fort at the clinic. She said you wouldn't call me out here unless I could help. And believe me, I want to get to the bottom of this case, as you can imagine. Bruce MacFarland was under my care when he died," Louise said. She was glad that the two autopsy rooms along the hallway were empty. "This is my first time here."

"It's nothing to write home about. We've been promised a new facility for years. Now they're saying 2022. This building is seriously limited. We're going to get eight autopsy rooms in the new facility. And a more secure evidence storage area."

Tina ushered Louise into an office connected to a cluttered lab. "Even though we have a clear idea that the immediate cause of death was an air embolism, I need to cover all the bases before I sign out my final report. I've been given all MacFarland's medications that were found at the house."

"And he was taking lots of them. I had just reviewed them in the clinic with the MacFarlands a few days before he died. He was also taking a lot of vitamins and supplements. I was wondering if any of those caused his coagulation and blood sugar labs to go haywire."

"That's why I called you out here to take a look." About fifteen medication bottles of various shapes and sizes were lined up on a steel table in the lab.

"Over here are his prescribed medications. They correspond to what we saw in his medical record from the hospital," Tina said, pointing to the right. "Then over here, we have the vitamins. I had my assistant examine the pills in all the bottles and make sure they corresponded to their pictures on a pill ID website. The prescription meds all check out. But look at these over here." She indicated a bottle labeled thiamine one hundred milligrams and another for sawgrass ten milligrams. "You have to look carefully."

Louise peered at the samples of pills laid out in front of each bottle. The thiamine was a beige, round pill marked T-100. Tina picked up another one that appeared identical. Louise read the lettering. "WRF 10. Jesus, warfarin ten milligrams. That's a big dose of anticoagulant!"

"And look over here. These are from the sawgrass bottle. They're both oblong, scored, peach-colored tablets. Except about half of them are identical looking tablets of glyburide twenty milligrams," Tina said.

"Holy shit, Tina. If he was getting extra doses of those two meds on a hit or miss schedule, it would explain his seesawing labs. I've been trying to figure out what was going on ever since he became my patient. Those two drugs are responsible for his hemorrhage and hypoglycemia when he was admitted," Louise said, shaking her head. "He was being poisoned!"

"Does this make sense with his clinical course since you took him on?" asked Tina.

"It sure does. But who would do this?"

"It's another avenue for Detective Sudhan to explore. I'll let her know this afternoon. Thanks for coming out, Louise."

On the drive back to the island, Louise was furious with herself about the vitamins. *Damn it. I should have looked in those bottles myself. Whoever messed with his pills has been trying to kill him for months.*

Chapter 10

Friday, January 31, 2020

Marnie took a deep sigh of relief. The study at the VA in Aurora was on autopilot. Marnie's colleague, Allison, was excited that the data collection would be completed this spring. She was also happy to hear that Marnie's pregnancy was going well and looking forward to seeing everyone in the summer. Allison seemed more worried about the news from China and a possible pandemic than the rest of the government. *Pandemic. I can't add that worry to my pregnancy right now.*

Louise had called her and brought her up to date on the information from Dr. Tina Garcia. Marnie had tried to reassure Louise that it wasn't her fault that someone had been trying to poison Bruce MacFarland. The questions were who and why.

Marnie's research into Bruce had revealed that he was a controversial figure. His most active years had been from 1995 to 2010. His biggest case had been the Durst murder investigation. He had been instrumental in collecting evidence that was presented at trial. The acquittal must have disappointed him.

As the original Maceo crime family powers waned in the 1980's, the Mexican drug cartels moved into Galveston. By the mid-nineties drug related crimes such as assassinations, human trafficking and kidnapping were on the rise. In 1996 it was disclosed that the Gulf Cartel had paid law enforcement in the seven figures for protection.

Starting then, most of MacFarland's arrests seemed to be for mid-level gangsters and drug traffickers. His clearance rates were high— *too high?* He seemed to have some inside dope on the criminals, but he never quite nailed the bigger fish. When murder was involved, the medical examiner was almost always Dr. James Melvin—just as it had been for the Wood's case. *Amazing what you could find out from public records thanks to the Freedom of Information Act.*

Louise had told Marnie that Melvin and the MacFarlands remained close friends. She also mentioned that Bruce had been telling many tales about his time as a detective. *Too many tales?*

Her phone rang. *Iliana.*

"Hi Iliana. What's up?"

"Hi Marnie. I just wanted to confirm our dinner tomorrow. Six thirty?"

"Great! What can I bring?"

"Yourselves. Bob is cooking enough food to feed an army. Good Dutch food for pregnant people."

"Wonderful. Glad my morning sickness has finally passed. See you tomorrow."

I hope Iliana is in a talking mood. I want to pick her brain about the MacFarlands and Melvin.

***

Sudhan's morning began with a departmental meeting to discuss staffing for the upcoming week of Mardi Gras celebration. She was glad that her detective status got her out of patrol duty on the seawall on those crazy nights. Nonetheless, she anticipated that an increase in cases resulting from bad behavior would land on her desk. She wanted to keep the MacFarland and Wood cases on track when Mardi Gras mayhem hit Galveston.

She returned to her office and closed the door. She loved having her own office. It was nice to have a window, even if she looked out at the parking lot. The only greenery was provided by the weeds growing through the cracks in the pavement. She looked at the collage of photos on the wall. It contained an old-fashioned photo of her grandparents during a visit to Pakistan, their ancestral homeland. Her great-great-grandfather came to America in 1890 to help build the railroad. Between her Pakistani and her Texan Mexican ancestors her family could claim US citizenship for longer than most of those who considered themselves 'real Americans'. Growing up, she winced when people told her to go back to where she came from. As an adult, her response was more direct. Polite and educational, but direct.

She took a deep breath and returned to the files on her desk. Detective Bruce MacFarland and Dr. James Melvin had been quite a team. They shared many cases involving cartel turf battles. MacFarland's clearance numbers attained legendary status in the department. She remembered her fellow cops talking about them in her early years on the force. *Those old timers are long retired, but MacFarland's case numbers are still quoted.*

Torres's arrival was a welcome break from her research. As usual, he came to their morning powwow with fresh kolaches and hot coffee.

"Thanks, Torres. We're going to need these fine sources of energy if we plan to make serious progress on MacFarland."

She brought Torres up to date on the discovery of medication tampering that Dr. Garcia had uncovered. Torres let out a soft whistle and shook his head. "Could this get any more complicated?"

"I'm afraid so," Sudhan said. "The way I see it is that someone was trying to kill him with his own medications. When that didn't do the job, either that person or someone else killed him in the hospital. Let's start with the pills. Who had access to them?"

Torres took a gulp of coffee. "At the MacFarland house we have Yvonne MacFarland, of course. You've already taken her statement. Then there's the sister, Betty Fortenberry. She said she came up from Matagorda as soon as she heard. But was she a frequent visitor? And then we know that Dr. Melvin spent a lot of time at the house talking to Bruce." Torres paused to review his notes. "A young man, Foster Small, does odd jobs for the MacFarlands and is in and out of the house a lot. They all would have had access to the pill bottles since most were in the kitchen or bathroom. Betty was with me when I collected them."

"There was another visitor." Sudhan shuffled her notes. "Remember the real estate agent? On the twenty-fifth, two days before Bruce was murdered. Taylor Wood,

Sand Dollar Estates. Have you been able to talk to him yet?"

"He's on my list." Torres said. "I called the agency and left a message. I'll swing by and see what I can find out today."

"And where are we with the hospital and the imposter lab tech?" Sudhan asked.

"Dead end, I'm afraid. The hospital has no idea who he was. IT has no hits on the system to indicate MacFarland's wristband was scanned. Also, no orders in the system for the lab at that time."

"He? Do we know it was a man?"

"The nurse who caught a glimpse is pretty sure," Torres said. "I talked to a security guard I've known from when I came to the ER almost every night in my street cop days. He said it was a zoo that night. Staff and families were coming in and out. Anyone could have come through those double doors at the ambulance bay. Someone dressed as a lab tech suddenly appearing in that chaos wouldn't arouse any suspicion."

"Most likely someone who knew his way around the hospital."

Torres nodded. "Looks that way. Hospital admin has its panties in a knot about the security breach. My guy says they now have a guard stationed at all the ER doors now. All night."

"What are they saying about MacFarland's IV regarding the tampering?"

"Pretty tight lipped on that. I'm glad we talked to the nurse right after the murder. I think the admin came down on her for voicing her suspicions without having the hospital risk managers talking for her."

Sudhan stood up. "Let's divide and conquer. I'm going to pay a visit to the MacFarland home and talk to Betty. I'd like you to track down this Foster fellow as well as Taylor Wood."

"What about Dr. Melvin?" Torres asked.

"I'm going to give him a call and set up a meeting. Let's touch base later."

***

Wanting an unguarded interview, Sudhan visited the MacFarland house without calling ahead. When she got out of her car, she saw Yvonne's sister coming out the front door. Glad for this opportunity to speak to Betty out of Yvonne's earshot, Sudhan intercepted her.

"Hello, Betty. I stopped by to give y'all an update on our investigation. I hope this isn't a bad time."

"Well, actually, I just convinced Yvonne to lie down and I'm sneaking out to get some fresh air."

"I could use some of that too. Police work involves more desk time than most people realize. May I join you?" Sudhan noted Betty's sturdy physique. Such a contrast to Yvonne who looked as if a stiff breeze could knock her over.

"Sure thing. I'm headed to the beach after I get my sunglasses." She reached into the driver's side of an ancient Subaru parked in the driveway.

Sudhan turned around and matched Betty's stride.

"I understand you live in Matagorda. We used to stop there on our way to Corpus Christi when my son was young. He loved the aquarium."

Betty smiled. "It's our pride and joy. I like to

drive down there myself. I volunteer and help with the school groups that visit."

"Ben loved the tide pool. He picked up every creature he was allowed to. Probably some he wasn't. If you have time to volunteer, does that mean you're retired?"

Another smile. "Oh yes. Thirty-five years on my feet as a nurse was plenty, let me tell you. But I do find that I have time on my hands since my husband passed eighteen months ago. When I get cabin fever, I hop into my car and drive up here to visit. I always feel better when I'm in motion."

Sudhan believed it. She had to work to keep up with Betty. They reached the seawall and descended the steps to the beach. Sudhan was surprised to see Betty kick off her shoes and roll up her pant legs. She marched right across the narrow beach and up to her ankles in the water.

"I can't resist the feel of the wet sand between my toes," Betty said as she made a right turn along the water's edge.

Sudhan was not inclined to put her feet in the water on this last day of January. She kept apace a few yards away from Betty and had to raise her voice over the hum of the waves rushing around Betty's legs.

"It's nice that you're close enough to visit," Sudhan said.

"Oh, yes. It's been good for both of us, really. I get a change of scene and Yvonne gets, I mean got, a break from Bruce's abuse. Yvonne said his behavior improved when I was around. The poor thing."

"Abuse? Was it physical?" Sudhan asked.

"No. Not that I ever could tell. Purely

psychological. He was a first-class bully and made Yvonne's life miserable. The only time I saw the two of them enjoying each other's company was when we played bridge. So, I encouraged frequent bridge games."

"You need a fourth for bridge, right?"

"Jim Melvin was our fourth. You must know him. He was the chief medical examiner for years. I loved playing with that man," Betty said. "I guess we'll need a new fourth now. Do you play, Detective?"

"No. I've tried, but my brain doesn't work that way." Sudhan laughed. "Too much strategy for me."

"Well, I love it. I had just come home from my Monday bridge round robin at the Senior Center when Yvonne called me about Bruce being in the hospital. By the time I got myself up here, he was gone."

Sudhan decided it was time to dive in. "Betty, as you are aware, we have evidence that someone tampered with Bruce's medications." She had to shout to be heard over the breeze. "Do you have any idea how that could have happened? Have there been any other people with access to the house that we're unaware of?"

Betty stopped walking. The water swirled around her feet. "Believe me, I've been giving that a lot of thought. Yvonne has a woman clean for her every week. She has a key, as a matter of fact. And I hate to mention it, but that young man Foster has been helping them out more and more as Bruce was failing. He certainly is in and out of the house all the time."

Sudhan saw that they had walked as far as the next stairway to the top of the seawall. She looked at her watch. "I need to get back, so I'll leave you to your walk. Please let Yvonne know we're working hard on Bruce's case. I wish I had more to tell you. And if anything occurs to you, please give me a call. My card is at the house."

"Thank you, Detective. I will. As I tell Yvonne, "Truth will out."

Sudhan turned to walk across the beach to the stairs. She had to trudge through the soft brown sand. Sitting on a bench to shake out her shoes, she watched Betty proceed down the beach. She slipped her shoes back on and began walking back to her car. Betty had conveniently provided an alibi for the night of the murder without being asked. She would check it out. *'Truth will out.' Betty and Shakespeare have it right.*

***

Betty continued her walk after Sudhan left the beach. She enjoyed these rare moments of solitude as she supported Yvonne through the nightmare of Bruce's death. It was at times like these that she let herself recall the unexpected and passionate interlude she had experienced not long before. She blushed to think that it had started during the last weeks of her husband's life. There had been so many doctors, nurses and therapists involved in his care. Friends tried their best to support her as well. Yet, she never felt so alone.

There was one person who registered her pain and suggested she needed a break from the bedside. She was happy to accept the invitation to walk along the Matagorda shore. They had taken their shoes off to walk at the water's edge. They didn't speak. Their shoulders touched as they walked in the frothy surf. Betty was comforted by the close presence of another person. When they rested on a bench at the end of the pier gazing at Matagorda Bay, they found each other's hands and pulled each other closer. *I had no idea that was what I needed.*

Soon they were meeting for trysts up and down the Gulf Coast. They took their time. Betty craved physical contact and sexual release. They used their hands, lips, and tongues in ways she had only read about. When, in the past, she had made overtures to her husband that didn't involve the missionary position, he had not responded. *Who would have guessed there was still time for two senior citizens to experience such passion?* They adjusted for stiff joints and found positions of comfort in which they sated their desire. Their lovemaking was urgent or leisurely, depending on their needs.

Betty was brought back to the present when a dog raced past her in a futile attempt to catch one of the tiny gray birds pecking at the sand. *Yvonne would know exactly what kind of bird it is. Time to get back and check on her. Time to sort out what life has in store for both of us.*

***

Torres drove over the short causeway to Pelican Island north of Galveston Island. It was mild enough to drive with the window down. He was headed to the campus of Texas A&M University at Galveston, where Foster Small had asked to meet. He parked in the visitors' lot and followed campus signs to their designated meeting place at the clock tower. Torres was fifteen minutes early and pulled out his notes to review.

Mrs. MacFarland had provided Torres with

Foster's phone number. She explained that Foster worked for Didier LaSalle at Feathers, a birding store. It was there that she had met Foster when he offered to help with some maintenance around her home.

Foster sounded nervous when Torres called to set up the appointment. That didn't surprise Torres. A call from a police detective would put anyone on guard.

Torres decided to call Didier while he waited. He introduced himself and explained that he was working with Detective Sudhan on the MacFarland case.

"Pleased to speak with you. Louise mentioned that she knew you when she was working in the ER. How is it working with Sudhan?"

"Never a dull minute!"

"I'm not sure I'll be much help to you," Didier said. "Bruce and his wife were good customers and avid birders. Especially Yvonne. But I didn't know them otherwise. What would you like to know?"

"We're interviewing anyone who had contact with Mr. MacFarland in the recent past. Apparently one of your employees has been doing some chores for the MacFarlands. Foster Small, right? Can you tell me a little bit about him?"

"Sure. I hired several of the kids from the college to help in the store. Foster is my number one employee. He's reliable, responsible, and great with the customers. I've been considering bringing him on full time after he graduates."

"Seems like a good kid," Torres said. "He should check out fine."

"He is a good kid. But I'll be honest with you. He has a history." Didier paused. "I'm sure you could find this out. He was up front with me. Foster got into trouble in high school. Mostly drug-related petty crimes. Apparently, that's all behind him. He said a stint in rehab saved his life. The counselors helped him get his GED and got him to understand how his rough childhood had messed him up. Now he's in college and working on a degree."

"Good to know. I'm about to meet him on campus in a few minutes. Thanks for the information."

When Torres hung up, the clock tower began to chime the hour with a melody. He looked at the clock face trying to catch the tune it was playing. He was still concentrating when Foster walked up to him.

"Detective Torres? I'm Foster." He followed Torres's gaze to the clock. "It's playing the Aggie War Hymn. They don't want us to forget we're Aggies, even if we're not at the flagship campus. And even if the only sports going on here are intramurals."

Torres chuckled. "Thanks for meeting me. It's my first time on campus. Looks like a cool place to go to school."

"It is. I'm taking a light load since I need to work to put myself through college. I should have my degree in three more semesters," Foster said. "You said you have some questions for me regarding Mr. MacFarland? Man, I can't believe what I've been hearing. You guys think he was murdered?"

"That's what it looks like. We're talking to everyone who had contact with him recently. I understand you've been helping around the MacFarland house."

"That's right. Mrs. Mac, I mean Mrs. MacFarland, needed a lot of help as Mr. MacFarland's been having some health problems. And I can use the extra income." Foster looked at his feet. "If you're talking to me, you probably have me as a suspect considering my history. Those records are supposed to be sealed, but I imagine you guys have a way to get to them. Anyway, I've been up front about my past. I told my boss at Feathers and Mrs. Mac."

"Listen, man, we're talking to everyone who had contact with the victim. That's our job," Torres said to put Foster at ease. "I'd just like to ask you a few questions."

Foster shrugged. "Okay, shoot."

"We found out that before Mr. MacFarland was murdered, someone had messed with his medications. Complications from that are what sent him to the hospital on Monday night."

"You think I …"

"Like I said, we're asking everyone. Did you see anyone or anything that could help us figure out how his own medications almost killed him?"

"No. All I know is that he had pill bottles in the kitchen and more in the bathroom. Lots of pill bottles. I never touched them and never saw anyone other than Mrs. Mac or maybe her sister giving Mr. Mac his medication."

"How did Mr. MacFarland get along with Yvonne's sister? Betty, right?" Torres glanced at his notes.

"Hard to say. He was rough on Mrs. Mac. Maybe a little easier on Betty."

"How was he with you?"

"Me? I think he resented the fact that I was doing the odd jobs he used to do. He was often critical."

"To the point of being insulting?"

"No, nothing like that. Just gruff and ungrateful," Foster said. "I chalked it up to him being so sick. I know Mrs. Mac appreciated my help."

"I'm sure she did. And still does. Were you there the day that Mr. MacFarland was taken to the hospital?"

"No, sir. Not that day."

"How about the night he was in the hospital? Can you tell me where you were?"

"In my apartment, studying for an economics exam. I live alone, so…"

Torres noted Foster's defensive posture and decided to hold off on further questions. "Thanks for talking to me, Foster. Here's my card in case anything comes to mind."

Foster appeared relieved that the interview was over. He took the card and glanced up at the clock. "I need to get to class."

Torres smiled and nodded. "Sure thing. Take it easy."

Torres walked back to his car against the flow of students going to class. *Man, they look young. That kid was anxious. I wonder what he's hiding.* He would run his interview by Sudhan. She could decide if they needed to invite Foster to the station to give a formal statement.

Chapter 11

Saturday, February 1, 2020, and Sunday February 2, 2020

EJ collapsed in a beach chair next to Louise. She had been playing with Cora, Noah, and the three dogs. They took turns throwing driftwood into the water for the dogs to retrieve. Only Jack returned with a stick. Chico marched off with his and Harlee dashed between the two of them. The mild weather had continued, and Galveston beach goers were making the best of it.

"Thanks for coming by to see the kids, EJ. They've been missing you," Louise said.

"Same here. Chris and this internship have been keeping me busy. Especially the Wood assignment. Will you call her? Your pathologist friend at the ME's office?" EJ asked.

"All right, all right, I will. You're serious about this assignment, or about this young man?" Louise raised an eyebrow.

"Both, as it turns out. And don't give me that mom look. I'm proceeding carefully. At least with the assignment. I'll tell Ben about your help this evening. Our families are getting together."

Louise closed her eyes and welcomed the sun on her face. "I'll give Dr. Garcia a call on Monday. It'll cost you an evening of babysitting."

"Deal."

***

Chris, Marnie, and EJ arrived promptly at 6:30. Bob and Iliana met them at the door.

"I'm the unofficial bartender," Ben called from the great room. "Place your orders. Margaritas are my specialty."

Iliana's house was a new bungalow built just west of Sydnor Bayou.

"What a great place!" Marnie said. "Are you feeling settled yet?"

Bob and Iliana beamed. "We're so happy to be in new construction. We unpacked everything the first day! We had planned where everything would go before the move," Iliana said.

Bob added, "We had to do something with the two extra months the construction took. You're our first guests."

After a tour of the new home, the group settled in the great room which consisted of the kitchen, dining room, and family room. The floor-to-ceiling windows had an expansive view of one of the three lakes in the planned community. The rich smell of stew filled the room.

As she sipped her virgin margarita, Marnie said, "This reminds me of my neighborhood in Colorado.

Louise is always making fun of my suburban oasis but there's a certain amount of peace in a place like that. I used to send EJ out to play in the morning and not worry if she didn't show up till dinner—with strict instructions to stay out of the lake. But then again, I didn't have to worry about alligators."

EJ laughed. "I remember that. When I was six, you gave me lessons on what to say if someone tried to trick me into going into the lake."

"I can't imagine that, even at six, anyone could trick you into doing something you didn't want to do," Ben said.

"You know your research partner well. But aren't you glad you can trust me to do smart things?" EJ replied.

"How's the research into Mr. Wood's death coming along?" Bob asked. "He was such a well-respected man in the community. I wasn't the charge nurse in the ER yet, but I was on duty there. We were overrun with weeping, hysterical teenagers. The high school held a memorial." Bob shook his head. "There was a lot of speculation about just what happened to Mr. Wood that day on East Beach."

"Speculation?" asked EJ. "What were people saying?"

"People wondered if he had a heart attack and fell in. Others brought up the possibility of foul play. Then the horrifying report of a shark attack came out. His family must have been devastated."

"We've been looking into Mr. Wood's case," Ben began. "The obituary in the paper was written by his principal. She praised him for his involvement with troubled students, helping them stay in school and graduate. After the report that his death was caused by a shark attack, the story died. Around then, the paper and police records were all about drug cartel and gang related deaths. Some were solved but a lot must be cold cases."

Iliana nodded in agreement. "I remember this period."

EJ jumped in. "Wood's wife was apparently too distraught to contribute anything when she was interviewed, and his son was too young. As a matter of fact, I'm pretty sure that his son is back in town. We've met but haven't discussed this yet. I have an outing planned with him tomorrow."

"Whoa," said Chris. "Are you staying safe? Not being lured into any lakes?"

Marnie and Chris exchanged looks. Iliana made a slight frown as if she were thinking about saying something and then thought the better of it.

"I told her to be careful," Ben said.

EJ smiled. "We're walking the seawall in the morning and eating lunch at Garrett's Trattoria. Garrett promised me a fantastic meal."

"How is he doing?" Iliana asked. "I don't think I've seen him since the memorial eighteen months ago. We've been eating at home and saving our pennies to get into this house."

EJ said, "He seems good overall. Still missing Gen but apparently seeing a nurse at the hospital."

Bob smiled knowingly. "Julia. She's a nurse on the OB ward. I suggested his restaurant to her when she was looking for a caterer for the ward Christmas party. They hit it off."

"Chris and I met her late one night as the

restaurant was closing," Marnie said. "The four of us had a great time talking about politics. Luckily, we're all on the same side. She seems nice."

"Speaking of food, dinner is ready," Bob said. "It's a stew with chicken and vegetables in a rich gravy of vinegar, cloves, and laurel leaves. Hachee. We have waffles for dessert."

The warm stew was the perfect antidote to the cool front which had blown in. After everyone had sopped up their last of their gravy with the crusty sourdough rolls, Bob brought out a platter of waffles. Iliana placed melted butter, chocolate syrup and whipped cream on the table.

Everyone finished their second helpings and sat back with contented smiles. Chris said to Bob, "That was all just delicious. Thank you so much."

"You're welcome."

Marnie turned to Iliana. "Can we talk about murder now? I want to know what you can share about Mr. MacFarland."

Everyone looked at Iliana expectantly. "I can only share common knowledge. Though, I guess you, Marnie, already know that there was some tampering with his medications and supplements prior to his death. However, it has been officially ruled secondary to a cerebral air embolism. We're beginning to research who would have had access to his medication bottles. Another lead we're following is that there seems to have been a lab technician in his room around the time of his death. The hospital has no record of who that was."

Something tweaked in Marnie's brain, but she couldn't grab it. "Louise wants me to go to the funeral with her on Monday," Marnie said. "Will you be there?"

"Oh yes. The police always attend funerals of murder victims—especially if the murder victim is or was on the force. Interesting things often happen."

***

Sunday morning, February 2, 2020

Do you really need to work today?" Bob asked Iliana as he came into the kitchen. She was dressed in black pants and a fitted jacket worn over a gray herringbone knit top. She took a last sip of coffee and brought her cup to the sink.

"Just one interview. I've had a hard time connecting with Dr. James Melvin, good friend, and frequent visitor at Bruce MacFarland's house. He said he had time for me this morning."

"Is Torres going with you?"

"No. He's interviewing a few more people associated with the MacFarland household. We need to cover all the bases before we meet with the chief tomorrow morning." She gathered up her phone and keys. "Melvin likes to be in control. I think I can make that work for me."

Bob smiled. "My wily, detective wife. Makes me wonder what mind games you play on me."

"I got you to make dinner last night, didn't I?" she said over her shoulder as she headed out the door.

The drive to Dr. Melvin's condominium at Dorado Shores provided Iliana time to puzzle over the dinner conversation the previous night. EJ must have met the author of the letter about Luther Wood's death. That letter had raised the hackles of her chief as it accused the department of botching the investigation, albeit many years in the past. And Chris looked none too happy about EJ having a date with this T. Wood. Taylor Wood? I'll have to see what Torres has dug up on the charming real estate agent.

Iliana parked in front of Dr. Melvin's building. It was one of the newer towers on East Beach. She was buzzed in by the concierge. The plan was to meet in the building's lobby. Comfortable sofas and easy chairs were grouped in the tastefully decorated atrium. A wall of windows provided views of the gulf and salt marshes on opposite sides. Iliana turned from the gulf-side window when she heard her name.

"Detective Sudhan?"

"Dr. Melvin, thanks for meeting with me," Sudhan said, taking in the doctor's sallow complexion and two-day stubble. Nothing like his usual suave, camera-ready appearance, she thought.

"Of course, shall we sit?" He gestured to a pair of chairs. Once Sudhan was seated, he folded his tall frame into the other one. "I apologize that you had to ruin your Sunday to meet with me. I've been quite busy helping Yvonne with the arrangements. She's been overwhelmed, as you have surely noticed."

"Yes. She mentioned how helpful you've been. And what a good friend you were to Bruce."

"Helping Yvonne has kept me busy. But now, with no more immediate decisions to make, the loss of my best friend has washed over me." He let his hands drop between his knees. "I was working on his eulogy when you arrived."

"I'm so sorry. Yvonne said your visits were bright spots for Bruce as his world was closing in on him."

"I have so many recriminations," he said, meeting Sudhan's gaze. "I should have known…"

"Known?"

"Yvonne told me about the medication tampering. I can't understand how it happened. He deteriorated right in front of me. And I kept telling him he just needed a better attitude. I thought he had given up."

"Do you have any idea who might have been responsible?"

He slumped forward, elbows on his legs, eyes on the floor and shook his head. "No earthly idea." Dr. Melvin paused and looked up. "Have you discovered any evidence to suspect an intruder? I should have made sure Yvonne was putting on the alarm at night. When I asked her, she said she had forgotten all about it. Bruce had always been the one to set it at night and disarm it in the morning. Yet another thing she depended upon him for. Poor woman."

"Certainly, no sign of forced entry, and it's unclear at what point the medications had been disturbed. Bruce's health was failing for months, presumably from the tampering. His physician, Dr. Finnerty, has concluded as much."

"Dr. Finnerty, yes, I met her in the hospital. Another source of recrimination for me. I blamed her for mismanaging Bruce's case. A horrible thing to have done, one physician to another."

Sudhan was surprised to find herself feeling sympathetic to Dr. Melvin. She needed to redirect the course of the interview. "I imagine Bruce had his share of enemies, considering the number of arrests he made that led to convictions. Are you aware if he had received any threats?"

"You're right. Bruce's team put a lot of very bad people behind bars. This was before your time, I imagine. The turf battles between cartel factions were raging during the early 2000s. The murders kept us busy at the medical examiner's office, too. But to answer your question, no, I can't recall him ever mentioning any threats. Then again, his memory was not what it once was."

"Yvonne said he kept some case records in his file cabinet. Were you aware of this?"

"He shouldn't have been keeping records at home. But it wouldn't surprise me. Some of those cases were like trophies to Bruce," Dr. Melvin said.

Sudhan didn't respond, hoping that he would feel the need to fill the silence. Instead, he uncrossed his legs and began to stand up. "If you will excuse me, I need to get back to work on my words for the funeral. Unless you have any more questions, that is."

Sudhan stood to avoid him towering over her chair. "The night that Bruce was hospitalized, you were there with Yvonne. She told us you drove her back to the hospital when she received the call that Bruce had died."

Now fully erect, Dr. Melvin looked down at her, exhibiting a hint of the imperious posture she had anticipated. "Of course, I did. Yvonne was unable to rest so I gave her one of her prescribed sleeping pills. I didn't want to leave her alone. I slept on the couch."

When Sudhan didn't respond, he continued, "I

apologize for my tone. I know you needed to ask that question. Please forgive me. I've slept poorly since that night. I'm not myself."

"I understand, Dr. Melvin. Thank you for your time."

"Please let me know if I can be of any further assistance, Detective."

As she watched him walk to the elevators, she noticed a slight limp. He looked like a broken man.

***

EJ parked her mom's Audi near the Galveston Pleasure Pier. She spotted Taylor waiting for her. It was sunny and sixty-five degrees with a mild ocean breeze. *It wouldn't be like this in New Haven or Colorado.* She unloaded Harlee and Jack. They had a hard time not tangling their leashes into a knot. Their entire bodies wiggled with excitement.

"I didn't expect four-footed companions," Taylor said. Harlee and Jack entwined around Taylor's legs. Taylor bent down and gave them enthusiastic back rubs.

"They're my mom's dogs—and potential friend inspectors," EJ said.

"I hope I pass the test."

Jack leaned all his sixty pounds into Taylor. Harlee stood between his feet.

"Looking good so far," EJ said.

"What will we do with them during lunch?"

"Garrett has a small dog park attached to his restaurant. He said that reservations for the dog park fill up before his tables. I would have warned you, but I really didn't expect to bring them. My mom woke up not feeling great—again— and Chris had some work to do. When I stopped by this morning with my exercise clothes on, they attached themselves to me."

"Glad to meet them. If we walk east from here, we can get to Stewart Beach where they can go into the water."

"Good plan."

As they walked along the seawall, Taylor asked, "How's your internship at the paper going?"

"Well," EJ answered with a sly smile. "I've been given the job of investigating the letter you wrote about your father's death."

Taylor stopped abruptly. Then he smiled. "I guess my subterfuge wasn't very subtle. I want it on the record that I didn't know who you were when we met in the bar."

EJ looked at Taylor closely and thought about that night. Easier to believe him than to worry about it. Their conversation had been spontaneous.

"I can roll with that for now. You could have come clean during our text exchanges. But I did suggest this outing without telling you what I was working on— even if I also really wanted to see you again. We'll call it even."

"I'll just focus on the 'the really wanted to see you again' part. My employer did offer me a chance to work in Galveston. And I do want to figure out what happened to my dad."

Taylor gave EJ a thumbnail sketch of his time since leaving Galveston as a child.

"Sorry about your mom," EJ said. "Glad you had

your extended family in Dallas to help you."

Taylor was quiet. Then he asked, "Have you ever had a close relationship with a person with a serious illness?"

EJ shook her head no.

"It's exhausting. With my mom, her mental illness over the years often had me walking on eggshells. Breast cancer just added a whole other layer of problems. I went on a day at a time. Graduated, got a job. When she died last year, there was the guilt of relief—and then waves of loneliness and loss. Another reason I wanted a change of scenery. Also, it made me think that I should take up her crusade about my dad's death."

They had walked to the stretch of beach designated as a dog park. Letting them off their leashes, Taylor and EJ watched them frolic in the waves. Jack dashed into the ocean and then came out shaking off the water. Harlee walked along the edge of the water getting her feet wet. She tried to catch the waves in her mouth and appeared surprised when she tasted the salt water.

"Do you remember much around the time of your dad's death?" EJ asked.

"Lots. Tough to talk about it. I had the sheer overwhelming sense that my life had turned upside down. My dad kept our family functional. After his death, my mom vacillated between being catatonic and not being able to let me out of her sight. Until then I was just a kid who went to school, played sports, and rode bikes with my buddies. We hung out on the beach in the summer and fished. Then my world stopped."

"I didn't tell you the other night, but my dad died suddenly in a rafting accident two years ago while I was away at college. When you talk about your dad's death changing your life completely, I can relate. The totally unexpected loss of my dad brought me to a surreal place. It's taking me a while to adjust."

"Wow. Sorry." Taylor reached for EJ's hand. "We probably understand each other better than most." She felt an electric spark at his touch. She looked into his vivid green eyes. He smiled at her.

"Whatever brought us together, I'm glad it did," Taylor said.

They turned back to the ocean, gathered up the dogs, and headed back up the beach towards Garrett's Trattoria.

"Can we talk about your dad over lunch?" EJ asked.

"I'd like that," Taylor said. "I'll tell you what I remember about him and why, as I've gotten older that I agree with my mom. The story we were given back then doesn't hold water."

Glad to settle on the shady porch overlooking the dog park, Taylor and EJ ordered Arnold Palmers. After lapping up a lot of water, Harlee and Jack were also resting in the shade.

Garrett rounded the corner to their table and bent to give EJ a quick hug. EJ introduced Taylor. Garrett gave an approving nod.

"Taylor was actually born here, so I guess he qualifies for Born on the Island status, like you and me, BOI." EJ said.

Garrett smiled. "Welcome back. What brought you to your senses to return?" he asked as he settled into a chair at the table.

"Work. I'm in real estate. I needed a change of scene from Dallas." Taylor said.

"Good choice. Where are you staying?" Garrett asked.

"The company is putting me up at the Third Coast Hotel until I find a place."

"The Third Coast? I bet you've met my cousin then. She's the hotel manager."

EJ broke in. "Garrett has a cousin in almost every establishment along the seawall."

"You exaggerate. Only half." Garrett looked at the ceiling, making a mental calculation. "Anita is a distant cousin—kissing cousins, as we say. We're a big family. Let me know if Anita isn't treating you right."

A waiter beckoned Garrett, and he stood to leave. "Oh, the reason I came over here was to tell you what I chose for your lunch. I've prepared pan fried grouper with spring peas and tortellini after an appetizer of fresh oysters. How does that sound?"

"Delicious. Ok with you, Taylor?"

"Makes my stomach growl. My dad was allergic to seafood so I'm pretty much a novice at it. Not allergic though."

When Garrett left, Taylor said, "Actually my dad was allergic to a lot of things. He had bad asthma. Very allergic to bee stings."

"The police reports said he fell into the bay while fishing."

"He never fished."

"What do you think happened that day?"

"My mom said that he called to say that he planned to meet a student after school who was very distraught. She remembered him saying that he was going to take the student on a beach walk. Mom didn't know the student's name. She always made sure that he had his EpiPen and his inhaler with him. It was a warm winter, so a bee sting was a possibility, even in January. He was supposed to be home for dinner at seven and never showed up."

"What happened next?"

"When he didn't come home, my mom called the police. They were less than sympathetic. She felt that they thought that he was another Black man who had gone astray. Less than twenty-four hours later, pieces of his body started washing up. That's when my mom took to her bed. We could barely get her to the funeral a week later."

Taylor looked stricken as he told this story.

"Are you okay?" EJ asked. "I don't know what I was thinking about talking about this over lunch."

Taylor drank his tea and lemonade. "I'm fine. It's just weird talking about this with someone else. After a few months we moved to Dallas and my grandparents were afraid to ask about my dad. Must have been hard for them as well. They were always afraid to upset my mom."

EJ took a deep breath and took Taylor's hand, glad that this time the electric shock was more like a warm salve. "Let's table this for now. Tell me about Dallas. I've never been there for any period of time."

Over lunch, Taylor described his life and family in Dallas. EJ nodded and smiled, still holding Taylor's hand intermittently. Taylor turned to EJ.

"What was it like growing up in Colorado?"

EJ looked over at the pups, now playing with the

other dogs. "Carefree? I remember my childhood as a kaleidoscope of outdoor activities with my parents. Walking, hiking, skiing. I missed having siblings, but the neighborhood was full of playmates."

"Were you rebellious?" Taylor asked with a smile.

"The first conflict with my mom that I remember was when I was eleven. I wanted an expensive pair of embroidered jeans, and she said no. I got so mad at her I slammed my bedroom door in her face. She firmly opened the door and said that no one slammed the door on her. I could get mad but not slam the door. We could find a compromise when I calmed down. Later we agreed that I could manage my own clothing allowance. I didn't want the jeans once it was my money."

Taylor laughed.

"That was probably the biggest fight we ever had. Not much compared to what you dealt with."

Taylor looked at EJ. "If I had known you then, I would have been green with envy for your home life."

"When my dad died, my mom was paralyzed with grief. She walked around in a daze for two months. I told her that I felt like I was losing her as well as Dad. She looked hard at me and apologized. She pulled herself together." EJ didn't add all the ups and downs that they had had since then. "This pregnancy was a shock for me. Not sure I want a sibling now. Mom has moved on in her life much faster than I have. A new relationship and a new child. I feel expendable."

"You sound angry."

EJ nodded. "I guess I am. That's the first time I've admitted it. It's just that things have been changing so fast in what's left of my family. Too many unknowns ahead."

"I'll vouch that unknowns are scary. I think that's why I need some closure on my dad's death. The official story makes no sense."

"Ben and I agree. Hopefully the three of us can find out what happened."

Chapter 12

Monday morning, February 3, 2020

Sudhan and Torres met at 8 a.m. to compare notes and prepare for their meeting with the chief. Both were dressed more formally than usual. They planned to go directly from the station to MacFarland's funeral.

"How was your weekend?" Sudhan asked as they walked from the breakroom to her office, steaming mugs of coffee in hand. Torres and his partner George often headed to art exhibits and plays in Houston.

"Too short. The case kept me busy. I probably wasted time going down a rabbit hole. The MacFarland's housekeeper, Adelita Morales, doesn't have a cell phone and Yvonne doesn't have her current address." Torres sipped his coffee. "Eventually I found her, and she agreed to talk. She's worked for them for over twenty years, cleaning once a week. She does have a key, and she was able to show it to me. Then she started crying."

"This is where the rabbit hole appeared?"

"Before I could ask her what she knew about Bruce's medications, she asked me if my visit was about her grandson, Carlos. Apparently, he's been in trouble. He's affiliated."

"Which gang?"

"She had no idea. But he's stolen cash from her purse in the past. He could have made a copy of the key. I doubt a teenager would have the wherewithal to know how to mix up Bruce's meds in a way that would make him sick. But he could have given a copy of the key to someone higher up the gang chain of command. I still need to find the kid. He bounces around from relative to relative."

"And Adelita? What did she know about Bruce's medications?"

"Nada. She said she never touched them, per orders from Yvonne. I believe her."

Leaving the question about Carlos open, Torres reviewed his interview with Foster. Sudhan said she would think about bringing Foster in for a statement. Then, she filled him in on her interviews with Betty and Dr. Melvin.

"Dr. Melvin was evasive on the possibility of Bruce having enemies. He confirmed that Bruce kept records of some of his arrests at home. We need to review those. See if the crime scene guys picked them up. If not, let's pay Mrs. MacFarland another visit to collect them."

"Will do," said Torres, scribbling a note to himself.

"What about Taylor Wood, the real estate agent?" Sudhan asked.

"I talked to the broker at Sand Dollar. He has no

concerns. He can document that Taylor was at work at their Dallas agency until two weeks ago when he arrived here. It's unlikely he's been in town over the time frame to mess with the pills. I ran him through the system, too. He's clean. I still need to talk to him. I couldn't pin him down over the weekend. I guess it's a busy time for real estate folks."

Sudhan looked at her watch. "Not much to hang our hat on, is it? Let's fill in the chief. Remind me to tell you something I might have learned about this Taylor Wood later. I'm not ready to bring it up with the chief yet."

***

"Hi, Louise," Dr. Tina Garcia answered her office phone. "Are you calling about MacFarland's post report? I released what we have to the police on Friday."

"Yeah, I spoke to Sudhan. She's trying to figure out how the pill tampering fits in. There are several suspects. I still can't believe it," Louise said. "But I'm calling about something else. Well, someone else. And maybe it's related after all."

"I'm not following you," said Tina.

Louise gave her a summary of the Wood case, Taylor's letter and EJ's project, including the fact that Bruce MacFarland was the detective on the case and Dr. Melvin was the medical examiner and performed the autopsy.

"That was before my time in Galveston," Tina said. Louise noted her cautious tone. "You said that was one of Dr. Melvin's cases? 2002? Let me see what I can pull up." After a pause, "Here it is. Cause of death,

in next to Louise. "Galveston PD is present in force. Looks like lots of MacFarland's neighbors are here as well as Yvonne's friends from the birding community."

Louise pointed out Mrs. MacFarland to Marnie as she was being escorted to the front of the church. The altar was barely visible under the array of flowers in vases and wreaths. "Who is that with her?" Marnie asked, taking in the tall man at Yvonne's side. She noted his slight limp.

"That's Dr. James Melvin, the retired medical examiner I told you about. The guy who gave me a hard time at Bruce's bedside," Louise answered. "The woman with her must be her sister. Sudhan told us she was in town."

They watched Dr. Melvin deposit Yvonne and her sister in the front pew then took his seat with a group of his colleagues. Dr. Tina Garcia was among them.

"Not much of a family, is it? No other MacFarlands?" Marnie asked Louise.

"You're right. Yvonne told me they hadn't been blessed with kids. Her words, not mine." Louise said, grinning as she thought about providing soccer treats. Marnie looked somber as she thought about her miscarriages—five missed 'blessings'.

Chris turned around and looked at a group of men filling the pews in the back. "There's a contingent from the hospitality consortium here as well as several members of the DA's office."

Besides healthcare, which included the medical school and the Gulf National Lab, tourism was the biggest employer in Galveston. "Personal or professional interest on their part?" Marnie whispered.

Chris raised his eyebrows and gave a shrug.

Didier said, "The last few times I saw Bruce he was going on about his cases. I remember him mentioning that there were a lot of ways to improve a policeman's salary. He called it 'special overtime.' A few of the attendees might want to know that their secrets are safe."

The priest, who knew Bruce well, gave a brief sketch of Bruce's life and his years of service to the community. His ill health had not deterred him from attending Sunday mass. Dr. Melvin gave a eulogy laced with anecdotes from their joint careers and described how much he would miss him. Yvonne wept openly and leaned against her sister for support.

Iliana joined Marnie's group as they gathered in the reception area after the service. "I wonder how his body was released so early from the investigation?" Marnie asked.

"It's easier to release a body if there is going to be a burial versus a cremation and MacFarland is going to be buried in the Old City Cemetery. Believe me, we have taken every conceivable sample of his tissues during his autopsy."

"Speaking of autopsies, I spoke with Tina earlier today," Louise said to Iliana. "She's willing to reexamine Luther Wood's evidence if the case is reopened."

Iliana nodded. "I just need to square it with the chief, but I don't expect any pushback."

Yvonne and James Melvin approached the group. "Thank you for coming today," Yvonne said. "I'm sure Bruce is smiling down on us." Louise squeezed her hand in response.

Dr. Melvin looked vaguely familiar to Marnie.

"Have we met?" she asked. She noticed his intense green eyes and straight athletic bearing when standing still. Dr. Melvin smiled at her. "No, I would remember such a beautiful mother-to-be."

Marnie smiled back. "It seems like you and Bruce were very close."

"We worked on a lot of cases together over the years—successfully I might add. I will miss him."

Yvonne gently tugged James's sleeve. "We must see our other guests. Again, thanks for coming."

Louise looked after Yvonne as she continued to circulate. "She looks better than when Bruce was alive. At times I thought she would collapse from the exhaustion of caring for him. He may have been a good friend to Dr. Melvin, but he was tough on his wife.

"There are those on the force who were not sad when he retired. He was a mixed bag," Iliana said. "As we all are. Still there were rumors about his ethics."

"I wonder if those rumors extended to Dr. Melvin," Marnie said.

Chris had fallen into conversation with another group passing through the vestibule. Marnie didn't recognize any of them. That was nothing new. Chris knew half the population of Galveston, either from his school days or his career as a journalist. Two attractive women continued talking to him as the others made their exits. Marnie was aware that he had an active social life before they met but hadn't asked for details. One of the women straightened Chris's lapel as she spoke to him. Marnie approached and took Chris's hand.

"There you are," Chris said, and gave her hand a squeeze. "I want to introduce you to a couple of members of the Ball High School class of 1996. And more specifically, my co-stars in Grease."

"The way I remember it, Chris, you had a bit part. I played Rizzo and Vera played Frenchy." The woman extended her hand to Marnie. "I'm Anita Martin. Vera and I were hoping to meet you and welcome you back to the island. Chris told us you went to medical school here."

"Congratulations on your pregnancy. When's the big day?" Vera asked.

"Pleased to meet you both," Marnie said. "My due date is March 21 and I'm ready for it."

"Well, I hope you feel as good as you look," Anita said before she and Vera continued to embarrass Chris with reminiscences of high school hijinks. *Was Chris blushing?* Marnie made a point of smiling. After a few minutes she noticed Louise waving to her and pointing to her watch.

"Chris, it looks like Louise and Didier are getting ready to go," Marnie said. She turned to the ladies. "It was nice to meet both of you. And get some insight on my partner's high school days."

"I'm sure we'll be seeing each other again. Small island, right?" said Anita as she gave a quick wave to Louise. "Tell Louise hi for me. We ran a few 10ks together a while back."

"I will and I'll hope to join you when I get back in running shape."

"Cool," said Anita. "I'm managing the Third Coast Hotel. Let's get together for a drink when you're ready to get out of the house. I'd love to show y'all what we've done to the bar and restaurant."

"I run the day spa at the hotel," Vera added. "Please come see me when you want to relax. We offer a pregnancy pampering package." She and Anita turned to leave, waving at another group.

"Funny how funerals bring old friends together." Chris looked on as his classmates started laughing with another group. "Those two are having the times of their lives."

***

After the funeral, Chris, Didier, and Louise returned to work. Marnie went back home to tackle her 'Before the Baby is Born' list. Furniture ordered, birthing class scheduled, Aurora study on autopilot.

"Good time to take a short walk," she said to her pups. They jumped off the couch and ran to their leash drawer.

Walking around historic Galveston always settled Marnie. It was warm and sunny. She checked the weather in Colorado—thirty degrees and snowing. *I can't believe that I miss that, but I do. She rubbed her stomach. At least I can walk without fear of slipping here.*

"Thinking about being here when EJ was a baby," she said to Harlee and Jack. They wagged their tails in agreement. "Not that you were here. Twenty years and a lot of living since then. Hard to believe that my second pregnancy would bring me full circle geographically but to another life entirely than the one I thought I would have. Man plans and God laughs.

"But dinner time never waits. Let's head home."

Chapter 13

Monday afternoon, February 3, 2020

Dr. James Melvin pulled off his dark tie as soon as he returned home from Bruce's funeral. He looked at the funeral program. Bruce MacFarland looked back at him. *He looks a hell of a lot better in this picture than in the open casket. Must have been taken at least ten years ago.*

"We had some good times together, didn't we, buddy?" he said aloud.

The décor in his tenth-floor condominium was sparse. He preferred a few well-made pieces of furniture to the clutter that people his age accumulate. The past was the past and he had few good memories to hold onto. But today was different. Bruce's death had brought the past front and center. *Who would think that their boondoggle would end this way?* He poured himself a whiskey, downed it quickly and poured another. Darkness had gathered when he slumped into a chair facing south, gazing at the horizon.

He had few memories of his life before arriving in the US from Belarus at the age of nine, but one memory remained sharp. He had fallen off a high, grimy snowbank in Brest where he was engaged in a snowball fight with neighborhood kids. He was terrified and in pain. At the hospital an x-ray confirmed a broken femur. When the cast was removed, his right leg was half an inch shorter than the left. When his mother complained, she was told that at least he had two legs and could work for the good of the people in some capacity.

After his injury healed, his family escaped across the Polish border to Warsaw, then on to Gdansk where they were smuggled onto a cargo ship heading to the United States. They settled in the Belarusian community in Chicago, aided by Uncle Yakov who had made the trip ten years earlier.

Yuri Malekov became James Melvin. His limp prevented him from participating in sports, so he channeled his energy into his studies. His desire to help patients avoid a disability like his led him to choose a career in medicine. He married Layla, a nurse, introduced to him by Uncle Yakov.

After medical school, he accepted a coveted position in a general surgery residency. James was crushed when he was cut from the program in his third year. The program, like many surgical residencies at that time, was based on a pyramid model. He assumed the decision to cut him was based on an unspoken prejudice related to his disability. Or was it his Eastern European roots that rankled the White surgical faculty? The sting of rejection lingered but he pivoted to a pathology residency to complete his training. If he couldn't help living patients, he would find answers for the dead and their families.

During his first job at the Chicago Medical

Examiner's Office, he noted the elevated status of the chief medical examiner, often interviewed in the press and on television regarding high-profile murders. He wanted a piece of that. In 1996, now 42, he accepted a position in Galveston as assistant to the chief medical examiner. Five years later the chief succumbed to an aggressive cancer and James was promoted. Although Galveston was a sleepy backwater compared to Chicago, there were plenty of lurid crimes that brought his office into the limelight.

Layla did not like Galveston. She became progressively more depressed and resentful. She missed her tight knit community in Chicago. When their son finished middle school, she returned with him to Chicago. After a year of separation, they divorced. James sold the family home, taking only a few things for himself. The rest was shipped to Layla.

He remained in touch with his son, Mark. It was difficult to maintain a meaningful relationship or create memories. But he went above and beyond the terms of his divorce agreement in financial support for Mark. As a single physician with a high profile in the community, he had no problem finding female companionship. None of his liaisons led to long-term commitment. He was always the one to break things off when he grew bored or suspected his companions of gold digging. He had money to spend and preferred to spend it discreetly on luxury travel and make conservative investments. The former for him and the latter as a way of providing something in his estate for his son.

Chapter 14

Tuesday, February 4, 2020

At noon, Ben and EJ drove to the Galveston Police Department. The duty sergeant greeted them with a smile.

"Your mom said to expect you. Go on back to her office. You know the way."

EJ followed Ben down the hall to Detective Sudhan's office. The small room was only large enough for a desk and two chairs. Sudhan sat behind her desk and Torres occupied one of the chairs. EJ and Ben stood in the doorway. Torres glanced at Ben's and EJ's Bay City Daily press IDs.

"Hi, Ben. Journalism? Not police work, not medicine?" Torres asked.

"I'm not so sure yet, this is just an internship for us," Ben said and introduced EJ to Torres, explaining the family connections. "We thought we'd invite my mom out to lunch."

"Well, isn't that nice of you. And a pleasure to meet you, EJ. Chris and I go way back. It wasn't that long ago that he was a reporter nosing around the station," Torres said. Then addressing Sudhan, "I should have more information on some loose ends at the hospital on the MacFarland case by the end of day."

"Hold up a second, Torres," Sudhan said. "Which one of you wants to update Detective Torres about the Wood case? I spoke to Louise yesterday about reopening it. I got approval and requested the evidence be transferred to the ME's office for a second look. You two don't need to bribe me with lunch. You can reward me with lunch, instead."

EJ and Ben took turns explaining the story.

"Is this the case that the Bay City Daily ran the letter about last week?" Torres asked.

"Yes. Which reminds me," Sudhan said. "Have you got any tips?"

"Nothing helpful yet," said Ben.

Torres turned back to EJ and Ben. "Did you say that MacFarland worked that case? It was before my time in Galveston. MacFarland had a knack for getting in the middle of some nasty cases. That guy had quite a reputation around here."

"That's what we've heard," said EJ. "He was involved in an impressive number of arrests around the time Mr. Wood died and he kept quite busy clearing cases for years."

"How can I help?" asked Torres.

"To speed things up, we need someone from the department to head out to Texas City where the medical examiner's office has an overflow storage unit for evidence," Sudhan said. "You'll have to sign for it and check all the boxes to maintain the chain of custody. Then get it into the hands of Dr. Tina Garcia."

"Sure thing. Which one of you budding journalists

want to ride along on a visit to the morgue?"

"Count me in," said EJ. Ben nodded in agreement, although not very enthusiastically.

"I'll pick both of you up here in an hour. That should give me time to finish up with IT at the hospital."

"And time for me to claim my reward," Illiana said. "I'm in the mood for a bahn mi. Let's go, kids."

***

Torres pulled up in a department issued unmarked car. EJ and Ben were ready and waiting by the door. EJ slipped into the passenger seat and Ben took a seat in the back. Although the car looked like a well-worn sedan on the outside, EJ noted a complicated radio system and a computer attached to the dashboard.

"How do you like my ride?" Torres asked.

"I didn't know they still made Buicks," Ben wisecracked.

"We get junkers like this from the pound when the owners fail to pick them up. Then our mechanics give them a good going over and make some modifications," Torres said, indicating the electronics.

"Off to Texas City?" EJ asked.

"Yup. It's about a fifteen-minute drive. And not a very scenic one." Torres said as he pulled out.

Torres peppered Ben and EJ with questions about college life as they crossed the causeway to the mainland. He turned off I-45 onto Route 197 headed to Texas City. EJ took in the marshy wetlands as they gave way to enormous refineries and chemical plants. Huge spherical tanks loomed over the landscape.

"I've never been here before," she said.

"It's definitely not the part of Galveston County that the tourist board advertises," Ben said. "Kind of a hellscape."

They drove through the small downtown area of Texas City. When Torres stopped at the red light, EJ spotted a sign for Texas City Memorial Park. Statues and an obelisk were visible, surrounded by neat flower beds.

"Memorial for what?" she asked.

Ben was ready with the answer. "We learned about it in school. It sets another sad national record for Galveston County. The first being the Great Storm of 1900 that still ranks as the worst natural disaster in our history. In 1947, a ship caught fire in the Texas City harbor and caused a string of massive explosions. I think over five hundred people died. It's still considered the deadliest industrial accident in US history."

"Why the anchor?" EJ asked.

Torres said, "Apparently the blast was so strong that the anchor flew from the boat that exploded about two miles away. Windows were blown out back on Galveston Island, ten miles from here."

"And guess who came to the rescue of the injured, orphaned, and widowed? Sam Maceo, at the time our beloved Mafia boss. He staged a huge benefit at one of his nightclubs and donated all the proceeds," Ben added.

Torres was shaking his head. "You don't have to scratch too deep below the surface to discover the influence of organized crime around here. The Maceos knew how to keep the politicians and citizens happy while they ran their rackets in plain sight. Once the Maceos either died, went legit or moved to Las Vegas, they were replaced by the Mexican drug cartels."

"I bet you've had some run-ins with them," EJ said.

"More than you want to know. When I got here from Dallas in 2005, I learned that there was a smooth transition from the Maceo family to the cartels. And along with it, payoffs, and protection rackets in our police department."

"Like cops on the take?" EJ asked.

"Oh yeah. I heard stories. But that all got cleaned up when the old guard on the force retired and our local pols started paying attention."

EJ and Ben exchanged looks. Torres drove on. On the north side of town, he pulled up to a cinderblock building surrounded by a chain link fence that was topped with barbed wire. At the gate, he rolled down his window and spoke into the squawk box. The gate swung open.

"Better leave your Bay City Daily IDs in the car. I'll say that you two are with me on a ride-along," Torres instructed.

To EJ, the balding fellow who met them at the door appeared to be close to eighty. He surveyed the three of them as Torres politely explained the nature of their business.

The attendant turned his back to them and walked into an anteroom of the storage facility without another word. They followed. He went behind a counter and pulled out a document that he had apparently prepared ahead of their arrival.

"I'll need your IDs. Nothing and nobody comes in or out of here without me making a record of it," he growled, still avoiding eye contact.

"Understood," Torres said pleasantly. "Chain of custody and all."

After Torres, Ben, and EJ signed, the attendant initialed in multiple spots. Torres was provided with a copy of the paperwork. The attendant lifted a plastic container the size of two shoeboxes from under the counter. It was sealed with a bright yellow sticker that announced: WARNING Police Seal Do Not Remove. He scanned the barcode before handing it over.

Torres checked the name on the label and read aloud, "Luther Wood, January 11, 2002. Yup. This is it. Thanks for your help, sir."

"That's it then," the attendant said. He pushed a button unlocking the entrance to let them out. As they made their way to the car, EJ turned to look back and saw the attendant at the door. He was making a call on his cell phone.

With Torres in the lead carrying the evidence box, EJ said to Ben, "That was creepy."

"Yeah, and we haven't even gotten to the morgue yet."

"Do you know that guy, Detective Torres?" Ben asked once they were back on the main road.

"Nope. I got his name on the evidence document though. I imagine he was on the force at one time. Maybe he got this job to supplement his pension."

The refineries, chemical plants, and industrial parks stretched on until they got to their destination at the office of the County Medical Examiner in La Marque.

Torres needed to put the evidence box directly into the hands of Dr. Tina Garcia. After identifying themselves at the front desk, they were cleared to walk back to Tina's office. Both autopsy rooms were in use. EJ looked in the first room through the small window on the door and saw two people in full protective gear with bloody gloves exploring their patient's abdomen. She could see the deceased's feet extending outside of the field where the pathologists were at work. She was hit by a pang of sadness seeing the painted toenails. Ben kept his gaze laser focused on Torres's back until they arrived at Dr. Garcia's office.

While Torres organized the forms for signature, Tina greeted the interns. "Hi Ben, your mom said you would be dropping by. And you must be EJ Miller. Louise told me about your project. It sounds like you two are digging deep. I can't promise you I'll be of much help. It all depends on the condition of the evidence."

"It's nice to meet you, Dr. Garcia. We really appreciate you helping us out." EJ glanced at the container. "Any idea when you might have a chance to look at all this?"

"I've got some time this week. Let's hope this box has a thumb drive with the photos on it. My report will go to your mom, Ben, since she's the one who reopened this case."

"Ok, then. I've signed off everywhere I need to. I'll get these two back to the island before they come up with another errand for me," Torres said. "Let's hit the road."

***

When Chris arrived home at 7 p.m. Marnie put the news on pause and called out from the den. "I'm in here, watching TV."

Chris smiled to see Marnie looking relaxed with her feet up in the recliner and the dogs lying next to her on the couch. "Quite the domestic picture. Sorry I'm late."

"No problem," Marnie said. "I decided that we would have leftovers tonight since Rosa had the afternoon off for a dental appointment. I made a plate for myself but there's plenty for you."

"Sounds delicious. I was waiting for some proofs from my new hire in advertising, Charlotte Reeves, but she said it was going to take another hour. She said that she'd bring them by around eight."

"Glad to have you home for an extra hour. I know that running a newspaper isn't a nine to five job." When Chris was in the kitchen, Marnie thought of the promise she had made to her therapist. *Tonight might be the perfect time to tell him.*

An hour later, amid a downpour, the doorbell rang. "Come in, come in," Chris said to Charlotte, who, despite carrying an umbrella, was dripping wet.

"I'm going to get everything wet. Except the proofs. They're in this protective portfolio."

"Don't worry about it. This foyer was built with Galveston weather in mind."

As Charlotte shed her raincoat and umbrella, Marnie came into the room, followed by Jack and Harlee who enthusiastically gave Charlotte the smell test.

"Excuse my dogs. Their boundaries are a little weak." Marnie smiled and extended her hand. "I'm Marnie Liccione."

Taking Marnie's hand, Charlotte said, "Charlotte

Reeves. No problem about the dogs. I have a Heinz 57 mutt named Scooter." She turned to take in the home. "This is lovely. I'm a Galveston native and I always love a chance to see these historic homes," Charlotte said.

"Thank you," Chris said. "The renovations took years but we're glad to have it done before the baby is born."

Charlotte looked at the winding staircase going up from the foyer. "It looks like you placed the spindles according to the new codes. No chance of the baby falling through them."

Marnie laughed. "We had no idea that a baby would be in our lives when Chris coordinated the renovations, but he was conscientious about following new codes for everything. Finding more spindles to match the antique ones was a scavenger hunt."

Hugging Marnie close, Chris said, "Actually since Marnie's daughter was almost twenty when we met, I thought more about grandchildren than children. Let me go to my office to look at the proofs. Why don't you give Charlotte a tour of the house?"

Marnie smiled at Charlotte. "Would you like to see it?

"Oh yes!"

Marnie led Charlotte into the dining room. "This room has most of the original wainscoting. However, Chris gutted the kitchen. He rebuilt it with streamlined efficiency and modern appliances including an induction stovetop. We have a housekeeper—more like an abuela, Rosa, who loves all the new gadgets and quartz countertops."

Marnie continued the tour of the main floor from

the library, study, guest bedroom, bathroom to the sunroom. "I mostly use the sunroom as my office," Marnie said. "We plan to use the guest room as a downstairs nursery."

They continued upstairs where Marnie showed Charlotte the bedrooms with ensuite bathrooms and a playroom. One of the bedrooms had been turned into a nursery with a palette of yellow, blue, and white.

"I love the color scheme," Charlotte said. "I also love this rocking chair. Do you know the sex of your baby?"

Marnie rubbed her stomach. "A boy. We think his name is Jon."

"It's amazing to think of being able to grow a new person, isn't it? I'm for reproductive freedom but also pro-child. Every child should be a wanted child."

Somewhat surprised by Charlotte's forthright comment, Marnie said, "My feelings exactly."

Chris joined them when they went downstairs. "Sorry, that took me so long. EJ called while I was uploading the proofs and sending them to the night crew for inclusion. They looked great."

"I'm sorry for the delay. I'm afraid I ruined your evening," Charlotte said as she gathered her things.

"Not at all. It's a pleasure to meet you. I hope we see you around," Marnie said, thinking that Charlotte might become a new friend. "You should bring Scooter over for a playdate soon. The dogs and I are interested in making more friends in Galveston."

After Charlotte left, Marnie asked, "What did EJ say?"

"She said that she and Ben had reviewed the

police investigation of the Wood case with Dr. Garcia. Sudhan hadn't given them any information on new evidence."

"Do you think it's easier or harder to pump a detective for information if she's your mother?"

"If you were the detective, easier. From Iliana, I'm not sure," Chris said.

"Do you have a minute to sit and talk?"

"Of course."

As they settled back in the den, Marnie took a deep breath and glanced at Chris. "My therapist has been after me to tell you the details of EJ's birth."

Chris looked alarmed. "This sounds ominous."

"I was home alone on the third day after she was born, and I started having severe bleeding. It was terrifying—apparently my uterus had failed to continue shrinking. When it happened, it was so sudden I couldn't even get to the phone. Gen came by to say hello and found me in a pool of blood. When I was rushed to the hospital, they wanted to do a hysterectomy. I didn't want EJ to be an only child, something I always hated, so I refused. I told Adam to consent only if it was an absolute necessity. He helped the medical team make second-by-second decisions."

"Wow, how come you never told me?"

"It didn't seem relevant to our relationship until I became pregnant. Very unexpectedly. When Adam and I tried for our second child I had five miscarriages. Possibly related to my postpartum complication. Life went on and I just put it out of my mind until eight months ago. I never thought this pregnancy would work."

Chris looked at Marnie with tears in his eyes.

"Now I understand what you've been going through. I wondered why you seemed to be keeping your distance."

"Since passing the thirty-week mark, I've been thrilled with visions of our future together. Starting with meeting our son. But still, my postpartum period scares me. I don't want to be left alone for the first couple of weeks. So, work as hard as you need but know that you will be more homebound after the baby comes."

Chris drew Marnie, belly, and all, in for a tight hug. "Oh baby, I'm so sorry for your worries. I wish you'd told me. I'm going to make sure that the three of us get through this."

With tears running down her face, Marnie melted into Chris's embrace. She hadn't realized how keeping this burden to herself was weighing her down. Her therapist had told her to tell Chris. *I need to listen to her more.*

Reaching for tissues, Marnie shared them with Chris. As they blew their noses and dried their tears. Chris took a deep breath. "It's been a long and busy day. Let's head to bed."

"I'm exhausted," Marnie said. "But relieved."

Chris hugged her all the way upstairs.

Chapter 15

Wednesday, February 5, 2020

At 10 a.m. Ben and EJ arrived at the police department. Ben had a bouquet of roses. Sudhan smiled at the open bribery. "I'll give Tina a call and see if she had time to look at the evidence."

Tina answered her phone on the first ring. "I was just about to call you."

"Great minds think alike. The cub reporters you met are in my office," Sudhan said. "Do you mind if I put you on speaker?"

"No problem. But I would prefer that this conversation not be recorded."

Sudhan shot a look at Ben, and he clicked off his phone. EJ got ready to take notes.

"You really made me hit the books on this one," Tina said. "We got very lucky with the condition of the evidence. If Mr. Wood's body parts were in the water, they weren't there for very long."

"Interesting," Sudhan murmured.

"I'll try to summarize. Sections of tissue from all the available fragments of his body were taken and microscope slides were made from each. One of them contained material from his throat around the area of his voice box. It showed an impressive amount of edema, or swelling, and congestion. All of which indicates a sudden reaction to something."

"Reaction? I'm not following," Sudhan said.

"Suggestive of an allergic reaction. Like the kind of fatal reaction we see when people are highly allergic to peanuts or insect venom. Anaphylaxis. A hypersensitivity reaction that causes the airways to swell and cuts off respiration. This reaction causes the circulatory system to go into shock. Basically, it's sudden death due to an allergic reaction."

EJ was scribbling furiously.

"But like I said, these findings are suggestive. The only test we can hang our hat on to diagnose anaphylaxis is a tryptase level. That requires a frozen serum sample which we don't have. Then, this is where we got lucky. One of the slides came from a fragment identified as an 'internal organ.' Meaning it was probably a mushy mess to the naked eye and hard to tell which organ it was. But the slides helped us out here. Under the microscope, it's easy for the trained eye to determine tissue type. Several slides from this fragment were from Wood's spleen. The tissue showed an unusual infiltration of mast cells and eosinophils."

"Of what cells?" Sudhan asked. "Come on Tina, you're talking to lay people. Help us understand the significance of these findings."

"That's what I'm getting at. We sometimes see

those cells in the spleens of patients who have had an anaphylactic reaction. Without a tryptase level, it's about the only way we can be sure of the diagnosis. We don't see anything like this in drownings or shark bites." Her excitement came through over the phone.

"Meaning the cause of death doesn't appear to be caused by a shark attack?" EJ asked.

"Exactly. Now bear with me a minute more while I tell you about shark attacks. We all know how rare they are. I had to do some digging in Australian literature. They have more experience with fatal shark attacks down under. I looked at tons of photographs from autopsies. Shark teeth sometimes show up in the victim's tissue. The teeth marks are characteristic. And guess what? Neither teeth marks nor teeth are noted in any of the photos of Wood's body parts. What the pictures do show when I look with a magnifying glass, are blunt force hacking marks perhaps from an ax. And saw marks on the bony fragments."

Illiana looked at Ben and EJ. "Tina, how are you going to read this out?"

"I'm going to correct the record and list the cause of death as an anaphylactic reaction and make note that the body parts were mutilated with tools postmortem." Tina paused. "It's an answer for the family. I'm sorry it's such a grisly one."

"Thank you for your help, Tina. It looks like a new case just fell into my lap."

"Yeah, it does," Tina replied, and before hanging up she added, "EJ and Ben, proceed carefully. There could be a lot more to this story."

***

"Does this mean we're going to blow this case wide open?" EJ asked Ben as they settled into their desk chairs in adjacent cubicles.

"I don't know," said Ben. "What about Dr. Garcia's warning to 'proceed carefully'? Not to mention what my mom said before we left."

"About Luther Wood's case being reopened? That's exactly what we wanted to happen."

"No, not that part. The part about this all being a police case now and that we need to let the police do their work. I think we need to talk to Chris about how we should proceed as reporters. I'm sure I don't need to tell you that my mom will not be giving me, or us, any special treatment."

"Point taken. I hope we get the byline when this story goes to print. I'll text Chris to see when we can meet." EJ tapped on her phone. "In the meantime, we can get caught up on our research about Bruce MacFarland's activity around the time of the Wood case."

Ben began scrolling through notes on his laptop. "Not to mention his untimely death. Do we dare go there?"

"I sure hope so." EJ's phone chirped. "Chris says tomorrow at nine. He wants a draft of our background articles. He added a slightly smiley face emoji for some reason. Maybe trying to be ironic?" They laughed. "We better get cracking. I don't think he'll give us a green light on MacFarland until we get our first assignments turned in."

At 5:30, EJ pushed her chair back and stretched.

"I hit the wall. I think I have enough copy to show Chris. How are you doing?"

"Same. I've found lots of material on Galveston circa January 2002. It was relatively quiet on the hurricane front that year. But lots of local political jockeying. The hotel consortium was busy debating bringing gambling back to the island. It got heated."

"Okay. I'm sending him my draft." EJ pushed send and closed her laptop. She looked at her phone as she gathered her belongings and dashed off a text reply to Taylor. *He must have read my mind.* "Ben, I'm off. See you tomorrow."

Once in her car, she put the address on M street into her GPS and pulled out of the lot, trying to avoid the potholes. She'd heard talk in the break room that they were really sinkholes due to the frequent inundations that weaken the sandy ground all over the island. If that was the case, EJ hoped she wouldn't be swallowed up by one before getting Luther Wood's case solved.

She drove along the I-45 access road, heading east. It soon turned into Broadway Avenue, taking her past taquerias, pho cafes, car repair shops and every imaginable religious denomination's place of worship. She turned south on 12th Street through a jumble of bungalows and apartment complexes until she reached her destination. Taylor had warned her that the MacFarland homestead needed a major update. *He wasn't exaggerating.*

She parked on the street and walked up the short driveway to the rambling ranch house. A young man with a ponytail was pulling weeds in the front garden. He stood up straight and wiped the sweat from his brow as EJ walked up the cracked concrete path.

"Hi, this is the MacFarland place, right? I'm meeting a friend here," EJ said with a smile. "Have you seen Taylor? Taylor Wood? He's Mrs. MacFarland's realtor."

Foster paused for a moment before answering. "He's inside with Mrs. Mac trying to help her get this place ready to show. As am I." He held up his gardening tool and grinned. "I'm Foster."

"Nice to meet you. I'm EJ," she said. "Wait. Have I seen you at Feathers? Didier LaSalle's birding store?"

"That would be me. A little better dressed than I am today. You know my boss?" He pulled out a tissue just in time to catch a loud sneeze. His eyes were watering. "Sorry, allergies. Even in the winter."

"Gesundheit," EJ said before once again explaining the family and friend connections. It was becoming a routine as she met new people in Galveston. "I'm working as an intern at the Bay City Daily. My mom's partner is the editor there."

Foster nodded. His eyes locked on EJ as Taylor came out the front door.

"Hi there," he said as he slid his arm around EJ's waist. "Glad you got off in time to see the place. I see you met Foster. I don't know how we could get this place ready to show without his help. Do you want to come in and meet Mrs. MacFarland and look around? See what I'm up against?"

Foster laughed, acknowledging Taylor's plight. "Nice to meet you EJ."

"Same here. I'll look for you next time I'm in Feathers."

Taylor opened one of the massive wooden double doors and led EJ into the foyer. Her gaze immediately fixed on a floor to ceiling mural of a Tuscan garden scene. She was about to ask if this house had belonged to one of Galveston's mafiosi before coming into Bruce's hands, when Mrs. MacFarland entered the great room from the kitchen.

"Mrs. MacFarland, this is my friend EJ Miller. EJ, Mrs. MacFarland. We were just talking about repairs that need to be done and maybe some staging of the house before it goes on the market," Taylor said.

"Pleased to meet you, EJ," Yvonne said. "It's so nice to have all you young people around. It helps take my mind off …"

"I'm sorry for your loss, Mrs. MacFarland," EJ said.

Yvonne blinked back tears.

After a moment, Taylor said, "I asked EJ over to look at your home. She has a real eye for décor." He gave EJ a subtle wink.

"Taylor is trying to convince me to have a decorator stage the house. He says that staging can add $40,000 to the asking price. But I just don't know if it feels right. I do know Bruce would never let that happen if he were here."

"I'm sure this is overwhelming," EJ said, looking left and right. "This house has good bones. Maybe storing a few larger pieces would allow potential buyers to imagine their furniture in these lovely rooms." She stopped there, having exhausted her knowledge of real estate talk and staging.

"I have a few more rooms to photograph," Taylor

said. "Can I give EJ a quick tour, Mrs. MacFarland?"

"Certainly, dear. I'll look over the information you gave me while you finish up. Maybe you're right about staging."

Taylor used his phone to snap some pictures. To EJ's surprise, there were more murals. And some of the bedroom ceilings were decorated with cherubs. The paintings looked amateurish. "Is Mrs. MacFarland the artist? These are dreadful!" she whispered to Taylor.

"No idea. I just know I'll have to do some fast talking to get her to agree to cover them," he whispered back. Then in a normal voice, "This is the study."

"The paneling is beautiful," EJ said as she looked around, glad that she was ready with a compliment as Yvonne had joined them.

"This was Bruce's favorite room. You could call it his man cave." She pointed out an enormous, mounted fish. "He was so proud of that marlin. He managed all our finances from that desk over there and filled those file cabinets with paperwork he brought home with him from work. Now I'll have to manage for myself and deal with all his files." Her voice became shaky.

"One day at a time, Yvonne," said another woman who had entered and put her arm around her shoulder. The cluttered study was becoming crowded.

"I know, Betty, I know." Yvonne introduced her sister to EJ. "Betty has been my rock."

"We all need someone to rely on in times like this," Taylor said. "And please take your time with any decisions." Both older women smiled at him. "I think I have enough pictures to get started. I'll be back tomorrow to take some measurements and talk some more."

"Thank you for letting me see your beautiful home, Mrs. MacFarland. I'm sorry it's under these circumstances." EJ edged out of the study.

Taylor and EJ slipped out the front door. There was no sign of Foster. They headed to their cars, both parked on the street.

"I was about to start laughing." EJ grinned.

"I like to make you laugh."

"Let's meet at Garrett's, the place where we had lunch. I have something important to tell you. And it's not about interior design."

"Something important? Tell me."

"Not here. Trust me. See you at Garrett's." She was no longer smiling.

***

Garrett's Trattoria was hopping. The wait for a table was an hour. When Garrett saw EJ and Taylor standing in the foyer, he waved them over. "I have a private table in the back by the kitchen. If you're willing to take that, you can avoid the wait."

EJ gave Garrett a hug. "Thanks! We're starving."

"Can we let you choose our meal again?" Taylor asked.

Garrett smiled. "Love to." He headed to the kitchen.

EJ and Taylor ordered beers.

"What's up?" Taylor asked.

EJ reached across the table for Taylor's hands. "We got the police to request a review of your father's autopsy results. You were right. There was no shark attack." She stopped and watched Taylor as this settled in.

"How *did* he die?"

EJ told him what she had learned from the pathologist.

Taylor let go of EJ's hands. He leaned back in his chair, his shoulders slumped. "Wow, it's hard to believe that the answer was right there all these years. And nobody would even look."

"I'm sorry that this happened to your family. The police have reopened the case. It's a cold case but at least it's open."

Taylor sat quietly looking at the floor. When he looked up, he said, "I've kind of lost my appetite. I need to move. Can you make my excuses to Garrett?"

No problem. If you want, I can square with him and walk with you."

Taylor smiled sadly. "Thanks, EJ, but I need to be alone. Maybe we can walk tomorrow?"

"Text me."

Garrett came over to the table when he saw Taylor leave. "Lovers' quarrel?"

"Not lovers and not a quarrel. Taylor got some sad news. Do you mind boxing up our meals? I'll take Taylor's to my mom and make her evening."

"Gladly. Give her my best."

Chapter 16

Thursday, February 6, 2020

Chris, EJ, and Ben sat at the table in the conference room, laptops open. Chris continued to read and occasionally typed a few words. EJ caught Ben's nervous glance.

This was the first assignment they had received. When they started at the Daily, their days consisted of rotations through the various sections, meeting the editors, observing the workflow, and getting an idea of what went into publishing a daily newspaper.

Two semesters of journalism were required for internship at The Daily. Experience on a college paper was looked upon favorably. Ben had been the sports editor at the Rice Thresher. EJ had taken journalism as an elective, with only the vaguest idea about her post college career path. She was quite sure she was accepted at the Daily because of her connection to the managing editor.

Chris looked up and took a sip of coffee. "Not bad. Good start, both of you."

EJ and Ben sat back, relieved.

"I'm reviewing your work to make sure your leads make sense, and your stories are fair and balanced. From here they go to the copy editor. That's where both of you'll see the red ink."

Chris turned to EJ. "I like the way you used some quotes from the archives. Citizens were clamoring for more police intervention to take down the meth labs in their neighborhoods. You could put more emphasis on the fact that Galveston has long been a hub for distribution of drugs for Mexican cartels. The Gulf Cartel has been running protection rackets very similar to the ones the Mafia had in place back in the 1950s. Nice touch mentioning the involvement of the MS-13 gang. It might be a good hook to mention their penchant for murder by dismemberment in relation to Luther Wood's death."

"Yeah, I'll make those additions. I wasn't sure how far to go with the gruesome details."

Chris went back to reading. "We should also highlight what you have here about Black citizens complaining about police brutality. It looks like we reported it and then looked the other way for a long time. Let's bring that forward.

"Ben, you did a good job profiling the business and political power brokers on the island during our time frame. Good pick up on the local battle about gambling. Bringing it back to Galveston comes up every few years and gets people riled up on both sides. I recognized several names from the 2003 hotel consortium that sound familiar today. Maybe family members? Cross reference the names you mention with current local pols and hoteliers." Chris shut his laptop. "I'd like those revisions by noon. Then I'll send your pieces over to the copy editor. Any questions?"

"I guess we'd like to talk to you about next steps

regarding the Wood case and the letter. Have you talked to Sudhan about the autopsy findings?" EJ asked.

"She gave me a heads up," Chris looked at EJ. "And asked me to make sure we didn't get ahead of ourselves on that just yet. She wants to discuss the findings with the remaining family. That would be this young man, Taylor, that you've been seeing, right?"

"Of course, right," EJ said quickly. "Makes sense."

"As for next steps, I'll have Tom forward you all the responses we got after publishing the letter. It will be a good exercise for you two to sift through them. Apparently, there was skepticism about the shark attack from people who knew Luther Wood. Plus, a fair number of loony conspiracy theories to wade through. But who knows, maybe you'll find something of interest there. I kind of doubt it, but more eyes never hurt."

EJ and Ben walked down the hall to their cubicles.

"That went well, don't you think?" she asked Ben.

"Definitely." He paused. "You already told him, didn't you? Taylor, about the autopsy results?"

"I thought he needed to know what I knew. But now I realize it was impulsive of me."

"How did he take it?"

"That's what worries me. I think the brutality of it fed the fire for revenge that's been smoldering all these years. Now that he knows *what* happened, I'm afraid of what he might do when he finds out *who* did it." EJ sighed. "We're meeting for lunch. I'll suggest we go together to talk to your mom. She'll be mad at me for jumping the gun."

"Let me know if you need back up." Ben said with a smile. "I doubt it's the first-time information leaked from the police department."

Chapter 17

Thursday, February 6, 2020

Marnie sat in her sunroom drinking her second cup of coffee—decaf. *I'm thirty-two weeks into this pregnancy.* She rubbed her stomach. *Hard to believe that we made it.* She glanced at the clock. *I have fifteen minutes until I need to leave for my appointment. Why is it so hard to get out of this chair and get going? My counselor will be glad that I told Chris about my postpartum bleed. Still, sharing is hard.*

Her phone rang. "Hi Louise, what's up?"

"Just calling to see how you're feeling and if you heard any updates on the Wood case."

"I'm feeling fine. Trying to get up the energy to go to therapy. But to the other half of your question, yes, EJ told me the case has been reopened and gave me the details of the autopsy. Do you think this death relates to MacFarland?"

"I wonder," Louise said. "Didier told us that Bruce was talking more and more about his old cases. Apparently he was the lead detective on the Wood investigation which we now know was mishandled—

probably intentionally."

"I must run to make my appointment. Shall we meet for lunch? Maybe invite Tina?"

"Good idea. I'll text you the details. See you later."

Marnie took a deep breath as she sat in her car outside her therapist's office. She had started seeing Dr. Rogers shortly after relocating to Galveston. *I felt like I was coming apart. New relationship, difficult pregnancy, new house, loss of my professional status. Too much.*

Dr. Rogers was warm, supportive, and skilled. She was also no-nonsense. She told Marnie that there was no need to work with people who basically liked their lives but wanted to complain. That's what friends were for, she said. If Marnie wanted some help in figuring out where she wanted to be in a year, how she would stitch the new pieces of her life together, Dr. Rogers was there to listen and guide.

It's just exhausting though. As doctors, we're quick to recommend therapy. I can understand why people find it hard to follow through—emotionally and financially.

The forty-five-minute appointment went quickly. Marnie told Dr. Rogers about her conversation with Chris. How it had lifted a burden from her.

"I'm so happy for you, Marnie. I'm glad you're feeling comfortable enough to share the responsibility you've taken on with this pregnancy. You've said before that since Adam died you felt you couldn't count on anyone but yourself. Life isn't like that. We must be prepared for being alone, but we must count on those around us. It's the human condition. We live, we rejoice, we mourn, together. Endings and beginnings." She smiled. "These next few weeks will go fast. I'm eager to meet this new baby. Continue to take care of yourself. I'll see you next week."

As she left the office, Marnie felt a sense of peace that had eluded her since her move. It's going to work out. She was glad that she had a lunch date. And a mystery to solve.

***

At Oscar's Seawall Grill Tina, Louise, and Marnie sat at a table looking over the Gulf. The sea was calm and deep blue. A rare occurrence in Galveston where the silty Gulf water was usually a light shade of brown. Seagulls squawked as they dove for bait near the pier.

The women placed their orders and sat back in anticipation of their meal. "Trust your patient to open a can of worms for my department," Tina said, looking at Louise.

"Ok," Louise said. "Lunch is on me. What can you tell us?"

"Since you were the primary doctor for Mr. MacFarland, I'll let you know what we didn't find. His drug screen was negative except for a small amount of morphine that can be explained by his hospital medication orders. Apparently, it had been administered earlier in the evening when he complained of pain."

Final cause of death?" Marnie asked.

Microscopic evidence of excessive air was found in his brain. Air embolism. The hospital administrators are very concerned. They want it documented that the central line showed signs of tampering. An accidental embolism puts them at risk."

Their waiter arrived with their lunches. They compared notes on their orders before continuing the conversation.

"Sudhan told me that there was an unidentified lab technician in his room that night shortly before he died," Louise said.

"A technician with syringes? That could explain it," said Tina.

A vague memory tugged at Marnie's brain. Shaking her head to clear her thoughts, Marnie said, "I have to say that, because of EJ's interest in Taylor Wood, I'm more interested in that case. What can you tell us about Luther Wood's death?"

"I'm afraid that information is confidential," Tina said. "The timing of its release will be up to the police."

Tina looked up from her plate and nodded as a man approached their table. "Hi Dr. Melvin."

"Hello Tina. Are you ladies having a good lunch?"

Louise's back stiffened at the salutation. "As a matter of fact, yes. A working lunch."

Dr. Melvin smiled. "How is the beautiful expectant mother?"

Marnie locked eyes with Dr. Melvin and smiled back. "Enjoying my lunch."

"I will leave you to it then." Dr. Melvin turned and walked away.

Marnie stared after him and turned to Tina. "How did he get that limp?"

"Oh, I think it was from a childhood accident.

When he was still working, he wore a lift in his shoe to hide the limp."

Marnie nodded and continued to study him as he walked away.

Louise looked at her watch. "Lovely as this is, I need to get back to work. I'll pay on my way out." She reached over and squeezed Marnie's hand. "Glad your appointment with Dr. Rogers went well. Talk to you soon."

After Louise left, Marnie turned to Tina. "What's your take on Dr. Melvin?"

"He's smart. Worked hard. Kept his department under tight control. There were rumors about ethics."

"A ladies man?"

"In Galveston a single man in his sixties with money has a big field."

"Any long-term relationships?"

"Not that I've heard about. Now I need to get back to work. Good to see you, Marnie. You really do have a pregnancy glow."

"Thanks. I'll be happy to have a baby and the tired look of a new mommy."

***

After running a few errands, Marnie was relieved to pull into her driveway. *That took longer than I thought it would. I'm exhausted.* She was surprised to see a strange car next to EJ's. She was even more surprised when she went into her kitchen and found a tall young man with vivid green eyes looking at her from the open door of her fridge.

"Oh hi! Didn't mean to startle you. I'm Taylor. EJ said to get a couple of beers from the fridge and meet her on the porch. She took the dogs on a run."

"Hi. I'm Marnie." She couldn't suppress a grin at Taylor's discomfort. "And this is my fridge. It's very nice to meet you."

Taylor smiled. "I guess we should have warned you. EJ left you a voice message about what was happening, but I guess you didn't get it."

Marnie looked at her phone. She hated beeping interruptions, so she usually kept it on silent. Sure enough, there was a voicemail from EJ. "I missed it. Glad not to have to walk the dogs though. Let me grab a seltzer and join you on the porch."

Marnie was glad to sit on the porch which looked out upon the native garden, with a few exceptions, that Chris had installed. The imported daffodils were in full bloom. Chris promised bluebonnets in March.

"I really can't believe that I'm enjoying seventy degrees and sun in early February. Too many winters in Colorado."

"I've never been to Colorado. EJ has great stories about it."

"You're in real estate, right?"

"Yes, though to be honest that isn't why I'm here."

"EJ told me about your father's death."

"We just came from the PD. I sort of broke down and started yelling at them. I know that these weren't the police in charge of the original investigation but…EJ took me for a walk to calm down." He looked up at Marnie. "I really want someone to pay. Whoever murdered him and whoever covered up the crime."

"I can't say I blame you one bit."

Regaining his composure, Taylor said, "EJ thought we could rustle up something to eat here."

"It's the least I can do since I ate your dinner last night," Marnie said smiling. "Rosa left a casserole for dinner tonight. I'll put it in the oven. There should be plenty since I'm still full after lunch at Oscar's. You can wait here. I'll be right back."

When Marnie looked back at Taylor from the doorway, he had his head in his hands. Grief radiated off him.

"Hi Mom," EJ said as she entered the kitchen with the dogs. She went to the sink to wash her face and hands. "We did a quick mile. I assume you met Taylor?"

Harlee and Jack were jumping up and down around Marnie like Tiggers on pogo sticks.

"Calm down, goofuses. I've been gone for a few hours not overnight. Let me get your dinners."

"I'll feed them, Mom, while you get our dinner going. I'm sure some food will help settle Taylor too." EJ added in a whisper, "He was so angry. Scary angry."

Marnie put the casserole in the oven and sliced some cheese and vegetables. She added crackers to the appetizer tray and handed it to EJ. "Take this out to him to tide him over. I'll be out in a minute."

EJ and Taylor were deep into conversation when Marnie returned to the porch.

"No, Taylor, don't go. Stay for dinner." EJ looked pleadingly at her mom.

"What's going on?" Marnie asked.

Taylor stood up and began to pace. "Thinking

about what happened has me all churned up. I can't believe that all these years, nobody listened to my mom. I knew Bruce MacFarland was the detective on my dad's case," he blurted. "I've had my eye on him since I got back to Galveston. I was walking back and forth outside the hospital the night he died. I don't think it's a good time to meet Chris."

Marnie and EJ exchanged looks.

Marnie quickly said, "You may be right about that. He wasn't editor for most of the time your mom wrote the letters. But anyway, he's not going to be home for dinner. He has a board meeting."

EJ chimed in, "Let's get some food in you and talk about what we know and what we don't. And you can tell us about your dad. We've heard such wonderful things about him, but all second hand. He sounds like a very special man."

Taylor softened and smiled. "I'd like that. I'd like to tell you about my dad."

Chapter 18

Friday February 7, 2020

Ever since her therapy appointment Marnie's mood had been better. *I can feel my depression lifting.* She heard the hummingbirds buzzing in her garden. *I could offer them a boost for their migration north. Instead of thinking—too much work-- I could go to Feathers for feeders.*

As she parked in front of Feathers, she noticed the new storefront. *Very inviting. I haven't been here since Didier remodeled.*

A tall young man with a blond ponytail and lightly tinted glasses greeted her. "Hi, I'm Foster. How can I help you today?"

"Hi, I'm Marnie. I want to put out a hummingbird feeder, and maybe a squirrel-proof bird feeder."

"There really isn't a completely squirrel-proof bird feeder but this green one over here is the best we have. The weight of the squirrel shuts off access to the bird seeds."

"It looks sort of tricky to install."

"I, with my boss's permission, have a side hustle doing installations."

Marnie smiled. "Didier is smart to offer that service."

Just then Didier came into the store. "Marnie! Great to see you. You look fabulous!"

Marnie leaned over as he kissed her on the cheek. "Compliments are always welcome. I love the new storefront."

"Thank you. I see you and Foster met. We've been so busy that it's great to have steady help."

"I understand he installs in his spare time."

"For you, whenever you want."

"I'm off tomorrow afternoon," Foster said.

"Perfect. I do have a question for you, Didier. Why, if we are instructed to never feed wildlife, is it ok to feed birds?"

"Good question. The answer is not straight forward. Pros about feeding the birds is that it makes up for loss of natural habitat and helps survival of migratory birds. Cons are that it has birds congregating which increases the risk of spreading diseases. We recommend that you clean your feeder every two weeks and hummingbird feeders at least every week. We don't recommend bird feeders to people with outdoor cats."

Marnie laughed. "Good thing my kitty, Mateo, is hanging out with a house sitter in Colorado. She turned to Foster. "How about tomorrow afternoon at two for the installation? Here's my address."

"I'll be there."

After Marnie completed her purchase and left the store, Didier said to Foster, "You forgot to take your sunglasses off again indoors. Our customers will think you've been enjoying some herbal medicine."

Foster laughed. "I keep forgetting to take off these new glasses. They lighten up so much when I'm indoors."

***

Friday evening, EJ was excited to see Taylor. She had almost gone home with him the night before, but they had decided to give themselves twenty-four hours to cool off. Every time they touched, she felt an electric buzz. She had parked at the Third Coast Hotel, where Taylor was staying, and met him at the bar. She loved this old hotel with its panoramic view of the Gulf. He smiled when he saw her and put down the flier he'd picked up regarding the hotel's history.

"I've ordered us top-notch margaritas and nachos. I hope that's not too presumptuous."

"Great choices."

As they talked about Galveston and its quirky history, EJ focused on Taylor's broad and easy smile. They laughed about the Ghost Bride, supposedly seen from time to time in the window of Room 501, waiting for her fiancé to return from the sea. She loved the twinkle in his eyes when he talked about his extended family in Dallas and the crazy cookouts they had. The margarita was helping loosen the tension EJ had felt all week.

They took sips of their drinks. EJ noticed a woman approaching from behind Taylor. She was smiling directly at her.

"Hi, would you be EJ Miller?" the woman asked. Before EJ could put her drink down and answer, she continued. "I'm Anita Martin. Cousin Garrett told me your friend was staying here. Taylor, right?"

EJ and Taylor swiveled on their stools. "Oh, yeah. Garrett told us you were the manager here. A distant cousin?" asked EJ.

"Kissing cousins is what we called it." Anita laughed and tossed her dark hair back. Looking directly at Taylor, she continued, "Garrett says you're in real estate? I hope you're ready for a roller coaster ride on this island."

Taylor met her gaze with a smile and shrugged. "I heard it can get wild but I'm going to give it a shot."

Keeping her attention riveted on Taylor, Anita continued, "Well you're young enough to roll with the punches. Good luck to you. And let me know if I can do anything to make your stay here more enjoyable. This is my direct line." She handed Taylor her business card. "Pleasure to meet you both."

Anita turned and walked toward the reception desk. EJ noticed Taylor taking in Anita's full figure. Her shapely legs and curvy butt were accentuated by a tight dress and stiletto heels.

EJ laughed. "I think Anita was more pleased to meet you than me. She looks ready to show you more island hospitality than Garrett expected."

"There's only one woman on this island whose hospitality I'm interested in." Taylor slid his stool closer to EJ and pressed his leg against hers. "Ready to walk to the Pleasure Pier?"

"Yes." EJ gathered her light jacket, and Taylor helped her put it on. His hands lingered on her shoulders.

As they walked along the seawall, the wind picked

up and the temperature dropped. Taylor moved close and put his arm around EJ. "Not too cold?"

"Way too cold," EJ said. "Let's go back to your room."

"Should I take that as an invitation to do more than talk?"

"Absolutely."

Taylor used his key card to operate the elevator to the tenth floor. When he got to his room, he smiled. EJ felt a flush of happiness and a warmth wash over her. It had been a long time since she had felt this way.

The room was a small suite with the bed tucked behind a half wall. *Very neat and clean.*

"Would you like a beer?" Taylor asked.

"Sure."

"I bought some of the lagers you liked just in case the evening went this way."

EJ sat down on the sofa in front of the TV, flattered by his attentiveness.

"Nice room."

"I get a good rooming allowance from my company and felt that, since I would be in Galveston for a bit, I should enjoy myself. My family never stayed in nice hotels when I was growing up."

EJ thought about all the sweet trips she had had with her parents. *Different worlds.*

"Anything you want to watch?" Taylor asked as he held the remote.

"The Rockets? They're playing the Denver Nuggets tonight."

Taylor obliged. As they sat close together, EJ leaned over to Taylor and put her head on his shoulder.

He turned his head to her and placed a gentle kiss on her lips. She met him eagerly.

His left hand traveled up her back and caressed the side of her breast. EJ moaned encouragement. His other hand went to the back of her head, and he pulled her in close. Their tongues explored each other's mouths. Hot and heavy.

EJ stood up and pulled Taylor into the bedroom.

"We both want this right?" EJ asked.

"Very much."

"Give me a minute." EJ went into the bathroom and undressed. She slipped her long t-shirt back on and entered the bedroom. Taylor had turned down the bed and was lying under the sheet.

"You're beautiful," he said.

"Compliments will get you everything." EJ slipped under the sheet.

Taylor rolled over on top of her and gently slipped off her t-shirt. He nuzzled her neck and kissed her lips. His kisses traveled down her neck and to her breasts. He gently sucked her nipples. His hands caressed her stomach and traveled down between her thighs.

EJ felt her excitement grow. *This feels so good.* She placed her hands along his back and slid them down his firm hips. She could feel his erection, large and taut between them.

Taylor slid his hand between her thighs. She was warm and wet. He turned halfway away and started to put on his condom. EJ reached down to help. Then she rolled on top of him and let her breasts rub his chest. Their eyes were open and locked on each other.

Slowly EJ lowered herself onto him. She wanted

to fill a void inside her. As their rhythm grew more intense, Taylor pulled EJ close and flipped them both over. EJ locked her legs behind his back and lifted to meet his thrusts. Then all senses dimmed, and she gave herself over to her orgasm. As she started to climax, Taylor let himself follow with primal thrusts.

As they lay still, their breathing quieted. They remained in an embrace, not wanting the moment to end.

EJ was first to break the silence. "More fun than a hot dog on the pier? All puns intended," EJ said.

Taylor pulled her close and nuzzled her neck. "Yes, but now I'm starving."

EJ checked her watch. "Let's grab a quick sandwich downstairs. Then I should go. My mom's been trying to pull herself together lately and I want to see her before she goes to bed."

Taylor smiled. "It's been a while since I had to worry about a mom."

"It's weird living so close to Chris and Mom. But it is convenient. It's just that a lot is going on right now and I don't want to increase Mom's anxiety. I want it to be easy for you and me to be together."

"I'm all for that," Taylor pulled her close for one more long kiss.

***

That same evening Chris and Marnie, and the two dogs, were cuddled on the recliner sofa in front of the TV. They were watching the local news, weather, and sports. A story about the murder of a young man concluded that his death was retribution for a gang member's arrest. The victim was made out to be a snitch.

"Is it my imagination or is Galveston just as crime ridden now as it was when the mob was in control," Marnie asked.

"Not a chance, figures show that…" Chris began.

"Do I hear EJ's car?" Marnie interrupted and turned toward the window facing the garage.

"Where did you say EJ was?" Chris asked.

"She's out with Taylor."

"What do you think about that?"

"I'm afraid that she's in love and I can't say that I really trust the guy. He's carrying a lot of baggage. I'm hoping that as more is revealed about his dad's death, he'll be able to meet you. If it hadn't been for you, the case wouldn't have been re-opened."

"Still, I understand his anger."

"I just hope he can channel it constructively."

Chris nodded and shrugged. "I'm going to head upstairs. It's been a long day." He gave Marnie a kiss on her forehead. "I'll leave you and EJ alone to talk."

EJ called out, "Hi Mom, Chris? Where are you?"

"I'm in the TV room," Marnie answered.

When EJ came into the room, Marnie noticed a rosy glow. "Looks like you had a nice time," Marnie said.

EJ blushed. "We did. Had a hot dog on the pier and then walked to his hotel. Talked about a lot of things unrelated to the investigation. He's wondering how long he wants to sell real estate and what he might do next."

Marnie was sure they did a lot more than talk.

"Are you taking precautions?"

"Are you asking if we are being smarter than you

and Chris?”

Marnie was stung. “I guess I am.”

“The answer is yes.” Changing the subject she said, “He’s thinking he might come to New Haven for my graduation ceremony this spring. He’s never been to the East Coast.”

“EJ, I like Taylor, but we don’t really know him that well. Try not to get too involved until these cases settle out.”

EJ nodded. “May be too late for that. I do trust him.” EJ smiled. “I’m sure you’ll get there.”

Chapter 19

Saturday, February 8, 2020

When she came down Saturday morning, Marnie found Chris removing a batch of Rosa's previously frozen cinnamon rolls from the oven.

"Mmm, the smell of those rolls baking woke me up."

Chris pulled Marnie into a hug. "Sorry—not sorry—about that." He kissed her behind her ear.

Marnie leaned into him. "You're forgiven—not forgiven."

They took their coffee and rolls to their breakfast nook which shared the view of the back yard with their porch. The birds were already busy.

"Early birds catch more than worms," Marnie said.

"Whose job will it be to clean the bird feeder every two weeks?"

Marnie put her finger to her nose.

"You aren't pulling the finger-on-nose, not-it gag, are you?"

"You're it."

Chris groaned. "What time is the feeder getting installed? Any chance we could hire Foster to clean it biweekly?"

Marnie laughed. "I'm sure we can. Anything on your agenda this weekend?"

"I need to spend a few hours at the paper. I plan to do that at some point today. Tomorrow is our monthly dinner with my folks."

This time Marnie groaned. Chris's parents had been wintering in Galveston since they moved north several years ago. "Do we have the ground rules established?"

"No talking politics. No rubbing your stomach. No telling you what you should or shouldn't eat."

"It's funny that the only time your parents eat together is once a month with us. Actually, it's funny that they're still married."

"Don't ask me to explain it. When my mom went full on MAGA, Dad had to move out. But neither of them sees the advantage of a divorce. I've resisted requests for separate meals, but it may become necessary after the baby is born."

"I'm not sure I can handle your mom without your dad."

"A problem for another day," Chris said. "What's on your agenda?"

"I'm relaxing. Doing some last-minute online shopping, getting diapers etc. The growing rumbles about a possible pandemic have made me nervous. I want to be sure to be stocked up just in case things are hard to get for a few weeks."

"You always said that your granddad called you a

nervous Nelly."

"He was in no position to talk. He died with enough toilet paper to last a year."

***

Foster arrived promptly at 2 p.m. He knew the historic area of Galveston and the restored Victorian mansion on 18th Street stood out among its neighbors. Marnie met him at the door and walked him around to the backyard.

"Lovely place," Foster said, pushing his sunglasses up to get a better look at the screened-in porch.

Marnie noticed his dark green eyes. "Thank you. All the restoration took a toll on the yard, but Chris hired a good grounds crew. He's trying to make sure that the new plantings are native. I've restricted my favorite non-natives to pots and planters." Marnie pointed to a spot not too close to a tree to discourage squirrels but close enough to bushes that the birds would have a good resting spot. "We thought the feeder would work well here."

"I agree," said Foster. "Have you considered a water feature? It's handy for the birds to have a place to drink and bathe. We have one that circulates the water and is easy to maintain."

"Good idea. We wanted to hire you to keep the feeder clean so maintenance of a water feature would fit in well. I have a pond at my home in Colorado. I love it but I don't want to take on such a big project here." Marnie rested her hand on her stomach.

Foster smiled. "I'm working on my Tourism and Community Development degree at Texas A&M-

Galveston. Taking on maintenance projects helps bolster my education fund."

"We wanted the hummingbird feeder close to the window by the porch and the sunroom. I can manage its maintenance. I'll leave you to your work. Just knock if you need anything. I should tell you that a friend is bringing her dog by for a playdate today. He'll be in the backyard with my dogs."

Marnie heard Charlotte drive up as she walked back to the house. She met her in the front yard.

"Hi there," Charlotte said. "Lovely day we're having. If this weather continues, Mardi Gras next week will be wild."

"It'll be my first Mardi Gras in Galveston in a long time. Come on in. Jack and Harlee can meet Scooter and then we can let them outside."

The three dogs did a circle greet and then started to play. Marnie turned them loose in the yard. Charlotte did a double take when she saw Foster working in the backyard. "Looks like you're getting a bird feeder installed."

"Oh yes, from Feathers." Having noticed Charlotte's double take of Foster, Marnie asked, "Do you know the installer?"

"Foster, right? I've seen him at Feathers. I remember him from high school. He was a freshman when I was a senior."

They watched EJ walk across the backyard. She stopped and said hi to Foster. They chatted for a few minutes. EJ waved at Marnie and Charlotte and continued to the side entrance of the house.

From the screened porch, they watched the dogs

take off in a mad game of chase. Charlotte waved at Foster. "The dogs seem to be having a blast," Charlotte said. "Can I come back in a few hours to pick up Scooter? I have some errands to run."

Marnie nodded. "A few hours should give them time to wear themselves out. Excuse me. I need to talk to EJ for a minute."

"I'll show myself out," Charlotte said. "I'm just going to say hi to Foster. Say hi to EJ for me."

EJ walked from the kitchen to the porch, meeting Marnie on the way. "Hi mom," EJ said with a smile. "I came to see if I could take you and the pups for a walk around the neighborhood."

"Luckily, we can leave the dogs to play and enjoy a walk with just us. Charlotte brought her dog over for a playdate since she doesn't have a yard. I think they'll be exhausted after playing. I'll change into the walking shoes that still fit."

While waiting for her mom, EJ looked out the large picture *window. She saw Foster and Charlotte deep in a conversation. Seems like those two have a history. Charlotte looks upset. Ex-lovers?*

***

As she approached Foster, Charlotte said, "What are you doing here?"

Foster looked up from digging his post hole. He frowned. "What does it look like? Putting in a feeder."

"But why here?"

"Look Charlotte, you know that I do these odd jobs for Feathers for extra money. Marnie came into the store and bought one yesterday."

Charlotte saw Marnie and EJ leave on their walk and gave a wave. She turned back to Foster. "It's just that this is where the editor of the newspaper lives. Have you been following the story?"

"Of course, it's our history. No longer dead and buried. So to speak."

Charlotte put her hand on Foster's arm. "It was an accident."

Foster laughed harshly. "Being raised by a crazy uncle who hated any person of color was an accident."

"I'm sorry. I'm sorry I left you there."

Foster put his arm around his sister. "You didn't have a choice. I was glad you got out. He would have molested you. At least he only beat me up."

"I should have told my adoptive parents. They would have told social services."

"Social services knew what was going on. They were under pressure to keep foster payments to a minimum. Keeping me with Uncle Kevin as a family placement saved the state money."

"What should we do about the investigation?"

"I'm tired of feeling guilty about this. I was wondering about calling the anonymous tip line."

"Oh Foster, I think they'll find you. Reporters investigate."

"Maybe, but if they do, don't worry. I'll keep you out of it, Sis. No point in both of us getting pulled into this mess." He gave his sister a hug.

"Let's think about this," Charlotte said.

***

After the walk, EJ went on a run and Marnie checked on Foster. "Is everything working out?"

"Doing fine." Foster sneezed loudly and blew his nose. "Man, my allergies are bad this year. It was fun to see Charlotte again. She said she would be back around four."

All three dogs were resting in the shade. Marnie set out some water for them. "We have a pet door so they can come in when they want. I'm sure Scooter will figure it out and follow them in. I'm going inside to do some work."

"I'll finish up and let you know when I'm done."

"Sounds good. Let me know what I owe you before you go."

After Foster left, Charlotte returned.

"Come in and have a cool drink. The pups are resting after their second big play."

"I'd love to have a glass of water."

As they sat and watched the dogs stretched out in the shade, Marnie said, "I think that is a look of utter contentment."

"Do you think we ever attain that state?" Charlotte asked.

"Not often enough."

Charlotte sighed. "I certainly don't remember enough moments like this. My parents died when I was eight. Eventually, I ended up in foster care—a good home—and they adopted me. There wasn't a lot of money, but they helped me get through college.

"I'm sorry about your parents," Marnie said. *My world seems full of orphans.*

Charlotte smiled wistfully. "They had their struggles. I was lucky to end up in a loving family." Charlotte sighed and stood. "Ok we're off. Have a good weekend and thanks for the playdate."

"You're so welcome. I'm home a lot for a while so let me know anytime you and Scooter want to visit."

Chapter 20

Sunday, February 9, 2020

Chris and Marnie sat across from Raymond and Chelsea Hill. The dinner at the country club's formal dining room was characteristically stuffy.

"Oh Henri, this prime rib is divine," Chelsea said to the maître d'. "I love it when the old favorites are served."

Henri looked at Marnie and Chris and smiled. "And how are your meals?"

Marnie took a small bite. "The trout almondine is quite good."

Chris said, "Your food is always excellent. How are you?"

"Keeping the peace." Henri surveyed the room. A sign in the lobby reminded members that hats must be removed before entering the dining room. It was an attempt to keep political theatrics to a minimum. "We have patrons of both political persuasions at the club, but we do ask them to keep a civil tone here." He looked sharply at Chelsea who was wearing a bright red scarf with little MAGA imprints discreetly blended into the background.

Chelsea laughed. "It's the quietest scarf I have."

Henri nodded to Raymond. "Let me know if you need anything,"

As Henri left, Raymond muttered, "My wife to become sane again." His comment was drowned out by the voice of a man approaching their table.

"Good to see the owners of our own 'fair and balanced news' enjoying a quiet meal."

Raymond stood and shook hands with the well-dressed man with a deep voice. "Nice to see you again, Parker." He turned to the table. "You know Chris and Chelsea. Let me introduce Chris's partner, Marnie Liccione. This is Parker Dodge, head of the Galveston Hotel Consortium."

Chris started to stand but Parker said, "Don't let me interrupt your meal. I just wanted to compliment you on publishing the letter about Luther Wood and the follow-up stories you've been running. A fascinating story. Good to meet you, Marnie."

Marnie noticed that Parker's smile didn't reach his eyes. She got the feeling that he wasn't all that glad the Wood case was back in the spotlight. "Nice to meet you as well."

Parker nodded to the group and left.

Chelsea said, "That reminds me. I really want to throw y'all a huge baby shower so that you can meet more of our friends."

Inwardly Marnie cringed thinking about a room full of Chelseas. "That is so nice of you, but we really have all the things we need."

Chelsea looked deflated. She took a sip of wine

and turned her attention to her son and husband.

Raymond asked Chris, "How is the investigation into the Wood case going?"

"Was he the Black man who got killed by a shark?" Chelsea asked, her voice rising an octave.

Raymond shot her a look. "I never was satisfied with the police report on that. I think they wanted to bury the case. And I'm not alone with that suspicion. The description of the body in multiple pieces washing up on shore doesn't fit with a shark attack. Too much like Robert Durst's mutilation of Morris Black."

"Turns out you were right, Dad. We now know that that isn't what happened. We have some good leads. The police have reopened the case." Chris said.

"Well, I'm sure that the police can't solve all these gangland killings," Chelsea said.

Marnie couldn't contain herself any longer. "Luther Wood was a well-respected teacher at the high school. I've met his son who is a very nice young man."

Chelsea shrugged.

Marnie wanted to add that Taylor and EJ were dating but decided it would just add fuel to the fire.

As Chris and Marnie drove home, Marnie shuddered. "That was a long evening."

"Thanks for putting up with them."

"Your dad is fine. Your mom…"

"She was always conservative. Grew up with money. Her family thought Galveston was a backwater and marrying my dad was a step down. Just like she thought my taking over the newspaper was a dumb choice. That may be one point that my parents agree on."

"What do they think about us having a baby and

not being married?"

Chris laughed. "On that point I think they are confused. They're excited about my starting a family but aren't sure about the way we came together—and think our not being married just invites trouble."

"What do you think?" Marnie asked.

Chris looked at her lovingly. "I think we should get married. It's fine with me if we sign prenuptials since we're both adults with assets. I like the idea of committing to each other and our baby."

Marnie gave Chris one of her best smiles. "I think that works as a proposal—just not an on-your-knees-with-a-diamond-ring proposal. And I'll say yes—but not until things settle down and our baby is here."

Chris grinned. "I'd say that was a qualified yes."

"I'm thinking of a quiet wedding with Louise, Didier and EJ. I want to avoid any political overtones."

Chris took a deep breath. "Let's decide the details later. My mom may come to her senses yet. I think that being able to identify with the country club MAGA crowd makes her feel like she fits in. The polarization in the country is pulling families apart. It may finally lead my dad to a divorce."

Marnie reached over and squeezed Chris's hand. "Glad we're on the same side of this divide."

Chris squeezed her hand back.

Chapter 21

Monday, February 10, 2020

 By 8 am, Chris, Ben, and EJ were secluded in the conference room at the Daily.

"We got a good response from your articles on Friday. Lots of comments on Galveston in 2002. Some people snidely remarked that meth now seems benign compared to fentanyl. We also got more emails with some tips about Luther Wood. I'm going to forward those to you two for follow up."

"Has Detective Sudhan said whether or not we can print the autopsy results?" EJ asked. "I was with Taylor when she told them to him."

"That's a go. We should have gotten it out this morning, but we can get it in the online evening summary. Reprint it tomorrow. EJ, you take the lead on investigating the tips."

"What else do you want for tomorrow?" Ben asked.

"Ben, with all the cases you two dug up, let's focus on the ones where Bruce MacFarland was the lead detective. Drill down on the time frame before and after he worked on the Wood case. Start a year before and then look forward a few years."

"I'm on it."

"Let's reconvene at two and see what you have," Chris said.

***

A call from Chris awakened Marnie from her afternoon nap.

"Don't know if you heard the news but there's a stand-off at an elementary school in Unidad, Texas, about forty miles southwest of here. I'm taking the reporting staff, including Ben and EJ, down there. We won't be back tonight."

"Damn, not another one. I'll turn on the news and check my computer. Keep me updated? Do you need anything?"

"Both EJ and I have go-bags in our cars. Will you get Rosa to stay with you?"

"I'll be fine, but I will let her know you're gone."

"Be sure the security system is on. There's a storm expected tonight."

"You're the one going into a combat zone. *You* be careful. Love you."

"Back at you."

Marnie got up slowly. She put her hand protectively on her stomach. "I'm sorry Jon for bringing you into this mess." *The US has two mass shootings a day. It's nuts. If people are so proud of their guns, they should be glad to register them and insure them—just like a car. This way is insanity.*

She reluctantly flipped on the news. The newsfeed was live. There had already been shots fired and probable victims. The gunman was sequestered inside, and the police were encircling the school. Worried parents were trying to push through the police lines as scattered shots rang out. Marnie felt nauseous.

"Let's go downstairs," she said to the dogs. "I need some coconut water and crackers."

When she got to the kitchen, Rosa came in the back door.

"So terrible, so terrible," Rosa said. She walked over and hugged Marnie. "Sit down. Tell me what you need."

"Your being here is great. Chris called. He and EJ will be gone tonight to cover the situation in Unidad."

"I will stay here and tuck you in. My niece, Anna, is coming in from Houston tonight and wants to stay at my house but I will make sure you are settled before I go."

Marnie looked out the window. "Storm seems to be moving in. Maybe we should walk the dogs around the neighborhood before it starts. All of us will sleep better if we move some — if we can sleep at all."

As they walked, they saw multiple police cars heading to the main road to the mainland. Helicopters were heading west. "Looks like they're calling in backup," Marnie said.

Rosa shook her head and made the sign of the cross.

The storm hit as Rosa and Marnie finished their pot pies. They had the TV on as they ate. The local police had taken forty minutes to enter the school building and kill the shooter. There were at least nineteen dead. The shooter was eighteen years old and had bought the gun legally. Marnie clicked off the news.

"I can't watch this. The storm is getting worse. Did Anna make it?"

Rosa nodded.

"You should go home."

Rosa looked at Jack who was pacing and whining. "He hates the storms. He is not going to let you rest tonight."

"I'm afraid you're right."

"Let me take the dogs tonight. Ana will love seeing them and you will be able to sleep better."

Marnie wavered. She was exhausted. Perhaps not worrying about Jack would be worth the price of not having their company. "Ok, but only if you'll borrow my car to go home. I don't want any of you walking in this rain. He does like to get into a small place during storms. Last time you were watching him in bad weather you said he loved your half bathroom. If that doesn't comfort him, give him his medication for anxiety."

"He will be fine. Set the security system when we leave."

Marnie checked the weather forecast. The storm was blowing in worse than predicted. Power outages were anticipated. Chris always kept the back-up generator ready. Marnie went into the garage to make sure she knew how to turn it on if needed. She came back in and set the security system.

At 9 p.m. with the wind howling and rain beating a relentless tattoo, Marnie climbed into bed and sent a prayer of protection to all those she loved. She fell into a deep sleep.

The next morning, she awoke slowly and stretched. There was a pale light spreading over the bedroom. She noticed that the house was silent except for the light patter of rain. She glanced at the clock which read 10 p.m. The overhead fan was off, and the house was chilly. The little light on the TV was off as well as all the other electronic blinks that disrupt the dark. *Damn. The absolute silence without the soft buzz of electricity makes the house eerily quiet.*

She stretched again under her blankets. Her baby started kicking. "Ok, ok. I'll get us some breakfast. Dang it's cold. Without power, the heat didn't come on last night." She grabbed her robe from the closet and picked up her cell phone. *Seven AM. Ten percent battery.* "And my phone didn't charge. I'll need to get the portable charger from my purse." She slipped her phone into her pocket.

As she slowly walked down the long winding staircase, careful to hold on to the banister, she reviewed what she needed to do first. Chris had been insistent that she learn the details. First was to open the garage door so that carbon monoxide didn't build up. Next was to prime the pump and push the start button. Once the generator was on, she would plug it in and flip the switch which fed the electricity into the house power grid.

Walking through the kitchen to the garage door, her phone buzzed. "Hi Louise, how are things at your end of the island? I've lost power." She stopped to flip the coffee maker switch on. Nothing happened. *Of course.*

She sat on one of the kitchen bar stools. "Glad to hear that you still have power. I might come over later today if our generator doesn't work well. Chris and EJ are out of town covering the school shooting."

She stood again and went to the back kitchen door and turned off the security system. *At least that battery back-up worked.* "They canceled school? I can hang out with the kids if you and Didier will be working." Still chatting with Louise, she opened the door to the garage. An arm shot out and grabbed her left wrist, yanking her into the garage. "Help!" she screamed as her phone hit the concrete floor and cracked.

Marnie was staring into the face of her worst nightmare. A tall man with a balaclava covering everything except his eyes. His green eyes. Then it clicked. She gawked, frozen.

"We meet again, lovely mother-to-be." His voice was deep with a slight foreign accent.

That reminder jarred her into defense mode. With her right hand, she reached for the baseball bat Chris kept by the garage door and swung it with all her might at the arm holding her wrist.

Her attacker dropped her wrist as he reached for the bat. "Bitch!"

Marnie stepped back into the kitchen, swung the door closed and bolted it. Still holding the bat, she headed for the stairs and the burner phone Chris kept in his nightstand. She could hear the attacker banging on the door with what sounded like a crowbar. Seconds later it was clear he had gotten through.

With one arm wrapped around her abdomen, she scrambled up the stairs as fast as she could. At the top of the stairs, her foot tangled in her long robe. *Fuck.* Righting herself, she looked back to see the cold dead eyes of her attacker at the bottom of the stairs.

He raised a gun and fired.

Screaming, Marnie ran into the bedroom, slammed, and locked the door, and went to the nightstand. She grabbed the phone and dialed 911. She reached a recording— "Please hold. Due to current weather conditions, we are experiencing an unprecedented call volume. If this is anything but an emergency, please hang up and call back. We will be with you as soon as possible."

Damn. Marnie slipped the phone into her pocket and grabbed the baseball bat again. She went to her doorway and stood to the side which would be opposite an open door. She heard footsteps on the staircase. The attacker slammed his shoulder into the door and burst into the room with a gun in his hand. With a fierceness that she didn't know she had, she cracked the bat over the attacker's extended arm. She heard the bone snap.

Her attacker screamed in pain and swiveled towards her. Despite his pain, he grabbed her bat with his left hand. They tugged on the bat until Marnie remembered her self-defense course. She shoved her end of the bat into his stomach, came forward and stepped on his instep. Then she kneed him in the groin. That move threw her off balance and she fell backwards.

Her attacker dropped the bat, went on his knees, and reached for the gun which had fallen into the hallway. Marnie quickly grabbed the bat and stepped into the hall. As he turned to fire, Marnie thought about her baby. With white hot fury, she swung the bat with all her force. Her attacker took several awkward steps trying to regain his balance. His limp caused him to stagger backwards into the antique stair banisters. His gun fired again as the banisters cracked under his weight. With a horrific scream, he fell to the first floor and lay still. Marnie slid down the wall and looked at the blood splatter on her clothes and her shaking hands. She heard her phone talking to her.

"Hello, hello, are you still there? This is 911."

"Yes…I'm still here." With a shaky voice she said, "I've been attacked. I think I killed him. I need an ambulance. I'm at 812 18th Street."

She felt her first contraction.

Chapter 22

Tuesday, February 11, 2020

Louise was screaming into her phone, "Marnie, Marnie, what happened?" Then the phone went dead.

"Shit." Louise ran upstairs to her bedroom, pulled off her nightgown and started dressing.

Didier stirred. Still groggy, he said, "What's up?"

"Marnie's in real trouble. I've got to go to her."

Waking up more fully, he said, "Wait a minute. You can't go alone. Power is out all over the island and trees are down. Let's wrap the kids in blankets and throw them in the car. You get Cora.

By the time their parents had awakened them and had them safely buckled in the car, Cora and Noah were wide awake. "Where are we going? I'm hungry. I need to go to the bathroom," Cora said.

Louise turned to the backseat. "Please listen carefully. Aunt Marnie is in big trouble, and I must get to her immediately. It's just a short drive and you need to keep it together. If you can't wait, we'll pull to the side of the road, and you can go."

Noah reached over and took Cora's hand. He

looked at her. She nodded. "We can wait, Mom," he said.

All the traffic lights were out and blinking red as they sped across the island. Didier reversed three times to avoid downed trees and blocked roads.

Louise called Chris. It went to voicemail. Next, she called EJ.

"Hi Louise, what's wrong? Chris and I are in Unidad."

"There's been some kind of accident. Your mom is in trouble and apparently her phone is dead. Didier and I are headed there now. I think you both should head back to Galveston."

"Oh my God, oh my God." EJ started crying.

She's had too many of these calls. "Listen EJ. Take a deep breath. She's alive. She's well. It's just that she may go into labor. I'll call as soon as I know more. You and Chris should head back. I couldn't get Chris to answer his phone."

"He sleeps like the dead. I'll get him. We'll be on the road in fifteen minutes."

"That's my girl."

By the time Finnerty-LaSalles pulled into Marnie's neighborhood. There were two ambulances in the driveway and police vehicles with flashing lights. Louise bolted from the car as soon as Didier brought it to a stop. "Go. I've got the kids," he said.

Louise ran to the first ambulance. She knew all the paramedics from her years in the ER. "Bert, who do you have?"

"Dr. Finnerty, we have a sixty-year-old male with severe head trauma. Blood pressure is high. He's unresponsive."

Louise nodded. "Stable?"

"Enough to transport."

"Okay. Go on."

Louise ran to the other ambulance. "I'm looking for Marnie Liccione."

She heard a faint voice from inside the vehicle. "Louise, Louise is that you? Oh please, thank God. Let her ride with me."

Louise looked at this paramedic and smiled. "Hi Greg. Ok if I go with her?"

"Love to have you, Dr. Finnerty."

Louise climbed in. She took Marnie's hand and glanced at the monitors. "You're doing fine," Louise said. "Blood pressure is up a little at 130/85. Oxygen and heart rate are good. No contractions currently. The monitor shows your baby's heart rate is stable."

Marnie grimaced and Louise saw the contraction. "How many have you had?"

"Maybe four? I don't have a watch, and I've lost track of time. The contractions started after our fight, which could have been five minutes or an hour. Is he dead?"

"No. Head trauma."

"Do you know who he is?"

"I didn't get a name. I'll let you know when I know. Chris and EJ are on their way. Let's concentrate on you. I want you to take slow deep breaths with me. Think about the calmest place you've been."

Marnie slowed her breathing and closed her eyes. "I'm in the mountains by an alpine lake. The air is warm. The sky is blue. I'm watching an eagle circle."

"Stay there Marnie. We're almost at the hospital."

***

Marnie lay on a gurney and was wheeled into the ER. *I hate this.* She closed her eyes against the lights and tried to go back up her mountain. She was transported immediately to Labor and Delivery. Louise followed the gurney.

As Marnie was transferred to the hospital bed and hooked up to monitors, Louise said, "I'm going to step into the hall and call Didier and Chris. I'll be right back."

Marnie nodded.

Chris said that they were twenty minutes out.

Didier said that he and the children were at the twenty-four-hour pancake house. Now that they knew that Marnie was safe, they could get breakfast. After the phone calls, Louise looked up to find Iliana Sudhan standing next to her.

Iliana touched her arm. "How is she?"

"Oh Iliana, I'm so glad to see you. Marnie seems stable. They're hooking her up to the monitors now. Do you know what happened?"

"I just arrived back from Unidad. Torres stayed here and answered the 911 call. He told me that when the police arrived at Marnie's they found a man lying on the first floor apparently having fallen through the second-floor stair railing. A gun, which had been fired, was near him. When they got upstairs, they found Marnie slumped against the wall in obvious pain with blood on her clothes. There was a bullet hole in the wall to her left."

"Oh no. Poor, poor Marnie. Who was the attacker?"

"When they removed the balaclava he was wearing, Torres identified Dr. James Melvin."

Louise gasped.

"I know. We had him on our suspect list in the MacFarland case. I don't know why he targeted Marnie."

"This is my fault," Louise stammered. She wiped her eyes as tears ran down her face. "I wanted to investigate what happened to MacFarland. Marnie was just doing some research for me."

Iliana patted Louise's arm. "We need to talk to her."

Dr. Ramirez, Marnie's OB-GYN, came down the hall. She smiled at Louise and Iliana. "Good morning. Glad I had inpatient duty last night. I'm going to go examine Marnie. I'll let you know when you can see her."

Ten minutes later, Dr. Ramirez waved Louise and Iliana in. "She's doing well overall. Her blood pressure is up a little, but the baby's heartbeat is strong. We figure that she's right at the thirty-three-to-thirty-four-week mark so medicines to stop the labor aren't indicated—especially with the borderline high blood pressure. We're going to keep her on bedrest with bathroom privileges and give her a dose of dexamethasone to help the baby's lungs get ready to breathe air."

Louise was glad to see that Marnie had been changed out of her bloody clothes and given a sponge bath. She reached for Marnie's hand, the one without the IV. "Chris will be here in fifteen minutes. I'm so sorry to have brought this tragedy to you."

Marnie gave Louise a wan smile. "Actually, I think we can blame my UTI."

Louise looked confused.

"I didn't remember it until last night. When I saw the green eyes through the balaclava, the pieces fell into place. The night I was hospitalized, I was restless and decided to walk the hall for a minute. A lab technician with green eyes visible above a mask bumped into me. I was so woozy from the UTI and medications that I thought the experience was a dream. He must be the hospital personnel who was seen in MacFarland's room. Who was he?"

Iliana stepped forward. "Dr. James Melvin. Remember, the retired medical examiner? MacFarland's friend that you met at the funeral?"

Marnie nodded. "Yeah. Then at the restaurant. Makes sense now that I think about it. He must have become afraid that I would eventually recognize him. Is he…?"

Louise shook her head. "He's alive. In the ICU. Bad head trauma from the fall. Unconscious."

Marnie grimaced as a contraction hit her. "I hope he dies."

Dr. Ramirez stepped forward. "I'm going to give you a mild sedative, Marnie. We'll let Chris in when he comes but I want to keep you quiet."

"Please let EJ in as well. She'll need to see that I'm fine."

Dr. Ramirez nodded and ushered Iliana and Louise out of the room.

***

As they walked back into the hallway, Louise answered Iliana's expectant look with a broad smile. "She's going to be fine. The baby also—may come early but should be fine."

"What a relief." Iliana smiled and turned to Louise. "Marnie's story of meeting Melvin at the hospital explains a lot. Since I'm here, I want to see if Dr. Melvin is out of surgery. Would you be willing to go with me?"

"Sure. Maybe I can get more information about his condition than you could alone. I've spent plenty of time in this ICU."

As they exited the elevator on the ICU floor, they saw Betty and Yvonne.

"Hello," Iliana said. "How is he?"

Betty spoke up. "Since we're not family, they aren't giving us much information. They've tried to contact his son but haven't had any luck."

"We'll see what we can find out," Iliana said. "We know that you're close to him."

Iliana greeted Marty, the officer who sat in the corner of Dr. Melvin's room. Louise turned her attention to the patient, moving in close to the bedside to see the monitor readings.

"Has he been awake, Marty? Said anything?" Iliana asked.

The officer shook his head. "Not really. He moans every now and then. That's about it."

"He's been extubated," said Louise. "That's usually a good sign. They're monitoring his intracranial pressure. High pressure in and around the brain can lead to serious complications."

Melvin's nurse entered the room, noted Iliana's badge, and didn't question the officer's presence. Louise was relieved that she knew the nurse on duty.

"Hi Darcie, can you give us an update on Dr. Melvin? Detective Sudhan asked me to tag along to help gather information on his status and prognosis."

"Dr. Melvin is beginning to wake up. He's opening his eyes and responding briefly to verbal stimuli. We don't know the extent of his brain damage. We're keeping a close eye on his intracerebral pressure postoperatively. It's been high."

"I never quite get adjusted to all the tubes and monitors," Iliana said. "Everyone appears to be more dead than alive."

"Blood pressure is stable. Pulse and oxygen levels are good, so he is breathing well by himself. Whether his higher brain functions are intact is an open question," Darcie said as she removed an empty IV bag and hung a new one.

Suddenly, Dr. Melvin opened his eyes and let out a loud groan.

"Get me out of here!" he croaked. His arms stiffened as he grabbed the bed rails. His complexion went from ashen to flushed.

Darcie rushed to calm him. "You can't get up Dr. Melvin. You need to lie still."

Louise noted a sudden increase in his intracerebral pressure. Darcie left the room to draw up a sedative to administer through his IV.

"They're going to kill me. I've got to get the files," he whispered with a hoarse voice, looking blankly from Louise to Iliana.

Iliana leaned in. "Who? What files?"

"They'll come after me if they find out …" Dr. Melvin gasped and went rigid. He began to convulse.

"He's seizing!" Louise called out.

Iliana stepped back from the bed and out of the way as Darcie and the ICU doctor rushed to Melvin's bedside and took over.

"We've got him, thanks," Darcie said to Louise.

Iliana and Louise quickly left the room and exited the ICU before speaking.

"Who do you think he meant?" asked Iliana.

"Don't know, let's talk later," Louise said as she saw Betty and Yvonne approaching from the waiting room. Betty appeared as unsteady on her feet as Yvonne.

Clutching Louise's arm, she asked, "How is he?"

Louise patted her hand. "It is too early to say. He's in critical condition."

Betty sagged onto a nearby chair. Yvonne patted her shoulder. "He's been such a good friend to our family. I can't believe he really tried to murder someone."

"That's not in question," Iliana said. "We will have to wait to see how he does before we know what his motivation was."

Louise looked at the two women. Their exhaustion showed. "You should go home and get some rest."

Betty took a deep breath and gathered herself together. "Thank you." She turned to Yvonne. "Let's go home. I have a feeling it will be a long couple of days."

After the sisters left, Iliana said, "That seemed out of character for Betty to be the one to collapse."

"I agree," Louise said. "We'll have to keep an open mind as to how that three-some relates to the case. Any ideas on why Melvin would have killed MacFarland?"

"I have some. I'm going to do some investigation

before I share them. Plus, we need more than Marnie's middle of the night encounter before we can nail him. She'll need to make a formal statement. Will you keep me posted on Marnie?"

"Will do," Louise said. "I'm going to check on her and make sure Chris is here. Then I'll meet up with my family at the pancake house."

***

Chris sat by Marnie's bed watching her sleep. *What a day. I can't believe how close I came to losing them.*

Marnie roused and stretched. She placed her arm protectively across her abdomen. When she saw Chris, she smiled. "The best way to wake-up is to see you here. How long have I been asleep?"

"Most of the day," Chris said. "Dr. Ramirez said that was the best thing for you. It looks like your contractions have stopped. Louise stopped in to see how you were. EJ was here—she brought me food. I sent her home to take care of the dogs and get some rest. How do you feel?"

"I feel great. Weird, right? This baby and I have been attacked twice, once in Colorado and now here. Two ICU hospitalizations. And we're still here. I think nothing is going to stop us now from a successful delivery."

Marnie pulled herself up to a sitting position. Chris adjusted her pillows. Marnie continued. "He's been checked out by so many ultrasounds that we know we're starting with a healthy baby. Life will throw us plenty of curve balls but, within a few weeks, we *will* meet our son." She reached for Chris's hand.

Chris's heart filled with relief. *This is Marnie I met.* He could see that her depression had eased. Her confidence was back.

"Do you think Dr. Ramirez will let me go home tomorrow? I hate being in the hospital."

"She said that you needed at least twenty-four hours without a contraction so that would be tomorrow afternoon. Also, Sudhan wants to talk to you. She told me that you think you saw your attacker in the hospital the night MacFarland died."

Marnie said, "I know it was the same person I saw at the hospital."

Chris gave Marnie's hand a squeeze. "By tomorrow afternoon I should have the house ready for you. You need to be on the main floor."

Marnie gave a sigh of relief. "I'm so glad that you're here. Tell Rosa I'll let her take great care of me. I'll be a model patient."

"I know she'll be happy to hear that."

"What's the latest about Unidad?"

Chris frowned. "Are you sure you want to talk about that?"

"It's your job. And I want to keep abreast of the news. I don't want to just sit here and worry about myself."

Chris updated Marnie on the details of the most recent mass shooting. He saw tears roll down her face. "I don't think this is good for you."

"No, I wanted to know. Do you think this country will ever update our gun laws?"

"Hard to say. It does feel like something has to give. But how many times have we said that?"

After a pause, Marnie said, "Can you get me some dinner? After that maybe we can watch a rom com until I fall asleep. Then you can go home and get some rest. I really want to go home tomorrow if I can. One thing I can tell you is that I won't leave my room tonight. I don't want any more accidental meetings."

Chris was shocked and then caught the mischievous grin on Marnie's face. *She's back.*

"No worries for you tonight. Until we know who or what motivated Melvin to try to kill you—besides his probable killing of McFarland—Sudhan posted a guard outside your door. When you get home, Sudhan is going to have a patrol car come around several times a day. Rosa has lined up relatives and workmen to be around the house acting as guards. We're all still suffering the shock of your near miss."

"I'm sure a lot of my adrenaline high is the result of being glad to be alive and for our baby to be safe. But I do think it's all going to work out. I trust you to take care of me as much as a person can. I love you, Chris. We have so much to look forward to."

Chris leaned over and kissed Marnie. "We'll have a wild ride."

Chapter 23

Wednesday, February 12, 2020

EJ was at the hospital early the next morning. Marnie was already up eating breakfast. "How are you feeling?" EJ was flooded with relief to see her mom's smile.

"Come here and let me hug you." Marnie pushed the tray table aside.

EJ was warmed by the request. It felt like coming home to hug her mom again.

"I want to apologize for my comment the other night." EJ said.

"We deserve it. I do want you to know that we weren't totally cavalier about our approach to unprotected sex. We both got tested and confirmed our negative status for sexually transmitted diseases. I thought I was too perimenopausal to get pregnant, especially after all the years of infertility. That's not a valid excuse but we weren't entirely foolish."

EJ smiled. "We've had a strange few years. I feel like it's been a while since you and I have been on the same page. I hate to admit to sibling jealousy, but I've been feeling tangential to all the changes going on."

"Oh EJ! I remember holding you in my arms for the first time and thinking no matter what happens you will always be my child, and I will always love you. You will always be central to me."

EJ sat on the side of the bed and took her mother's hand. "I'm glad that you and Chris are happy. I'm even glad to get a baby brother. I do have a lot of conflicting emotions about everything but when Louise called me and told me you were in the hospital I almost collapsed. On the drive from Unidad I was rocking and praying that you and baby Jon were all right. I realized how much I need you and how distant I've been. Judgmental, too. It's time for me to join this new family we have. Join as an adult and as a big sister."

"I'm so glad to hear you say that. I've hated the distance between us. You had to grow up fast after your dad died. I was such a wreck. I've had a few depressive episodes even before my parents died. That event triggered one as well as your dad's death. I think this pregnancy and move did it again. I went from mourning to a new relationship to pregnancy, leaving you…"

"You never left me, Mom. I always knew you were there."

"And I always will be." Both were wiping away tears.

"So, when can we bust you out of here?" EJ asked.

"All systems are go. I should be able to leave this afternoon. No contractions for twenty-four hours which means early this afternoon if my blood pressure is stable. Can I ask you to run a few errands for me?"

"Anything Mom. Anything at all."

***

EJ returned home to find the place full of workmen. Rosa had wasted no time getting her crew back together. A temporary stair rail was being installed. The main floor guest suite was being set up for Marnie. Everything she was going to need was going to be within easy reach.

Rosa asked, "Do you need breakfast?"

"I wouldn't dream of taking you away from this task."

"No, I insist. Everyone has their assignments. It will give me something to do. I find I'm constantly thanking God for keeping our Marnie and her baby safe."

EJ smiled. *A tragedy averted. About time for some luck.* She settled in the kitchen as Rosa made huevos rancheros. She hadn't realized how starving she was until she began to eat. "This is fantastic. Thank you so much."

"What are your plans today?"

"Mom is in a very good mood. She seemed more like herself than she's been since moving here. She believes the trauma stimulated some chemical release and she feels great. The contractions stopped and it looks good for her to come home this afternoon."

"Oh, the saints be praised."

"She asked me to run a few errands which I'll do after work. We're still trying to get to the bottom of Luther Wood's case."

"Be careful, my dear. Stories can have strange endings. I remember Mr. Wood. He taught one of my nephews—even inspired him to become a teacher. No one thought the shark attack made sense, but the police were different then. Rumors floated around about corruption."

"The review of Wood's autopsy confirms that something else was going on. Let me know when Mom gets home. Thanks for all that you do."

"You are a part of my family."

After giving Rosa a hug, EJ hurried off.

When she arrived at work, she noticed that Tom Assan was in charge. "Chris emailed over a set of instructions early this morning. Tough week for two of our reporters to be on vacation. He's hoping you have your write-up of Unidad ready to go in this morning's edition. I'm supposed to proof it."

"It's all set. I worked on it last night to keep my mind off my mom."

"I'm relieved that she is doing better. I assigned Sue, our local crime reporter, to write up that attack. She wants you to look it over. Ben's turned in an article about the storm and power outage. We're just waiting for yours and we can send out the electronic update."

"I'll send it right over."

"Chris also said that it was fine for Taylor to help go through the responses we received about his dad. He and Ben are working in the conference room if you want to join them."

EJ smiled. *Trust Chris to grease the wheels. He must be getting over his suspicions.* "I'll be there if you need me."

She stopped at her desk and sent her Unidad story to Tom. When she reached the conference room, she paused and watched Ben and Taylor through a glass partition. She sensed an air of easy comradery. When she entered the conference room, both men beamed at her.

"How's Marnie?" Ben asked.

"Doing well. The plan is for her to come home later today and take it easy. We're hoping for a couple of more weeks of pregnancy." EJ had already texted Taylor with an update. He had responded with relief and said he was taking vacation time to help work on the mystery of his father's death.

"That is good news," Ben said. "We've been going through the responses to the published letter. A few of them are crude. Some are racist. Most of them talk about what a great teacher Mr. Wood was."

"Those warm my heart," Taylor said. "Good to know that people remember him."

EJ squeezed Taylor's hand. "Any tips in the emails or letters that give us an angle on the case?"

"One of the letters suggested that it was a copycat killing orchestrated by the Durst family to make it look as if another person could have killed Robert Durst's neighbor, Morris Black. That seems like a stretch since Durst admitted killing the neighbor in self-defense."

"But his admission didn't come out until the trial in 2003," EJ said. "Maybe that *was* the motive."

Taylor shook his head. "I don't buy it. Mom said my dad was meeting with a student."

Ben said, "Could have been a victim of the wrong time, wrong place. He finished his meeting but was by the shore and the killer was just looking for a victim. Maybe the shock of being attacked caused the anaphylactic reaction."

"I don't know. As Black man in a White environment, he was always conscious of his surroundings. Not an easy man to surprise."

"What about phone messages?" EJ asked.

Ben's eyes lit up. "Mostly nothing but I saved one call to share with both of you." Ben pulled up the tip line on the computer, scrolled down and hit play.

Several clicks sounded.

"Uh, uh…I think Mr. Wood's death was an accident. He was very allergic to wasps. I think that it was covered up because the person who cut up the body had ties to the cartel and didn't want an investigation. The cartel leaned on the police department." The caller sneezed loudly. Click.

EJ and Taylor sat stunned.

"Who knew he was allergic to wasps?" EJ said, turning to Taylor.

"I don't know. Maybe lots of people? He always carried an EpiPen."

"It fits the autopsy results which suggested anaphylaxis. The voice from the recording. I've heard it somewhere before. That sneeze is distinctive!" EJ said.

"Hard to say. Sounded like they were trying to change it somehow. Maybe speaking lower than normal? It would be very helpful if you remembered where you heard it."

EJ elbowed Taylor. "No shit, Sherlock. It'll come to me."

Ben said, "If this is our go-to supposition, then we just need to find someone who was a student when your dad was teaching and who had a connection in the cartel. Maybe a gang member?"

"That really narrows the field," Chris said as he entered the room. The three young people looked up.

"Hi! What are you doing here?" EJ asked nervously. She got tense easily—always ready for bad news.

"Relax, EJ," Chris said "Everything is fine. I stopped by to check on things before going home. Rosa has everything under control. Marnie's champing at the bit to get released."

EJ breathed a sigh of relief. "She looked great this morning." Then looking at Chris, "Did you hear the recording?"

Chris nodded. "It might be a big break. My guess is that the caller was the student Mr. Wood was meeting or a close friend of that person."

"Do you know how many students there are at Ball High School?" EJ asked.

Chris smiled. "That's a question I should ask my interns, but as I remember around two thousand at the time."

"Cross referencing student names with known criminals sounds like a computer programming task," Ben said. "One of my many skills."

EJ grinned. "That's why I wanted you on my team." She turned to Chris, "I'll stay to work on computer searches. Then I need to run a few errands for Mom. She wants some bird seed from Feathers. I'll be home by five-thirty."

"Good to know. I'm doing some paperwork I can't put off, checking out the house, and then picking Marnie up at three. She said she would have a shopping list for me by then and would get settled while I did that." Chris nodded to Ben and Taylor and squeezed EJ's shoulder as he left the room.

With some to-go sandwiches the three of them worked through lunch and the afternoon, researching the current whereabouts of the students who attended Ball High School during the 2001 school year. It was a monumental task.

EJ said, "Maybe we should concentrate on those students that didn't graduate? Wasn't Your dad counseling troubled students? His death could have derailed the student from graduating."

As they scrolled through the list of students who received diplomas and compared it to the roster of starting seniors, EJ noticed the name of Foster Small. She pointed to it.

"That's interesting. Remember, we met him when he was helping at the MacFarlands?" Taylor said to EJ.

EJ said. "He also works at Feathers. I saw him a few days ago when he was putting up a birdfeeder for my mom. If I see him today, I'll ask if he remembers anyone struggling at school during our time frame."

By 4:30 no other names had jumped out at them. Ben was still working on the computer search program. EJ checked the time on her phone. "I'm off to Feathers. I'll check in with you two later."

On her drive, she tried to synthesize what she learned. If Mr. Wood was walking with a student and had an anaphylactic reaction, would the student have helped him with the EpiPen or been paralyzed with fright? Why not call 911?

Foster was at the checkout counter. "Hi, EJ," he called out. "I heard about Dr. Liccione. How is she doing?"

EJ smiled. "Much better, thanks. She's coming home for 'bed rest' and said she needs to be able to watch the birds at her new feeder. She asked me to stop by and grab some bird seed."

"Got some right here for you." Foster pulled a bag out from under the counter.

As EJ searched in her backpack for her wallet, she said, "I have a question for you. You probably heard we're investigating Luther Wood's death at the paper. A student might have been with him the afternoon he died. Do you remember hearing anything like that?"

When she looked up, she saw that Foster stopped what he was doing. He looked directly at her.

He said, "That was a tough time in my life. I really liked Mr. Wood. He was my teacher. He was trying to help me get my head on straight. No one else seemed to give a damn. It wasn't long after his death that I dropped out. I left and joined the military. Got into even more trouble."

"Oh, I'm sorry. I wasn't thinking how it was for his students."

"I would guess many of us had trouble that year. Hope you find the person you're looking for." Foster stood up and carried the bird seed to EJ's car. "Tell Dr. Liccione that I'll start the biweekly cleaning."

EJ thanked him and drove away.

Chapter 24

Wednesday, February 12, 2020

Marnie was safely ensconced in her bedroom on the main floor when Chris got home. "I've taken a shower and washed away the hospital germs," Marnie said. "I feel like a new person. I'm in my own nightgown and going to rest before dinner. What are you going to do?"

Chris told her about the tip line call. "I think I'll start by looking closely at the Mafia/cartel situation from 2001 to 2002. The caller suggested a connection. I wasn't in Galveston then and can use a review."

"It's great that you can do so much of that online—and stay close by." Marnie smiled.

As she settled into her bed, Chris planted a kiss on Marnie's head and headed to his home office. He looked at his desk. *Amazing how much paper can accumulate in only a few days.* After clearing the clutter, he did an online search for cartel activity in Galveston during the window of interest.

The cartels had taken over much of the organized crime scene in Galveston by the 1980s with the Pappalardo wing of the Maceo family running protection rackets for them. When Bruce MacFarland and James Melvin started working in Galveston in the mid-nineties, there had already been scandals involving police bribes and murder cover ups. After a period of calm, such activity started up again. Chris wondered if, by this time, MacFarland and Melvin were in place to benefit from the uptick. *Who would know what was going on then?* Chris pulled out his cell phone.

"Hi Garrett, do you have a few minutes to talk?"

"Busy preparing for the dinner rush. How's Marnie? I heard she got home from the hospital. Such an awful thing to happen."

"She's safely home and feeling better than before. Instead of waiting for disaster, she feels it's happened, and she and the baby came through it."

"That's great news. Do you want to come over at around eleven for a drink and a chat? My work is mostly done by then."

"That should work. Marnie should be asleep. EJ said she would stay in the big house whenever I needed to go out."

"See you then."

***

The restaurant was quiet when Chris arrived. A few customers lingered over their dinner. Garrett saw Chris and ushered him out onto the patio. It was one of those wonderful winter evenings in Galveston where a heat lamp was all that was needed to make sitting outside glorious. The day's traffic along the seawall had died down and the soft hum of the surf could be heard.

"What's up?" Garrett asked as he handed Chris a bourbon.

"Luckily, not Marnie. She's sleeping soundly— which has been a rarity in these last months of pregnancy."

"I can't believe you're going to be a dad. My kids are starting college."

"That's what you get for marrying your high-school sweetheart. But I might still be with Marnie when Jon goes to college."

Garrett smiled. "Well at least I get along with my ex. I thought Anita was going to snare you."

"I don't think she was over you. And hell, we were just kids. But interestingly, it's her side of the family that I wanted to ask you about. The paper got a tip that Wood's death might have some relation to the cartel in 2002. Do you think the Pappalardos were involved in providing protection for the cartels then?"

"Most of them had gone legit by then. But in families, there are always undercurrents and sometimes favors are called in. What was the tip?"

Chris told him about the anonymous call. "Supposedly the person who helped dismember Wood's body had ties to the cartel. But that person may have been low on the totem pole."

"That could be hard to suss out. Let me talk to Anita and see if she has any ideas. Okay if I call you tomorrow?"

"That would be great. Thanks for the drink. Sitting here is what I needed after the last few days."

***

After Chris left, Garrett checked his watch. A few

minutes before midnight. It was the next day when he called Anita.

"Hi, Anita, This is Garrett."

"Hi Garrett. What's up?"

"I just had a talk with Chris Hill. Did you see the newspaper article about Luther Wood's death that was published recently? He was wondering if any of our relatives had ties with the cartel at that time."

"Gosh Garrett. I don't keep up with all the ins and outs of the family. It seems like we had a few black sheep through the years who played fast and loose. I'm trying hard to avoid any contact with that part of our history. But yeah, I did see the articles about Mr. Wood's case being reopened. And I did read about Marnie's attack."

Garrett said, "I know. It's terrible. She's doing well, thank goodness. If you do hear anything about the Woods' case, will you let me know?"

"Of course. Say hi to Chris and let him know that I'm glad to hear Marnie is fine."

Anita hung up her phone as she pulled into her driveway. Once inside her condo, she kicked off her shoes. It had been a long day at the Third Coast Hotel. There'd been a high maintenance women's book group from Dallas that had required most of her attention, on top of finalizing the logistics for the evening's ghost tour. Time to unwind. Just as she sat down, her phone rang.

"Hi Mamma. Can I call you back? I just walked in," she said. Then, cutting her mother off, "Yeah, I know it's important. I'll call you back in ten."

"Harper!" she called. "I'm home." No response. Anita knocked on her daughter's door.

"Don't come in!"

This scene played out nightly. Anita had learned to leave Harper alone, knowing that, like a cat, she would emerge when she got hungry. Turning back to the kitchen, she sighed loudly and pulled a bottle of red wine out of the rack. She poured a generous glass, grabbed a bag of potato chips, and drifted into the living room. She sank into a sleek white chair and raised her tired feet onto an ottoman. The windows looked out over a grove of date palm trees that stretched to the Gulf. *I love this view. Even if it set me back an extra fifty grand.* The Regency was a new condominium complex built past the western end of the seawall. She and Harper had moved in after her divorce the year before. It hadn't been an amicable or financially rewarding separation. *At least that cheap son of a bitch gave us a waspy last name.*

Her phone rang again. "Hi Mamma." She put her phone on speaker so she could drink her wine and nibble the chips.

"Did you make the deposit?" her mother asked.

"Not yet. I told you I'd do it by Thursday and today is Wednesday. Jesus!"

"It's just that your dad and I are really worried about Uncle Vito. He's getting worse by the day. He needs supervision and Arbor View is the only place that will take him. But we need your help to pay the first month up front, the security deposit, and…"

"I know, I know." Anita's tone matched the exhaustion she heard in her mother's voice. Her parents had been caring for her great uncle, Vito Pappalardo, in their home for the past five years. Because of his behavior, *and his last name,* it had been difficult to find a senior living facility that would accept him. It hadn't helped that he had recently been arrested after he assaulted a parking meter attendant.

"Mamma, he didn't need to push that meter maid down and pull a gun on her. It hasn't helped us find a place that would take him."

Naturally, the entire scene was filmed by a passerby and shown on local TV affiliates. Captions read: "Vito Pappalardo, retired island Mafia capo, shows meter maid 'How we do business in Galveston.'"

The most common reaction was mild amusement. The article playfully mentioned the 'local color' occasionally provided by the aged gangsters. *Tell that to the meter maid on the sidewalk looking up the barrel of Uncle Vito's pistol.* The Pappalardo family learned that this type of local color was not appreciated in retirement communities.

"Mamma. I'll have the money soon. In the meantime, keep him out of trouble. Goodbye."

Anita took another sip of wine and closed her eyes. She was sick of living in a place where her family name was immediately associated with criminal activity. Her parents had been paragons of virtue, working seven days a week at their motel before retiring on their meager savings. But the fact that the Pappalardos were the wing of the Maceo crime family that stayed on the island when the others fled to Las Vegas in the sixties, always made people wonder if they had really gone legit. Were the hotels, restaurants, and service businesses the Pappalardos ran fronts for criminal activity? She lived under that shadow and felt contempt from those who knew her maiden name. *Basically, all the Born on the Islanders. And I don't want that for Harper. She needs to get accepted at UT and get an education so that she can get a good job someplace away from this goddamn island.* Maybe join a sorority for connections. Of course, she knew all that would cost money and she was already deeply in the red.

Harper snuck up behind her and grabbed a handful of potato chips. "When's dinner?" Anita jumped at the sound of her voice, then smiled at her willowy daughter. Anita would do whatever it took to make sure Harper escaped the suffocating environment of Galveston. Including talking to her cousin, Crawford, tomorrow. Even if there might be strings attached. Once she had Harper launched, she was desperate to get off the island herself.

***

Anita dressed carefully in a fitted suit over a filmy blouse and slipped on her signature high heels. She straightened her hair till it fell smoothly in dark curtains over her shoulders and applied a deep red lipstick. Using her God-given traits and some fashion sense had helped her in past negotiations with this relative.

Crawford Pappalardo was Anita's first cousin and ten years her senior. He ran a successful landscape design business. He had started out with a truck and trailer doing lawn care. After saving some money, he bought a nursery that had hit hard times after a hurricane leveled it. Eventually, he got into landscape design and began to make good money. The recurring tropical storms dependably ruined residential and commercial landscapes. Crawford hired talented designers and cornered the high-end projects. By all accounts he was an American success story.

"Hi Cousin Crawdaddy!" Anita called out as she entered the sleek showroom of Island Garden Designs on Post Office Street. Crawford looked up from the design sketches on his laptop. He smiled.

"Hey there, Anita." He took off his glasses, stood and greeted her with a chaste hug. "How are you and Harper? And your parents? I heard about Uncle Vito's latest shenanigan."

After chatting for a few minutes, Anita brought the conversation back to Uncle Vito. She explained the family's need for cash to get him into the one senior living facility willing to take him. She became emotional explaining the responsibility she felt for her parents and her attempt to give Harper a promising future. "I want to give her a chance to get away from here."

"I hear you. My kids are all in LA and Austin with no plans to come back."

Anita went on to explain. "I'm in over my head. The bank would never approve me for a loan. I hate to ask again, but is there any way you could help us out?"

"Hmm." He paused briefly. "If you're willing, there might be a couple of issues you could help us clean up. It wouldn't be a loan. It would be a payment from interested parties and worth more than enough to help your parents and give you a start on Harper's future options."

Anita left Island Garden Designs feeling relieved. By the time she was in her car, the relief she felt had been replaced by a wave of anxiety. To make things work out, she would be doing the bidding of the wing of the family still working with the cartels.

Chapter 25

Thursday, February 13, 2020

"Hi Rosa. How is everything going?" EJ said as she entered the kitchen the next morning

"Everything is going well," Rosa said. "Need breakfast?"

"No, I ate before coming over. Wanted to just check on Mom before going to work."

"Her friend Charlotte is with her now. She stopped by to drop off her dog for the day. Her house had some damage from the storm and workmen will be coming and going all day.

"Great. Have a good day." EJ walked to the bedroom. "Hi Mom."

"Oh EJ, I'm so glad you're here. You know Charlotte."

"Good to see you again. The newspaper has been keeping both of us busy," EJ said and quickly asked, "Have you lived in Galveston long?"

"I grew up here but left after high school, except for visits to my parents, I haven't been here much until a few months ago."

"I have a friend who went to Ball High School. Did you go there?"

Charlotte nodded,

"When did you graduate?" EJ asked.

The smile faded from Charlotte's face. "1999. Why?"

EJ made herself smile. "Oops. Didn't mean to interrogate you. I'm an intern at the paper and have been assigned to help with the investigation of the death of Luther Wood. I'm trying to interview anyone who went to high school around that time.

"Oh, yes. That was a tragedy for the whole school. I never had him as a teacher, but he was well-loved and respected. I was gone before he died."

"Did you know of anyone who had a significantly hard time with his death?"

"No, it seemed terrible for everyone."

Marnie glared at EJ.

EJ shifted gears. "I'm glad Mom has made a new friend."

Charlotte smiled at Marnie. "Every day Scooter wants to know if he can come over." Turning to EJ, she said, "It's been great to get to know your mom. You're very lucky. I lost mine when I was eight."

"I'm sorry," EJ said. "I know I'm lucky."

Charlotte shook her head. "Sorry, didn't mean to share that right now. Take it easy, Marnie. Glad you're home."

After Charlotte left, Marnie said, "What in heck was that all about?"

"Give me a minute. Let me make sure Charlotte's gone." When EJ saw Charlotte drive off, she returned to

Marnie. "I want you to listen to this audio clip I have of a tip line call."

Marnie gasped when she heard the voice. "The person sounds familiar!"

"I know, right?"

"Really bad allergies," Marnie said.

"It's an impressive sneeze. I think the caller was the student who was seeing Mr. Wood the day he died or at least knew that person."

Marnie looked at the clock. "Let's go to the sunroom. Maybe ask Rosa to make us some iced decaf coffee? She always wants to do something. You can bring me up to date and we can discuss what it means."

As they settled into the sunroom, Marnie watched the birds at the feeder. She thought about Foster. "Apparently, Charlotte and Foster went to the same high school. Foster has an impressive sneeze and a lot of allergies." She glanced at EJ.

"I think you're right. It does sound like him." EJ agreed. "By the way, the other day while I was waiting for you, I saw Charlotte and him in a tense conversation. Not what you'd expect from an ex-alumnus with no history. I thought they might be ex-lovers."

"Maybe there's a family connection? Siblings?" Marnie suggested.

"Why would they have different last names?"

"Charlotte told me that after her parents died, she was adopted. Maybe Foster didn't get adopted."

"That fits." EJ told Marnie about the conversation she had with Foster. "We need to research those two, their original family, and Charlotte's adopted family. I'll research the Smalls. Do you want to check out Charlotte and her adoptive family? If it's not too much?"

"I can use my brain, just not go running after bad guys."

"I'll go to the office and talk with Taylor, Ben, and Chris. Maybe we can all meet here for lunch since you're under house arrest?"

Marnie smiled. "I think Rosa will love having a crowd to cook for—just stop by and ask her on your way out."

EJ kissed her mom good-bye and spoke to Rosa who was excited to have a group for lunch. She quickly made plans for a taco buffet using some frozen barbacoa and put in an order for grocery delivery.

***

Crawford was as good as his word. Early the next morning he arranged to meet Anita for brunch at the Third Coast Hotel. He had a proposal. A person with knowledge of an affair was blackmailing a member of the Galveston Hotel Consortium.

"My guy is on the board of the consortium. Married with three kids."

"And the woman he's been meeting, is she the one shaking him down?"

"It's a bit more delicate than that." Crawford looked up at the ceiling for inspiration. "It turns out my guy plays for the other team sometimes."

"Oh."

"He says the blackmailer has access to hotel security videos showing his comings and goings with a young man. The victim won't pay the blackmailer, but he's willing to pay us a considerable sum to have those videos, and the blackmailer, disappear. Here are the dates and times." Crawford passed Anita a folded piece of paper. "Is this something you can make happen?"

"I can take care of the videos and probably find out who the blackmailer is. That's as much as I can do."

"You do that part. We'll take it from there. If this works out, we can discuss future projects."

Crawford gave her a peck on the cheek and left. Anita retreated to her cubby hole office behind Reception and closed the door. As general manager of the hotel, she had access to all security videos. With the dates and times given, she confirmed her suspicion. *Giles! This is going to be easier than I thought.*

As luck would have it, Giles was the front desk clerk on duty. When she noticed a lull at the desk, she invited the young man into her office. She had a still shot of Giles and a middle-aged man entering the main elevator on her computer, then footage from another camera, showing them entering a suite on the eighth floor.

"I'm not going to tell you how I knew you were playing this game *again,* Giles. I warned you! This man isn't a car salesman visiting from El Paso. This guy has family and powerful friends right here on the island."

Giles gulped. "How was I supposed to know? We didn't exactly share details about our lives. Threatening these johns with videos usually works." He had tears in his eyes. "Anita, I need this job."

"Relax. Here's how I'm going to help you fix it."

Anita went on to explain that she would delete the video evidence and assure her contact that the blackmail would stop. Giles could keep his job. Nobody would get hurt. She might need Giles' help in the future, depending on what Crawford has planned for her next project.

"But if you so much as breathe a word of this to anyone, I can assure you that the people you would be dealing with will not be as understanding as I am," Anita said and nodded her head toward the reception desk where a line was forming. "You better get back to work."

Anita grabbed her purse and jacket, brushed past Giles, and headed out the hotel's main door. The cool, salty breeze from the Gulf was refreshing. *Now all I need to do is find a patsy for Crawford. Whoever I choose might get hurt.* She took a deep breath and tried to banish this last thought.

When she informed Crawford that the evidence was gone and gave him a name, he deposited $20,000 in Anita's bank account. She used half of it to get Uncle Vito off her parents' hands. Now she could catch up on her bills and have a little breathing room.

***

The group at 18th Street gathered around the large dining room table with their taco plates and laptops. Rosa joined them.

Marnie started the conversation. "I'll go first with Charlotte Reeves. She is very much who she says she is. Her degrees check out. She graduated from Ball High School in 1999. Her adoptive family lives a quiet life in Galveston. They appear to have been her foster family but, of course, social service records are sealed. There is a public record of her adoption at age nine. The adoption record does reveal that her birth name was Small so we're on the right track. It looks like Charlotte and Foster are siblings." Silence fell over the group.

"You're kidding," Chris said.

"Nope. The story goes on. Charlotte Small, along with her brother, started at an elementary school on the east end of the island but disappeared from that school's record. A Charlotte Reeves appeared in the Galveston Independent School District in 1995. Chris, did anything strike you on her resume? Or at her interview when she was applying for her job at The Daily?"

"No, she was chirpy and friendly with solid recommendations from her previous job."

EJ cleared her throat. "My turn to pick up the story. Foster's is more interesting. Newspaper records report that the Smalls died in 1993 from drug overdoses. Foster and his sister went to live 'with relatives.'"

"Do we know who?" Marnie asked

"Ben researched that," EJ said. "Continuing with Foster, school records reveal that he finished at the elementary school where he started with his sister. Later, Foster collected a juvenile record with the police department, but it was sealed. He dropped out of Ball High School in 2002 and got a GED in 2008. He doesn't have a Facebook page or any social media that I could find. His military record reveals a general discharge which gives him a few GI benefits. He enrolled in Texas A&M-Galveston in 2016. Like his sister, this is very much what he claims."

"My turn," Ben said. "I was given the job of researching the Smalls. Starting with their parents' deaths, I was able to identify the relatives. Apparently, the dad's brother, Kevin Small, and his wife, took the children in. Kevin's wife filed for divorce in 1994. Social work reports are not available but old declassified records reveal that they received small monthly payments from the State of Texas until Foster entered the army. Kevin Small never seemed to hold a steady job but was able to buy his little house in Galveston East where he still resides. He has been arrested several times but never convicted. Chris took over the investigation of Kevin Small."

"I'm the only one who brought a show and tell." Chris produced a mugshot of Kevin Small on his computer. He passed his laptop around the table. EJ recoiled at the image of a disheveled thug with tattoos creeping up his thick neck. "There are strong indications that Kevin Small has ties to organized crime. Most of his arrests were for assault and battery. At the time of trial, the witnesses and victims either recanted their stories or disappeared. There was one charge of manslaughter but the evidence of the cause of death and the autopsy report disappeared. Bruce MacFarland was the chief detective of the case and Dr. James Melvin was head of the medical examiner's office—just as they were for Luther Wood."

"What do you think, Taylor?" EJ asked. He had been sitting quietly at the table, but she could see his hands clasping and unclasping in his lap.

Taylor said, "All of this matches up well with the tip. But if Foster and Charlotte are involved, why would either of them call the tip line?"

Everyone turned as two figures entered from the kitchen with Harlee and Jack dancing around their legs.

Chris stood up and placed himself between the newcomers and the table. The rest of the group was taken aback by the arrival of Foster and Charlotte. "Some guard dogs," said Marnie under her breath.

"They just know us," Foster said, patting their heads. He took a deep breath. "We can answer your questions."

"Have a seat." Chris, still appearing vigilant, indicated two empty chairs.

Foster spoke first. "I've been living with this story for a long time. When the letter came out in the newspaper, I thought that I could finally put this tragedy to rest. Charlotte has very little to do with what happened. I only told her after the fact. She helped me get out of town and into the army."

Charlotte squeezed Foster's arm. "When I told him about my conversation with EJ this morning, we agreed that we'd come over and at least tell Marnie the whole story and get her advice. It looks like our timing is good."

Foster straightened. "I was the student Mr. Wood was meeting the day he died. I'd always struggled in school but had never had the nerve to tell the school what was going on at home. My uncle, and guardian, was abusive and cruel. We told our social worker and showed her bruises, but she said we should just behave."

Charlotte said, "In first grade, my teacher saw my bruises and reported it to the school counselor. I told the counselor that Kevin was watching me bathe and that I would wake up at night to find him sitting on my bed stroking my leg. My counselor moved me to a vetted foster family. The Reeves later adopted me."

"I was not so lucky. I found out later that the social worker was under pressure to make as many family placements as possible to keep costs down. I was only three and had to learn to stay out of Kevin's way as much as possible. If he was drinking, his temper was explosive. I didn't have any lessons on how to control my own temper and so I was often in trouble in school. And that would set him off."

"We lost touch with each other until high school," Charlotte said. "I was an honor student and on the debate team. I tried to help Foster with his studies, but our two circles didn't overlap, and he was afraid that his group would contaminate me.

Foster looked at Taylor. "Your dad was the only person who tried to help me. The day he died he'd agreed to see me after school. I was so angry with Kevin that I was planning to kill him. Your dad calmed me down. Reminded me that I was almost out of Kevin's clutches. That I had my whole life ahead of me."

The room was silent. Taylor was frozen in place. EJ was pale. Marnie glanced at the two of them—*not what we thought their investigation would reveal.*

"Mr. Wood suggested we take a walk. I think he wanted to make sure I settled down before going home. We drove to a beach access parking lot close to East Beach. We walked on one of those raised wooden paths across the dunes and headed to the water's edge. That's when he told me he had a bad allergy to bees and wasps. He said the breeze at the shoreline would be brisk enough to keep them away. By the end of our walk, I felt a lot better. Like I could handle a few more months with Kevin."

Taylor sat with his arms crossed, staring intently at Foster. "Go on."

"On the way back to the car, we were crossing the dunes, walking single file on the walkway. One part of the path was overgrown with beach shrubs. I was in front and heard your dad call out. I turned around. He was batting a wasp away when another one stung him on the face. It turned red and swelled immediately. His eyes puffed up so much they were almost closed. He was gasping for breath and reaching for something in a pocket. I later realized it must have been his EpiPen. Before he could do anything with it, he collapsed."

Marnie felt tears streaming down her face and saw that everyone looked ashen. Rosa went to get tissues. Foster was shaking. He blew his nose and dried his eyes. Charlotte said, "You have to remember that there were few cell phones at the time, and neither Foster nor I could afford one."

Foster started again. He met Taylor's gaze. "By the time I got to your dad, he wasn't breathing as far as I could tell. I didn't know what to do. I was afraid to go to the police because of my history. I ran all the way home and found Kevin sitting in the garage, drinking. I explained what happened and he started laughing. He called your dad the n-word and said it served him right."

Charlotte sat shaking her head. Tears welled in her eyes.

Foster continued, "Then Kevin started thinking. He couldn't have me investigated because it would lead to an investigation of him. He already was on thin ice with his cartel bosses and couldn't depend on them to protect him if the police came snooping. He got agitated and said we had to get rid of his body right away."

Foster paused and took a deep breath.

"Go on," Taylor repeated through gritted teeth.

"It was starting to get dark, and the wind had picked up. It started to rain. He grabbed his chainsaw and made me take him to your dad. He made me help cut him up. I kept vomiting and he kept backhanding me. We threw your dad's body into the waves off the side of the jetty. Kevin said that if I ever told anyone about what we did that he would kill Charlotte and Mr. Wood's family. I believed him. The rain washed the scene clean."

Nobody moved. Marnie saw that Taylor looked both stricken and angry. He stood up and put both hands on the table, leaning towards Foster. "What happened next?"

Charlotte picked up the story. "Foster ran away that night and called me. It was impossible to report it to the police. Foster was still a juvenile—his eighteenth birthday was the following week. We knew what Kevin did for a living and that he'd throw Foster under the bus if the police got involved. We snuck into the house while Kevin was blacked out. Foster grabbed a few essentials, including his birth certificate. I drove him to the enlistment office in Houston. We sat in the car all night, until the office opened. We found him a place to stay for a week until his enlistment started."

"I didn't even make it through basic training. Too much PTSD. After discharge, I took odd jobs in the Houston area for a few years. Sold some weed. Got busted. I was lucky to get into a drug diversion program. It started my recovery. Charlotte and I kept in touch, but Kevin's threat hovered over us. It still does. But I can't keep this secret any longer."

Marnie could tell that Charlotte and Foster were

exhausted. She turned to Taylor and EJ. EJ had her hand on Taylor's arm. His expression had gone blank.

"Do you believe them, Taylor?" Marnie asked.

"I don't know. I've got to get out of here." He gently took EJ's hand off his arm and strode out the room. Marnie could hear his car start up and peel out of the driveway.

After Taylor left, Charlotte and Foster stood up. "We're going home now," Foster said. "You know where to find us if you want me to talk to the police."

Rosa stood up and started to clear the dishes. Ben and EJ helped her.

Chris said, "You need to go lie down, Marnie."

She nodded in agreement. After getting settled back in her room, she could feel how exhausted she was. Emotionally and physically. "What happens now?" she asked Chris.

"I don't know. A lot will depend on what Taylor wants to do. I think we should digest this information. Not the ending we thought we would get." He paused at the doorway. "Need anything?"

"No, I'm going to rest and then take a shower. Will you be staying close?"

"Yes, I'll work in my office."

"Tell Rosa we can eat leftovers. She can go home."

"Will do."

When Chris entered the kitchen, Ben and EJ were deep in conversation. Ben said, "It's quite a story. Front page news in a lot of places."

EJ shook her head. "It would destroy Foster and hurt Charlotte. What if Taylor doesn't want all this known?"

"I agree with EJ at this point," Chris said. "We can't do anything fast. We need to consider the consequences. We should alert Detective Sudhan that we have more evidence suggesting that MacFarland and Melvin were on the take. The timing is right for them to have been involved in the cover-up and shark attack story. I'll do that. Ben, you can have a go at writing up the story even if we don't publish. Keep it on a private disc. What are you going to do EJ, go look for Taylor?"

"I'm going to let him have some time by himself. I think he'll reach out to me when he's ready."

Chapter 26

Sunday morning, February 16, 2020

As Taylor waited at the school parking lot, he thought about his dinner with EJ Friday night. It had taken a day for him to calm down enough to call her. At the last minute he got a table at Garrett's for Valentine's Day—at 9 p.m. Trust Garrett to take care of them. They were quiet during the meal. He'd told her that he wanted to walk where his dad had walked the day he died. She'd said she'd call Foster and find out where exactly they had walked. They agreed to meet early Sunday at the school parking lot.

"I have a good reason for being late. I took a map by Feathers and had Foster mark it."

They drove in silence to the beach access lot which Foster had identified. The car bumped over the puddles and potholes to a parking place. Before they got out, Taylor leaned over and kissed her on the cheek.

"How are you feeling?" EJ asked.

"I feel dissociated. After all these years of wondering, I now know—or at least, I think I know what happened."

"I've only been wondering about your father's death for a few weeks, and I feel weird getting to the end of the mystery. I can't imagine how you feel."

They started off across the dunes. The walkway to the beach had seen better days. Many of the slats were missing and foliage grew through the openings. They continued along the hard-packed sandy path that continued across the dunes until they reached the open beach. Taylor stopped and stared at the gentle waves. *Hard to believe that it was just a tragic accident.* "I can't stop feeling that it was Foster's fault. If he hadn't needed help that day, maybe my dad would still be alive."

"If it helps at all, Foster feels horribly guilty. He told me this morning that he can intellectually understand that the death was an accident. He feels most guilty that he didn't come forward. He was, and is, afraid of his uncle."

Taylor nodded.

"They headed that way," EJ indicated the open beach extending eastward to the jetty at the far end of the island. Along the beach families were setting up picnics and flying colorful kites. Fishermen stood with their lines in the water. At the jetty, the gentle waves had become dark, swirling currents that crashed against the concrete block structure.

When they came to the spot that Foster had marked on the map, Taylor knelt and touched the sand. *Washed clean of any sins.* Taylor looked back toward the path through the dunes which nature was busy reclaiming.

Humans are only a small part of this island's history. His mind filled suddenly with images of his dad's body being desecrated. Taylor felt sick.

He grabbed EJ's hand and said, "I've seen enough. Let's walk back on the road. I don't need to repeat this path on the way back."

They decided to have an early lunch at the food truck park. They sat at a picnic table and shared a Cuban sandwich and an order of ceviche. As they were leaving, they saw Detectives Sudhan and Torres approach.

"Nice to see you," Sudhan said. "Gotta take advantage of weather like this."

"A working lunch?" EJ asked.

"We just came from the hospital. The plan is to disconnect James Melvin from life support today as soon as his son gets here from the airport. We thought we might as well eat."

"I can't say that I'm sorry for him after what he did to my mom. I hope she doesn't start feeling badly about it."

Sudhan patted EJ on the shoulder and then followed Torres to the food truck window.

"Where to now?" EJ asked.

"I'd like to talk to Chris and Marnie about what they think I should do."

EJ texted them and asked if she and Taylor could come by. "Chris and mom are home and said that we could come over."

As Taylor pulled out of the sandy lot in front of the food trucks, he was suddenly blocked on the side by a big Ford 150 pickup with two men in the front seat. A smaller Honda pulled in front of him wedging him in.

A large, heavily tattooed man exited the passenger side and gave Taylor a malicious grin. EJ gasped.

"Get out of the car and get into the truck. We're going for a ride. I should have taken care of you eighteen years ago—and ignored my little pissant nephew. Now that you were foolish enough to blackmail my boss, I'm free to take you out."

Taylor, confused, asked, "What the hell are you talking about?"

The large man guffawed. "Just get in the truck. Anita said that you were the guy blackmailing my faggot boss." He wiggled a handgun in the air then pointed it at EJ. "If you come quietly, she can stay in the car."

"Don't go, Taylor. That's Kevin!"

Looking between Kevin and EJ, Taylor hesitated. *Now I know how Foster felt.* When he opened his door, EJ jumped out of the car and started screaming.

"Help! Help!"

Kevin aimed his gun at her. Taylor shoved his door hard into Kevin's gut and kicked him in his groin. As he went down, Kevin's gun went off. The driver of the truck jumped out with his gun aimed at Taylor. Giles, at the wheel of the Honda, sped off.

Detectives Sudhan and Torres came rushing out of the parking lot, weapons drawn.

"Police, put your guns down now!" Sudhan yelled.

Kevin had struggled back to his feet and turned his gun on her. Torres took the shot. Kevin collapsed on the ground.

The driver of the pickup, looked at the odds, dropped his gun, and put his hands up. Shaking from adrenaline, Torres went around and handcuffed the driver.

Detective Sudhan called 911 for an ambulance and backup. Torres felt for a pulse on Kevin unsuccessfully but started CPR. The area soon filled with first responders. Sudhan looked at Taylor and EJ. "Are you two alright?"

EJ slumped back into the passenger seat. Taylor came around the car and knelt beside her.

"Will this nightmare never end?" she whispered.

"Well, we are down one more bad guy," he said.

Sudhan looked at Taylor. "You want to tell me what's going on?"

"It's a long story," he said. Taylor looked at the clear sky as the sun beat down and wiped sweat from his brow. "I know parts of the story, but I have no idea what Kevin was talking about. Blackmailing his boss? Me?"

"Let's all go back to headquarters," Sudhan said. "Torres needs to turn in his gun while the shooting is reviewed." She glanced at EJ. She was beginning to shake. "EJ needs a quiet place and a blanket."

"Can Chris join us?" EJ asked faintly. "He can put Mom on speakerphone."

"Sure."

Chapter 27

Sunday afternoon, February 16, 2020

Chris joined the two officers along with EJ and Taylor in a conference room. EJ was sipping on some orange juice. Taylor stood up and shook Chris's hand.

"Thanks for coming." Taylor said.

"Glad you called." Chris looked at EJ. "How are you doing, EJ?"

"Better than when I called you. My shaking has stopped. How is Mom?"

"She's beside herself with worry. I promised her we'd face-time this meeting."

EJ asked Sudhan, "May I step out of the room for a minute and call her? I think once she sees me, she'll feel better."

Sudhan nodded. "I'll go check on Torres and get started on the 'officer involved shooting' forms. She looked at her watch. "We can meet back here in fifteen minutes."

Chris and Taylor were alone in the room.

"Funny thing, we were just on our way to see you when we were attacked. We were going to ask you and

Marnie what your thoughts were on the best course of action after Foster's story."

"Marnie and I have been talking about it. A lot depends on how much you want known. And how much do you want Foster to pay for what he did."

Taylor snorted. "Today when I was faced with Kevin hurting EJ, I had my first real understanding of why Foster was so scared. He's a monster. I would do anything to protect EJ from him."

Chris put his hand on Taylor's shoulder. "Protecting those important to us often involves tough choices."

Taylor nodded. "I think we should tell the police the whole story except the name of the 'juvenile student.' Can we keep that person out of it?"

"As a journalist, I can claim qualified First Amendment rights to protect my source. Unless a judge feels that it's necessary for me to reveal my source, that should keep Foster out of it. I don't think Detective Sudhan will insist on going to court since we can make the case against Kevin without it."

When the group reconvened, Chris said to Sudhan, "I'm going to tell you the story of Luther Wood's death and dismemberment. EJ and Taylor know the story, so if you don't mind, I would like you to let them go to Marnie and reassure her in person that EJ is fine."

Staring pointedly at Taylor, Sudhan said, "As long as everyone stays in town in case I have questions, they can go."

Chris said, "EJ, clue Ben in so that he can finish the article on Mr. Wood's death. I'll look it over when

I'm done here."

EJ gave Chris a hug. "Thanks. I'll feel better seeing Mom also."

After they left, Chris filled in Sudhan and Torres on the whole story.

"Amazing!" Sudhan said, shaking her head. "But why did Kevin Small attack Taylor?"

"Taylor said that he didn't know. Kevin mumbled something about Taylor blackmailing his boss."

Sudhan said, "Foster's story gives us some solid leads to examine the cases shared by Melvin and MacFarland."

"I'll be on desk duty after the shooting. I can take a deep dive into the archives," Torres said.

Sudhan's phone buzzed. "This is Sudhan."

It was Deputy Jones calling from the hospital.

"Dr. Melvin has, um, passed away. The medical team disconnected him from everything. His son is talking to a chaplain about arrangements."

"Thanks. Ask him to stay put. I'm on my way."

***

It was a short drive from the police department to the hospital on the campus of UT Medical Branch. Sudhan walked briskly to the ICU. Entering Dr. Melvin's room, she took in his lifeless body, now resting quietly, detached from the hospital wires and tubes. A fortyish man dressed in casual clothes sat with his elbows on his knees, head bowed, as he answered questions about funeral arrangements. He looked up when he noticed the chaplain turn her attention to Sudhan.

"I'll only need a few minutes of your time, Mr. Melvin," Sudhan said after introducing herself and showing her badge. The chaplain excused herself and promised to return.

"It's Mark. Dr. Mark Melvin. I thought I would be talking to someone from the police soon."

"Let's go to the family room." Sudhan conducted him around the corner to the small room used for difficult conversations. Once seated she began, "I'm sorry for your loss."

"Thank you, but I'm sure there are others in Galveston who don't share your sympathy. Is the woman he attacked going to be alright? Did I hear she was pregnant?" He shook his head and looked back at the floor.

"Yes. It looks as if mother and baby will be fine."

"Thank God for that." Mark looked up. "People are saying he probably killed his friend, the cop. It's all a bit much to take in."

Sudhan explained that it was her job to collect evidence to understand why his father had taken the steps he did. She added, "There may be others involved who could cause even more pain and suffering."

"I don't know how much I can help you. My father's life in Galveston was a mystery to me, ever since my mother and I left. I was twelve. He was not an attentive father. At least not emotionally. He was very attentive in another respect."

"And what was that?" Sudhan asked.

"Financially. He paid for my education in private school, college, and medical school. He even subsidized my meager salary during residency. I finished my training with no debt. During our rare conversations he made it clear to me that his career down here had been very lucrative." Mark made a dismissive gesture to the window overlooking the medical campus. "Not sure how that was possible."

Sudhan winced inwardly at the casual slight of an institution held in high regard in Texas. She decided to move on. "Did he mention any outside business ventures or investments that might have augmented his salary as Chief Medical Examiner?"

"Never."

"How about female companions? Were there any women he might have been involved with?"

"Women? Not specifically, but he let me know he enjoyed the single life. Like he always had a hot, young girlfriend. It made me uncomfortable. I know he cheated on my mother and that was one of the reasons they divorced." He paused. "He was a complicated man. I'm beginning to learn that he had a complicated life in Galveston. Complicated and dangerous."

"Thank you for your time, Dr. Melvin. I'll let you get back to making arrangements." Sudhan gave him her card. "We may need your assistance tracking down his finances during the time he was supporting you. And by the way, what is your specialty?"

"I'll cooperate in any way I can," he said. "I'm a surgeon. My dad encouraged me to become a surgeon as soon as I was admitted to med school."

Chapter 28

Monday, February 17, 2020

Crawford's next call to Anita came early Monday morning. "Well, that didn't go exactly as planned. But I understand the powers that be are satisfied. They think the young man saw enough to be scared shitless and keep his mouth shut."

Anita smiled to herself. *'The young man' doesn't have a clue why he was attacked.* "Who was the guy that ended up dead?"

"A small-town goon, Kevin Something, who did some work for them. They were glad to get rid of him. Said he was becoming a liability. Anyway, want to meet to discuss another project? Are you interested?"

Anita's discomfort at the level of violence that went down was growing. At least he bought her story that the new real estate agent staying in her hotel was the one behind the blackmail. She sighed. "Yeah. Where should we meet?"

Five hours later, Anita slipped into a booth at the

Moody Gardens Hotel Lobby Bar to wait for Crawford. He had chosen the place and the time, 2 p.m. She took in the lush greenery and trickling water features. Aquariums, stocked with brilliant tropical fish, were visible from all parts of the bar.

Built in 1986, the hotel was part of a family friendly destination with a white sandy beach, waterpark, aquarium, and a rainforest. The last two were housed in pyramids. It was a far cry from Anita's Third Coast Hotel which prided itself on its historic relevance and understated elegance.

"Can I get you anything?" asked a waiter, appearing out of nowhere in the quiet bar.

"I'll have an iced tea. Sweet tea," said Anita, although she was thinking hard about ordering a drink. *Why did Crawford want to meet here?* She hoped her next assignment wasn't going to involve the powerful family and foundation for whom the sprawling facility was named. The Moody Foundation had provided scholarships to some of her classmates and Pappalardo relatives motivated enough to get an education and a ticket out of there.

She saw Crawford arrive and stood to catch his eye. He greeted her with a kiss on the cheek. "Like this place? I haven't been here for a while myself." He gestured toward the enormous pots of ferns and columns covered in well behaved vines. "We did the landscape design for this bar, inside and outside, after Hurricane Ike blew through."

"It's lovely."

Crawford asked after her family. Anita was happy to report that Uncle Vito was settling in at Arbor View.

"At least he hasn't pulled a gun on anyone yet." They laughed. When the waiter appeared again, Crawford ordered a martini. Anita said, "Make it two."

When the drinks arrived, Crawford laid out Anita's next project. The promised payout would be large enough to settle her debts and invest in Harper's future. She was relieved that it didn't involve the Moody family. But as Crawford laid out the nature and scope of the project her anxiety skyrocketed.

"I won't mince words, Anita. The people willing to pay for the right result here can be dangerous. They've ruined a considerable number of lives on the island, including those of some of our family members. Maybe you know some of this but let me start back in the eighties."

Anita sat back to listen. Parts of Crawford's story rang bells. She was only a kid then but remembered overhearing whispered conversations at family gatherings about arrests and disappearances of distant relatives and friends of friends. Her own parents never spoke of these things at home.

"Here's the short version of a complicated story from those years. The would-be movers and shakers in the hospitality business at that time decided to organize into a formal hotel consortium."

"The guy I helped out last time was in this consortium, right?"

"Right. But from the next generation. The guys who started it back in the nineties were feeling the pressure from places like this—clean, wholesome, and family oriented. They were still hoping to bring gambling back to the island and wanted to offer a classy, 'adult oriented' alternative. But they needed to make sure their ventures were clean and safe. At least on the outside." Crawford finished his drink and sat forward, hands cradling his glass and lowered his voice. "Do you see where this is going?"

"If 'adult oriented' means what I think it means," Anita said, using air quotes, "I'm guessing they offered some less than legal perks to their guests. Girls? Drugs?"

"You got it. And gambling." Crawford caught the attention of the waiter and indicated 'two more' with a victory sign. "And this meant coordination with an unsavory supply chain. The Mexican cartels had moved into the void left when most of the Maceos had died or departed."

"I remember lots of violence back then. Turf battles between the gangs. But…?" Anita wondered how this connected to Galveston in 2020.

"You're right. There was a lot of background violence. Our guys used that as a smokescreen while they paid off gangs to maintain supplies for their adult activities and cops to cover these activities up. Suffice it to say, the Galveston Hotel Consortium of the nineties engaged in some nasty behavior. Even extrajudicial executions."

Anita cringed and closed her eyes. *Where is this going?* "Isn't all that water under the bridge, so to speak?"

"Not exactly. That's the problem. A detective back then was very helpful to the hotel guys. When they needed someone to disappear or be taught a lesson, they would pay this cop to make the evidence look the way they wanted it to look. When murder was involved, as it often was, they made use of the services of the guy in charge of autopsies, the medical examiner."

"And this detective and medical examiner are still alive and well?"

"Not exactly. And that's the problem. The detective went senile. He was overheard bragging about some of the jobs he did. Calling them 'extra-curricular money-making opportunities.' He named some names and claimed that he and the old medical examiner stashed incriminating evidence that would cause major headaches for the older hotel consortium crowd."

Anita held her hands up, palms facing Crawford. "You are not going to ask me to kill these old guys. No way."

"Relax. Of course not. In fact, the detective is already dead, and the doctor is currently in a coma. Doesn't look like he's gonna make it. What I need from you is to get that stash of evidence. When we put the screws to the good doctor, he admitted that the files were in the hands of the detective's sister-in-law. An older lady named Betty Fortenberry. I'm going to tell you what you need to know about Betty and her whereabouts. You shouldn't have any trouble."

Right, no trouble at all. Anita swirled the ice in her empty glass. She was replaying Crawford's earlier comment that these people ruined lives and wondered what he meant by 'putting the screws' to the medical examiner. She wanted to disappear or wake up and realize this conversation had been a nightmare. *I need to get out of here.* Say thanks but no thanks.

But the temptation to put her financial problems behind her and launch Harper to a happy future won out.

"I'm listening."

Chapter 29

Tuesday, February 18, 2020

Louise hurried to her car in the parking lot of the Galveston Community Clinic. She held a medical journal over her head as protection from the light rain, waving to Connie Garcia as she ran to her car. She began her drive across the island to her parents' house to pick up the kids. *On time, for once!*

Her cell phone rang, and she picked up, assuming it was her mom. "Dr. Finnerty? This is Betty Fortenberry, Yvonne MacFarland's sister. I hate to bother you. Yvonne is having a hard time breathing. It might be anxiety, but I'm concerned because she says she has a tightness in her chest. Is there any way you could come by the house and look at her? I'm worried…."

Despite her concern for Yvonne, Louise cursed herself for giving out her number. "It sounds like she needs to go to the ER."

"I told her that and she's having nothing to do with it. I was hoping you could talk her into it."

"I'll do my best. Can you put her on the phone?"

After some rustling and whispers, Yvonne came to the phone. Her voice was tremulous. Louise thought she had been crying. "Dr. Finnerty, I hate to bother you. I think this is just nerves, but Betty, well, you know she's a nurse, she insisted."

Louise decided it was worth a short detour to the MacFarland's house to sort out the situation. She asked Yvonne to have Betty text her their address. She would call EMS herself when she got there if that's what was needed. She sighed and made a quick turn towards the seawall. The rain continued. When the Gulf came into sight, Louise could see the heavy gray clouds hanging low over the water. She felt chilled and turned on her seat warmer. She called her mom and explained that she would be delayed by her house call at the MacFarland home.

Louise parked in the driveway and ran to the door, grateful that it had been left open for her. She pushed the door open and looked down, considering whether to take off her wet shoes. She looked up to see Betty coming to meet her.

"Thanks so much for coming, Dr. Finnerty," she began. "Yvonne has me worried. Come on back."

Louise followed Betty toward the paneled den. Yvonne smiled weakly. "Oh, Dr. Finnerty, I'm so sorry to bother you. The tightness in my chest is gone now. I really shouldn't have mentioned it. To be honest, it's happened before but I was so busy taking care of Bruce and I just hoped it would go away. And it did."

"Well, that's good, but Yvonne, you really need to get this checked out. An EKG and some blood work can let us know if the pain is coming from your heart and how serious it is. I can drive you to the hospital, so you won't need to call an ambulance. Let me just ask a few more questions…"

Louise looked to Betty hoping she would chime in with support for the plan. Betty was standing frozen behind Yvonne's chair looking over Louise's shoulder, her eyes wide and unblinking. Louise turned to see what she was looking at. Anita Martin was standing outside the den. Her long black hair was plastered to her head and dripping down her low-cut dress. She was shivering. Louise could smell alcohol on her breath. She pulled a snub-nosed yellow weapon from her purse. Having seen police carry them in the ER, Louise recognized the taser. "Anita? What the hell?" Louise stood and positioned herself in front of the older women.

"I'll show you 'what the hell' if you take another step this way. And what the fuck are you doing here, Louise? I have business with Sister Betty. You know what I'm talking about, right, Betty?"

Yvonne gasped and grabbed her chest. Louise could tell the pain had returned. "I need to get her to the hospital, Anita. Let me get her into my car and you and Betty can talk about…."

"Yeah, right. Like you're not going to call one of your police buddies the minute you get out the door?"

Louise was terrified. *I need to cajole her like I did the uncooperative drunk patients in the ER.* "C'mon Anita, no one needs to get hurt here. Hand me the taser."

"Can't believe you're here, Louise. Like I really need another person to deal with?" Anita rolled her eyes. As Louise started to move toward her, she shouted, "Stay where you are!"

"Anita, please be reasonable." Louise inched forward into the foyer with her hand extended. Then, a crackling buzz and a jolt of excruciating pain hit her chest. She fell to her knees and slumped forward to the floor. It felt like a full body charley horse. She struggled to move. Anita took a step closer and pinned Louise's hand under the toe of her stiletto heeled shoe. Louise screamed.

"Shut the fuck up! Unless you want another jolt, shut up and listen," Anita ordered.

Louise's entire body was tingling. She turned her head back to the left. Betty was glaring at Anita.

"According to Betty, we need to take a trip to Matagorda. Isn't that right, Betty?" Anita said, taking her foot off Louise's hand. "Get up and get ready. Betty's gonna drive."

Louise tried to sit up but slumped back to the floor.

"What is going on here?" Louise asked, staring at the ceiling.

"I told you I'd get you the files as soon as I could leave Yvonne on her own," Betty said.

"It's gotta be tonight. I'm tired of waiting."

Betty sighed and said to Louise, "Basically, Bruce was on the take from some of Anita's upstanding relatives. He kept a file as insurance. At least that's what Jim Melvin told me."

Louise looked at Yvonne.

"I promise, I didn't know any of this, Dr. Finnerty."

Anita snorted. "You dumb shit, southern belle. Where did you think your cop husband got the cash for this house? And your cruises? Sister Betty certainly knew what was going on."

Yvonne started whimpering again. Louise turned to look at the hideous Italianate décor and murals. *Oh, Jesus. This is starting to make sense.*

Betty remained frozen in place and directed her words to Anita. "We better get going. It'll be a tough drive in this weather."

Anita pulled the taser darts out of Louise who was still too stunned to react with more than a flinch. She pulled Louise into a sit and then into a stand. Louise leaned against a wall.

Anita let the taser drop on the floor and pulled out a second taser from her bag and aimed it at Betty who backed up at the sight of it. She pulled zip ties from her huge purse, still slung over her shoulder. "Put them on those two," she ordered Betty. "Then give me your phone and Yvonne's."

Betty complied. Anita jammed her hand into Louise's back pocket and pulled out her phone. The three phones went into the purse.

Anita marched the women out the front door and into Betty's Subaru. When Betty turned on the ignition, Anita leaned over to assess the gas tank. "Full tank. Always prepared. Right, Betty? Is that what your friend, Melvin, taught you?" Betty made no response.

"Now, drive!" Anita ordered, sitting in the front seat, her purse in her lap, taser in her right hand. She pointed it at Louise in the back driver's side seat. "Don't even think about trying anything. And don't think this is the only protection I brought." She tapped her oversized purse.

***

Didier pulled into his driveway and made a dash to the house. He had led a weekly birding seminar at Feathers after closing time. The house was dark. *Strange.*

"Anybody home?" Only Chico rushed to meet him. "Where is everyone?" he asked the dog. He switched on lights and paced through the downstairs as he phoned Louise. The call went to voicemail. He called his mother-in-law, Nancy, and learned that Louise was making a house call on Yvonne MacFarland before picking up the kids.

"That was over two hours ago. I called her twice and texted. No answer. I'm beginning to get worried," Nancy said.

With his anxiety rising, his next call was to Sudhan. He gave her the timetable. "Iliana, I know it's only been a few hours, but I'm scared that this has something to do with MacFarland's murder after what happened to Marnie. This isn't like Louise. If she had to take Yvonne to the hospital, she would have called Nancy or me. Her phone goes right to voicemail."

Iliana didn't need convincing. "I'm still at work. Just about to leave. I'll swing by the MacFarland place."

"I'll meet you there."

***

When Sudhan arrived at the house on M street, she saw Louise's car in the driveway. She found the front door unlocked. Lights blazing in the hallway. Turning back to the driveway, she saw that Betty's car was gone. She scanned the hallway. Then she saw it in the corner. The bright yellow handle of a taser, copper wires attached to the silver barbs in a messy tangle. She called for backup.

When Didier arrived, Sudhan said, "Don't enter the house until backup arrives."

Didier stared at Sudhan, turned, and ran into the house. "Louise! Are you here?"

***

Louise felt nauseous in the backseat of the Subaru. Her tingling had resolved, but she couldn't concentrate. She looked at Yvonne, sitting next to her with her eyes closed, occasionally shuddering. Louise saw tears squeezing through Yvonne's lids. "Yvonne, are you okay?"

"No talking!" Anita barked.

I need a plan. Louise wished she could see Betty in the rear-view mirror. *What game is she playing?* Her thoughts were interrupted when Anita's phone rang.

"Hi, Harper. Did you eat? I left you a plate in the microwave and there's salad in the fridge." Pause. "I told you I wouldn't be home. Remember the yoga retreat Vera and I had planned?" Pause. "Yes, tonight. And no, you can't spend the night with Abby. It's a school night. You're seventeen and I'm trusting you to stay home alone. And remember you have a SAT review tomor–" Click.

Anita looked at her phone. "You're not going to hang up on me, you little shit!" she muttered under her breath then exhaled loudly. After texting madly, she pulled a flask out of her purse and took a noisy gulp.

She turned to Louise and said, "Kids, right? Wait

till your little ones turn into teenagers." Another swig. "I bet your parents have stories to tell about your teen years." Without waiting for a response, Anita turned to Betty and shouted, "Can this piece of crap go any faster?"

At the mention of her children and parents, Louise's stomach lurched. *How much does Anita know about my family? Is this her way of threatening us or is she just drunk and mouthing off?* The San Luis Pass came into view. They were at the southwestern tip of Galveston Island where a two-lane bridge connected to Follet's Island, the next barrier island in the chain along the Texas Gulf Coast.

Anita reached into her purse and dug out three cell phones, opened her window and tossed them into the roiling waves beneath them.

Louise watched her cell phone hit the water, fighting back tears. *Fuck. Didier can't track me by my cell phone now.* The drive progressed along the two-lane highways that connected Galveston to Matagorda. Night had fallen. The rain continued to hammer the car. Passing trucks sprayed water on the windshield which obliterated the view, forcing Betty to brake.

Anita called her daughter again. Apparently, the alcohol had made her forget that she was laying out her despair in front of the others in the car. "Harper, sweetheart, I need you to listen to me. I'm doing everything I can, so you get to have a better life than me. Isn't that what every mother wants? Just work with me and we'll both get a chance at a fresh start." She paused, teary-eyed. "Yeah, love you too."

Louise was desperate herself. She had to think of a way to get out of this situation. When they finally pulled into Betty's driveway, Louise's wrists were burning from the zip ties and every cell in the rest of her body ached. She could make out Betty's bungalow tucked close between neighboring homes. Yvonne was sitting still beside her, still shivering. "Yvonne, are you alright?" Louise tried again.

"I told you to keep your mouth shut," Anita shouted, having regained her composure and tough girl facade. She turned to Louise, then glanced at Yvonne. "She's fine. Let's go in. If your alarm goes off, Betty, the next sound you'll hear will be thirty thousand volts hitting your skull."

The women walked up the three steps to a covered porch. Betty, in the lead, opened the front door and led the group into the dark house. She turned off her alarm,

"Turn on whatever lights you normally would. We don't need your neighbors to get nosey. Then get me the file. I assume you have it in a safe." Anita trained the taser on Betty as she spoke.

"It's back here," Betty said.

Yvonne groaned and Anita turned in her direction. Betty made brief eye contact with Louise and nodded almost imperceptibly as she cast her eyes towards Anita. Louise wasn't sure what Betty was trying to communicate but she readied herself to act.

"This way." Betty headed down the hallway. Louise, Yvonne, and Anita followed close behind.

With the four of them in a line in the narrow hallway, Betty approached a closed door. Anita said, "Hold up, Betty." Anita turned. "You two, sit down and don't move." Louise and Yvonne still had their hands cuffed in front of them. Louise helped Yvonne slip slowly down   the wall and onto the floor, then slid down next to her.

"Go ahead, open it," Anita said to Betty, prodding her with the taser. As soon as Betty opened the door, she backed against the wall. Anita shrieked and lurched back as a large black cat jumped in her direction from the bathroom counter and streaked down the hall. Anita lost her balance as she tried to remain upright with her enormous purse in one hand and taser in the other, teetering on her heels. Louise swung her legs into Anita's calves. Anita toppled over, face down. The contents of her bag scattered across the floor. With Anita at ground level Louise was able to lunge over her, hoping to restrain her until Betty could assist.

Although hampered by the zip ties, Louise was able to grab Anita's hair and jerk her head back. Anita screamed. Louise held tight, keeping Anita's neck extended backwards in a painful, stress position. Louise felt as if they were in this posture for an eternity. Anita was bucking with all her strength and eventually turned over and got her hands around Louise's throat. She started to squeeze. Louise felt everything go dark. Then Anita screamed, loosened her grip, and went limp. Louise gasped for air. She saw Betty holding the taser and understood. Without missing a beat, Betty proceeded to inject Anita in the neck with a syringe. Completing that injection, she followed it up with another injection through Anita's sleeve and into her arm.

Louise scooted herself away from Anita's body. She watched as Anita's breathing slowed, as if she were relaxing. Her respirations continued to decrease. She was barely breathing. Her previously flushed complexion went ashen.

"Betty, what did you give her?"

"Fentanyl. And lots of it. Are you alright, doc? Yvonne?"

"Shit! Betty, she's dying," Louise croaked. "Call EMS before it's too late."

It was Yvonne who spoke next. "They're on their way." Yvonne was holding Anita's phone in her still-cuffed hands. "It's just like mine. I pressed SOS."

Louise looked from Betty to Yvonne. The sisters were staring at each other intently. The house lit up with red and blue lights as the first responders rushed in.

"Narcan!" screamed Louise. "She's been overdosed on fentanyl."

The paramedics were prepared. One uncapped a plastic container and sprayed it up Anita's nose. The second paramedic started an IV and injected more Narcan. Anita's breathing improved and she began to stir.

Two police officers arrived to find Betty still holding the taser, Yvonne and Louise with zip ties on, and Anita semiconscious on the floor. The used syringes were next to her. Anita's semiautomatic handgun, another taser, more zip ties and a flask were scattered on the hardwood floor.

One of the officers barked, "Don't anybody move!" Louise noticed that Betty was smiling, which struck her as odd. She followed her gaze to a tall bookshelf where a large black cat observed the scene.

***

Fifteen minutes later, a man Louise identified as a

detective walked into the house. "Would someone mind telling me what's going on here?"

"This one is the only one talking. Won't shut up." One of the first responding officers indicated Louise, still sitting on the floor. The two men moved out of Louise's earshot.

Paramedics placed Yvonne on a cardiac monitor and were performing an EKG. Louise strained to see it. The paramedic was immediately on his phone to alert the local ER that they were on their way. "We've got a sixty-six-year-old female with chest pain. EKG shows acute myocardial infarction. Vitals stable. Protocol in progress." Mercifully, they had snipped off Yvonne's zip ties before the police could object.

"I'll check on you as soon as I can. Hang tight," Louise called out to Yvonne as she was put on a gurney and wheeled to the waiting ambulance.

"Thank you dear, and I'm so sorry," Yvonne whispered.

A second team of paramedics crouched over Anita. "BP eighty over pulse. O2 sat marginal on non-rebreather. IV wide open. I'm giving her another dose of Narcan," the paramedic said to his partner. "Let's go. We can call the report to the ER en route."

The detective instructed two uniforms to accompany the patients. "Stick to them like glue. Nobody talks to them except the medical staff."

He turned his attention to Louise. Before he could speak, Louise began, "I'm Dr. Louise Finnerty, I live in Galveston. Please call Detective Iliana Sudhan at GPD while I try to explain this situation."

"I know Sudhan," he said. Then to one of the

cops, "Call Galveston PD and get her on the phone."

Louise began to recount the events of the evening. She hadn't gotten far when the officer charged with contacting Sudhan handed his phone to the detective. "Detective Sudhan, it's Marty Edwards in Matagorda. Long time, right?" He turned his back on Louise as he conversed. Without ending the call, he spoke to the officer, "Get these zip ties off Dr. Finnerty." Then he put the phone on speaker and handed it to Louise.

"Iliana?" Louise said. "Thank God they reached you!"

"Good to hear your voice, too," Iliana said. "I'm at the MacFarland home. Torres and Didier are on their way to Matagorda."

Louise couldn't contain the tears of relief that filled her eyes. "It was a nightmare, Iliana."

Detective Edwards looked on until she ended the call. He extended his hand to Louise and helped her up. "Please continue where you left off."

Then to the officer, "Keep an eye on that one." He jutted his chin toward Betty. "Take her down to the station. We'll question her there."

Sitting on the couch in Betty's living room Louise's account of the evening spilled out. Detective Edwards took careful notes. When Didier was ushered in, she rushed to him. Neither could say a word as they clung to each other.

Torres spoke to Detective Edwards. Louise heard them argue about jurisdiction. A call was placed to Sudhan.

After more back and forth, Edwards relented. "Fine, Torres, you can drive these two back to Galveston. Then to Louise, "Don't leave the island till we get this mess sorted out."

Chapter 30

Wednesday, February 19, 2020

Sudhan woke up to a sunny day and two more people of interest in the expanding web around Bruce MacFarland's murder—Betty Fortenberry and Anita Martin. She was trying to sort out the pieces as she drove to work. *James Melvin was our only suspect in the murder of Bruce MacFarland. Were Betty and Anita working with or against Dr. Melvin? From Louise's description of the abduction, they clearly weren't working together. Damn, I needed Melvin's side of the story. Too late for that.* Her phone buzzed. "Hi Torres, what did you find out?"

"Your buddy Detective Edwards talked to his chief who talked to our chief. Betty's being transported back to Galveston since she's a key player in the MacFarland case. When do you want to talk to her?"

"As soon as she gets back here. I imagine she's going to lawyer up. What's the status of Anita Martin?"

"I'm about to make another call to find out. She was admitted to the hospital down there. Apparently, Betty came close to killing her with all the fentanyl she injected. Where the hell would she get that stash?" Torres asked.

"Yet another question." Sudhan exhaled. "Let me know what you learn, and we'll take a crack at Betty."

As she entered her office, Sudhan made another call. "Louise? How are you doing? Did you get any rest?" Sudhan chatted with Louise long enough to be assured that aside from a hoarse voice her friend was recovering from the events of the previous evening. "I'll stop by on my way home from work."

Sudhan shook her head in disbelief. *First Marnie, then Taylor and EJ. Now Louise. Not to mention Yvonne MacFarland and Anita Martin. Looks like whatever MacFarland and Melvin were up to is causing plenty of collateral damage.*

***

Louise persuaded Didier to leave her alone for twenty minutes while he picked up the kids at school. When he left, her hand went to her throat, still bruised and sore. She heard a car drive up. *Too soon for Didier*. She stood and stiffly walked to the door to check the lock. A peek through the door's small windows brought relief. *Marnie!*

She opened the door to see EJ helping her mom out of the car. Louise went to Marnie and the women hugged each other hard, both with tears in their eyes.

Louise turned to EJ. "How are you doing? Didier filled me in on your attempted kidnapping. This investigation has been life threatening for all of us."

EJ replied, "It was terrifying. Luckily it was short-lived. I'm amazed you're functioning at all. The good news is that it led to a resolution of a lot of loose ends.

We can talk about it inside. Mom's supposed to be under house arrest with her feet elevated but I couldn't keep her home after she heard what happened to you."

Once settled, Marnie asked, "How are you doing, Louise?"

"I've been better," she said, rubbing her throat. "I think I need to find some scarves to wear when I go back to the clinic."

"You'll look like a chic French doctor," EJ said. "I'll make some tea. I know where everything is."

Marnie said, "Your abduction spooked us. These attacks on me, EJ and Taylor, and you make us feel like we stepped into a hornet's nest."

EJ returned with mugs of tea and a plate of cookies.

Louise told Marnie and EJ what happened at Matagorda. "I still don't know what's going to happen to Betty and Yvonne—or for that matter, to Anita."

EJ related the details of the shoot-out. "I've never been as scared as I was then. Thank goodness adrenaline kicks in and we can act before we think. It leaves a person shaking when it ebbs."

"Wait a minute—why was this Kevin trying to kill Taylor?" Louise asked.

Marnie looked at EJ. EJ nodded in agreement.

Marnie said, "We don't know what triggered Kevin to try to kill Taylor. Sudhan says that he had ties to the cartel. Maybe some remaining island Mafia, too."

"Like Anita's family? Damn, this is getting really twisted," Louise said.

"But let me tell the story of Luther Wood's death. Kevin was involved in that."

After Marnie finished speaking, Louise sank back in her chair. "Wow, that's quite a story. A series of tragedies and victims."

Louise was ready to shelve talk about their attacks and Luther Wood's tragedy. "Tell me more about getting ready for the baby."

"All done," Marnie said. "Once I told Chris about my fears of being left alone the first few weeks after what happened with EJ, he and Rosa organized a lot of assistance."

"Well, add Didier and me to the list. And you know you won't be able to keep my mom away."

Marnie smiled. "With the latest news on this virus from China, I'm beginning to hope that he comes sooner rather than later. I don't relish being in a hospital with a new flu-like illness hitting the country."

Louise nodded. "Talk of an epidemic makes me think of Gen's work at the Galveston National Laboratory. She thought it would be dengue. This new virus could be much worse."

EJ said, "Let's stop tragic speculation for a few hours. I'm excited about having a baby brother."

The three chatted happily about all the work that went into welcoming a baby into a home. Louise heard Didier pull up and she stood to greet them at the door. The presence of her family comforted her. The kids grabbed the remaining cookies and talked EJ into a game of Uno, leaving the adults to speak freely. Didier joined the women.

"Before we bring Didier up to date, I have some big news," Marnie said. "Chris and I decided to get married!"

After the initial shock, both Louise and Didier shouted, "Congratulations!"

"When did you decide this?" Louise asked.

"Ten days ago, to be exact. We're going to wait until things settle down and it's going to be small. We thought just you two and EJ. We told her a few days ago."

"We're so happy for you," Didier said.

Louise smiled at Marnie. "It is great news. We could use more of that around here."

After answering a few more questions about wedding plans, Marnie gave Didier a summary of recent events.

"Foster…?" Didier began but was interrupted by the doorbell before he could ask his question.

"Were you expecting more company?" he asked Louise as he went to the door. He carried a baseball bat behind his back. "Oh hi, Iliana. Come on in and join the party."

"I guess I'm not the only one wanting to check on you this afternoon, Louise. Hi Marnie." She waved to EJ in the kitchen with the kids.

Didier shooed a reluctant Chico off the remaining chair and Iliana joined the circle in the living room.

After reassuring Sudhan that Marnie and she were on the mend, Louise asked Iliana to fill them in on the aftermath of the scene in Matagorda.

"Whew, where to start? Torres gave me an update on Anita this morning. She's still in the hospital down there. Apparently, she aspirated after Betty injected her with fentanyl and has pneumonia. Torres said she had a neck injury and was going to get an MRI."

Thinking of the stress position she held Anita in,

Louise said, "I think I might have had something to do with the neck injury."

Iliana raised a hand to stop her. "I already forgot what you said."

Louise smiled. "Did I say anything?"

Iliana continued, "Torres says she's not talking much and says she can't remember what she was doing in Matagorda. Sounds like a convenient case of amnesia."

"How about Yvonne?" Louise asked. "I've been worried."

"Still in the hospital in Matagorda. Torres was able to talk to her medical team and learned that she had had a heart attack but was in stable condition. She's been very upset about the entire situation, especially about the involvement of her sister. Obviously, she's in no condition to be questioned yet."

"Definitely not," Louise agreed. Then to Didier, "Maybe you could ask some of her birding friends to pay a visit."

"I will," Didier said. "But is she under suspicion, Iliana?"

"Not yet, according to what Louise has been able to tell us about the events of last night. We're focused on Betty and Anita."

"What's the status of Betty?" Marnie asked.

"She's being held right now for attempting to murder Anita with a lethal dose of fentanyl."

"But can't that be seen as self-defense?" Louise asked. "Betty's attack is what saved my life."

"It's not that easy, Louise. As expected, Betty has engaged an attorney and isn't saying much. From what you told me, she knew a lot more about Dr. Melvin's and

Bruce MacFarland's extracurricular activities than anyone suspected. We'll have to find out the depth of her involvement."

"What about all that fentanyl in her possession?" Marnie asked.

"At least we have an answer there," Iliana continued. "Betty's husband died of pancreatic cancer about a year ago. During his last days, he was under hospice care at home. Since Betty is a nurse herself, she managed his pain medication. According to Betty, he passed away with quite a supply leftover. Betty did some fast thinking when Anita had you all at gunpoint."

"Taser point," Louise corrected.

"Yes, taser point. Still a form of assault capable of causing grievous harm." Iliana let out a soft chuckle.

The others looked at her. "What's so funny about grievous harm?" Louise asked.

"Nothing. I was thinking about the real hero of the night, Randy the cat. Apparently, Betty would leave the bathroom window open for him when she went out of town. She left food and water dispensers there. Betty hoped the bad weather would have caused him to come in. And if so, behave in his usual fashion and dash out as soon as Betty opened the door."

"That's exactly what happened. Like a 'cat out of hell'. The shock knocked Anita right off her feet. Probably helped that she was drunk." Louise shook her head. "It would be funny if it wasn't part of this twisted story where so many people have been hurt."

"As for Dr. Melvin," Iliana said. "While we didn't care whether he lived or died, it is unfortunate that we didn't get a confession from him to corroborate the findings at Bruce MacFarland's bedside the night of his murder and Marnie's recollection of the unidentified lab tech."

Marnie bristled. "It's more than a recollection! I'm sure the man who tried to kill me was the same person I ran into in the hospital that night. Dr. James Melvin!"

"Everyone in this room believes you, Marnie. But we don't have proof that he killed Bruce," said Iliana. "This is moot since he died before he could be tried."

Louise and Marnie locked eyes. Iliana looked from one to the other. She appeared to be about to speak when her phone chirped. "It's a text from Torres. Betty is proposing a plea deal. I need to go."

After Iliana left, Louise said, "James Melvin may never be found guilty in a court of law. Not for the murder of Bruce MacFarland nor for his attack on you but that doesn't mean he won't be found guilty as hell for both in the court of public opinion."

Marnie looked out the picture window which framed the west end marshes. "I think this island has a lot of secrets, but Melvin tried to kill my baby and me. I'm not going to let that be one of them."

Louise moved next to Marnie and gave her a hug. "I love this island. But it doesn't need that secret."

Chapter 31

Wednesday, Feb 19, 2020

Sudhan shifted emotional gears when she entered the department. Here her job was to solve crimes. She deposited her jacket and bag in her office.

"Ready for another round with Betty?" asked Torres. "I have her in the interrogation room with her lawyer."

"Just about. Before we start, I want to make sure we don't have any questions hanging that could trip us up. Were you able to confirm her alibi for the night of MacFarland's murder? Playing bridge in Matagorda?"

Torres consulted his notes. "Yeah. It checked out. Several members of her bridge club confirmed her presence."

"How about the kid, Carlos, the MacFarland's cleaning lady's grandson? Remember the grandma was afraid he could have copied the key and got into the house? Or handed it off to someone wanting Bruce dead?"

Torres flipped a few pages. "Got that too. His grandma must have been confused. His parents sent him to live with relatives out of state to get him away from the gang he was in. He spent the entire first half of the school year in Illinois. He could have copied the key before he left last August and handed it off, but that was before MacFarland's health took a dive."

"Unlikely that he was involved. Let's hear what Betty has to say and come back to Carlos if we need to."

"Do you know her, Betty's attorney?"

"We've crossed paths before. Megan Emerson is sharp. She doesn't let her clients waste time, neither hers nor ours. She must have got Betty to realize that attempted murder carries serious penalties. And that we have solid evidence for a conviction. Let's see what they have to offer."

Betty looked up as the detectives entered the room. She was dressed in orange jail scrubs that strained across her chest. She appeared fatigued but still focused. After a few preliminaries, including Sudhan's statement that the interview was being videoed, Betty's attorney began the proceedings.

"My client is offering to provide evidence in the form of emails and texts that will confirm the premeditated poisoning and murder of Bruce MacFarland by James Melvin. Additionally, she agrees to provide the police with the location of the files that Anita Martin was in search of on the night in question."

"In exchange for what?" Sudhan asked.

"That the charge of attempted murder be dropped. My client agrees to plead guilty to the lesser charge of assault and battery of Anita Martin."

"If you want me to take this offer to my DA, I'm going to need more information," Sudhan said.

Betty looked at her attorney, then to Sudhan, "If I may, I'd like to explain how we ended up here. It might take a while, but the evidence I have will allow you to close the case on the murder of Bruce MacFarland. In addition, I have information that will result in the correction of many wrongful convictions during the careers of Bruce MacFarland and James Melvin."

"Please go ahead." Sudhan nodded at Betty and her attorney.

Betty shifted in her seat. "When my husband was in hospice, I began an affair with Jim Melvin. With time I became privy to very damaging information related to the illegal activities of Bruce and Jim in their roles as detective and medical examiner."

"Damaging to whom?" Sudhan asked, still inwardly processing the upfront admission of the affair.

"Why did Anita want the files? Who was she protecting?" asked Torres.

"If you let me start at the beginning, most of your questions will be answered."

Sudhan exchanged looks with Torres, then responded, "We have all night."

Chapter 32

Thursday, February 20, 2020

Louise planned to stay home from work until Monday. The aftereffects of the taser had resolved—no more tingling or aching. Her neck was another story. The deep violet bruises looked worse. The morning routine with Didier and the kids kept her mind off the traumatic events of the last few days. She sensed his anxiety and reluctance to leave her alone.

"I was collateral damage," Louise said. "I showed up at the wrong place at the wrong time. Anita Martin had no choice but to rope me into her loony quest. And according to Iliana, she's in no shape to come after me." Louise hoped her tone was more reassuring than she felt. "I'll go with you to take the kids to school and then you can drop me off at Mom's house. I need some turtlenecks and scarves."

Didier nodded his approval of the plan. "I can catch up on a few things at Feathers, then pick you up. I'm sure your parents will be relieved to see you." He smiled. "Your mom does have an extensive wardrobe."

They packed lunch boxes and hustled the kids into the car. At the elementary school, Louise and Didier watched Cora and Noah find their friends. When the bell rang, the children lined up behind their teachers and followed them inside. Louise and Didier watched until the lines disappeared into the school, calmed by the routine. Normal life was coming back into focus. Louise took Didier's hand.

Nancy and Claude Finnerty rushed to the door to greet her. Their smiles faded as they took in Louise's battle scars. They hugged her cautiously. In the short time between Louise's call and her arrival, Nancy had laid out at least ten turtlenecks and as many scarves. Louise picked five of each, opting for the more subdued colors and patterns. For the rest of the morning, she allowed her parents to pamper her.

Around 11 a.m. she received a call from Sudhan. "Hi Louise, I hope you're on the mend. Do you think that you could come down to the station today? I need your help with Betty's account of events leading up to Matagorda." Sudhan recounted the interview in broad strokes for Louise.

"Geez. Quite a confession. Betty and Dr. Melvin! That never crossed my mind."

"I took her offer to the DA. Not sure what will be decided. We should know by later today," Sudhan explained. "In the meantime, I'd like you to verify some of the medical aspects of Betty's confession."

"Yes, let's bring this story to a close."

Didier arrived and stayed for lunch at the Finnerty's. Louise explained Sudhan's request.

"Are you sure you're up to it?" Nancy asked.

"Anything to put this behind me."

"Us," Didier added.

Didier drove her to the police station. "I guess you'll be safe here."

"Yes, dear. Hey, what do you think about the scarf? Is it too frou-frou?"

"I think the state of your throat calls for a bit of décor." He gently brushed her cheek with the back of his hand. "Call me when you get done."

Louise introduced herself at the front desk. Torres came out to greet her and escorted her to Sudhan's office. "It's good to see you up and around, doc. That was quite a mess down in Matagorda."

"I can't begin to tell you how happy I was to see you. Thanks for convincing the local police to let me go home and for bringing Didier along."

Torres laughed. "There was no holding him back."

Sudhan joined them. "Hi, Louise. Let's go into the conference room. I want you to watch the video of last evening's interview. Help us understand what Betty is saying about MacFarland's last few months. Your input will be important."

Once settled, Torres plugged in the laptop and pushed play. The lighting was not kind to Betty. She spoke directly to Sudhan and Torres, and occasionally to the camera. Her attorney remained off screen for the most part. Louise was spellbound by the story that unfolded.

Betty: I never expected to find romance and rediscover sex at this point in my life. Amazing sex! I felt like I was twenty-five again.

Louise glanced at Sudhan who smiled and raised her eyebrows.

Betty: It started shortly before the death of my husband. Jim Melvin had been a longtime friend of ours, through Yvonne and Bruce. He made visits to Hank's bedside at the end. When Hank passed, we progressed to secret liaisons and weekend trips. Great romantic stays at secluded resorts in the Caribbean. Jim wanted our love to be kept secret. I agreed with anything he asked. It was thrilling. Until it wasn't.

Betty recounted that after a year or so, the affair began to fizzle. Their lovemaking ceased. When Betty begged for an explanation from him, he became angry. Then, to Betty's surprise, he suddenly asked her if she wanted to spend the rest of her life with him.

Betty: Of course, I did. I was besotted. I would agree to anything. That's when everything went to hell.

Betty explained that Jim needed her help to protect their future. After more clarifications requested by Sudhan and Torres, it boiled down to the fact that Bruce MacFarland and Jim Melvin had been receiving payoffs from the cartel for years. They were paid to deep-six incriminating evidence of guilty parties or plant evidence incriminating innocent people. The sooner they cleared a case exonerating a cartel suspect, or convicting an innocent loser, the sooner they were paid. The remains of the island Mafia were the middlemen, arranging the hits and coverups and delivering the payoffs. During the raging drug wars, cases kept coming their way. The crimes were most often murders in which false autopsy and ballistic findings nailed the convictions.

Betty: As Bruce's dementia worsened, he began blabbing about some of these cases. He bragged about keeping a folder of evidence that he stole from the department. DNA had just become the gold standard. Bruce was an early adherent and kept blood-stained papers, scraps of clothing, even cocktail napkins. Word got back to cartel folks and mafiosi. They began to pressure Jim to silence Bruce and to retrieve the evidence he had stashed at home.

"Wait," Louise said, holding up her hand. "Who are these Mafia folks? I can understand the cartel, but the Mafia? I thought the Mafia families had cleaned up their acts or moved on from Galveston ages ago. I know there have been rumors, but they seemed more like colorful anecdotes than anything real."

"You might be surprised," Torres said. "Think about Anita Martin, nee Papalardo. What or who was motivating her to go on that rampage?"

"That's not a subject we need to address with Louise," Sudhan murmured. "The part coming up is where I need your help." She resumed the video.

Betty: Jim told me that we had no choice but to silence Bruce. Permanently. Then we could leave town or even the country. He said he had plenty of money saved offshore. He came up with the scheme to overdose Bruce on his own medication. Jim used his visits and frequent trips to the restroom to load up the supplement bottles with lethal doses of blood thinner and diabetes meds. It was my job to make sure Bruce stayed on his regimen. It was around that time that Jim asked me to get the file and take it to Matagorda for safe keeping.

Louise was shaking her head in disgust. "How could Betty have agreed to be an accomplice to her own brother-in-law's murder? She's a god-damned nurse!"

"Keep watching," Sudhan said.

Betty: When Bruce landed in the hospital the first time, I just couldn't go along with it anymore. After Jim's visits, I'd do my best to undo his handiwork with the pills. But they looked so closely identical, I could never get them all out. He was still having 'unexplained' symptoms and crazy lab results. Jim never knew what I was doing.

Betty recounted episodes of hypoglycemia and bleeding during those months. None were severe enough to be fatal but did result in trips to the ER and several short hospitalizations.

Betty: Jim decided on a more aggressive plan. He waited till Bruce landed in the hospital again. He had the whole lab tech scheme ready to go. He told me all about his plans. Even sent me articles about cerebral air embolism. I now realize he was trying to incriminate me as an accomplice. When I tried to talk him out of it, he threatened to kill me.

Here, Betty looked directly at the camera. Her face became blotchy, and she started to cry.

Betty: Not just me. He was going to kill Yvonne if I tried to stop him. Then, after he did it, he was scared the Liccione woman was on to him. I thought he was unhinged and paranoid, but he said she saw him in the hospital the night he killed Bruce and might eventually recognize him. None of this made any sense. I could only conclude that all his lies were getting twisted up. Then I heard about the attack on Dr. Liccione and....

Sudhan pushed pause. Betty's tortured features remained on the screen. "Louise, does this make sense to you? Did you note the swings in Bruce's blood tests? Do the symptoms correlate with what you observed about his medical ups and downs since you took him on as a patient?"

Louise couldn't look at Betty's image. She turned to Sudhan. "Her story corresponds perfectly with what I was observing during Bruce's medical spiral. And it corresponds to Marnie's conclusion about why he went after her."

Sudhan got up and turned on the lights. "I think that's enough for today. Thanks, Louise. I'll pass on your observations to the DA."

Louise stood and stretched, gingerly turning her head from side to side. She texted Didier that she was ready to leave. Turning to Sudhan, she said, "It's a lot to process. After listening to Betty, I can't help feeling conflicted. She violated the Nightingale Pledge she took when she became a nurse. Then again, she tried to mitigate the harm Melvin was causing. And she was trapped by Melvin's psychological manipulation, especially by his threat to kill Yvonne and her." She shook her head and added, "She saved my life by overdosing Anita."

"I hear you. Morally, Betty's situation is in the gray area," Sudhan said. "Legally she's guilty. Her willingness to hand over Bruce's files will help her case."

"And open a huge can of worms for our department.," Torres added, shaking his head. "Not to mention some prominent families on the island."

"Oh yeah, the files. Where did she hide them?" Louise asked. "Obviously it wasn't in the bathroom with Randy the cat."

"She put it in an old-fashioned safe deposit box at her local bank. It's been retrieved and is currently in the hands of forensics. They're having a field day. DNA analysis and genetic databases are much more sophisticated than when Bruce began his collection," Sudhan said.

"It turns out the legwork Ben and EJ put in searching for MacFarland's and Melvin's cases will give the department a head start on sorting all this out," Torres added.

"Never a dull moment," Louise said as she gathered her purse and coat. She received a text from Didier. He was waiting outside. She was pretty sure that Chris and his interns were already hard at work on the case. *But I'm ready to take a break.*

Chapter 33

Friday, February 21, 2020

With delicious smells coming from her kitchen, Marnie decided it was time to get up and do her hourly walk. "Hi Rosa, that smells great. Thanks for coming in on your day off."

"No problem. School is on vacation for President's Day weekend. I'm planning to be flexible on days until the baby is born and you're settled. I'll stockpile meals for a long vacation this summer." Rosa smiled. "I'm getting a jump on Mardi Gras cooking. Ash Wednesday is next week. I wonder if Louise is still planning on her party next weekend?"

"Oh, I hadn't even thought about it. I doubt that she has. Maybe I should suggest we have it here?"

Rosa glanced at Marnie's belly. "I think your baby has dropped."

Marnie settled onto a bar stool. "I did feel a thwump when I stood up this morning. I'm almost thirty-five weeks along. I think he'll do fine if he comes now. All the news about this virus they're calling Covid 19 makes me think that now would be great."

Rosa smiled. "He'll come in his own sweet time. But he strikes me as a smart and strong baby, so maybe soon. Anything else happening today?"

"Charlotte's coming over. She feels bad about her role in all of this."

"Poor Miss Charlotte. She was caught in a tough situation when she was young. I think her reputation as an adult is impeccable." The doorbell chimed.

Marnie looked at her watch. Right on time. "I've got the door," Marnie called to Rosa. She walked to the door with her hand under her belly. "Come in, come in." Let's go to the sunroom and watch the birds. Rosa said she would bring us some tea and cookies. How are you doing?"

"That's probably a question I should ask you. It looks like your baby dropped."

"I think he did. Not quite the feeling of carrying him between my knees but close."

As they settled on the porch, Charlotte said, "The truth is, I've been better. Both Foster and I have felt like a weight is off our shoulders but revisiting that time is painful. We've talked to the police. Detective Sudhan was understanding. She said that Taylor will have some input on whether charges are brought."

"It sounds overwhelming."

Rosa came in with tea and freshly baked chocolate chip cookies.

Charlotte managed a small smile. "Thanks so much."

Rosa nodded and left.

As they watched the birds and ate cookies, Marnie

looked at Charlotte. She looked exhausted. There were dark rings under her eyes. "I just want you to know that Chris and I understand your precarious position. We're here to support you and Foster as friends and as an employer."

Charlotte nodded. "That's so kind of you. I haven't been able to sleep. We don't know what Taylor is going to say. Our nightmare may not be over."

Marnie rested her hand on Charlotte's arm. "You need to take care of yourself and Foster. Speaking of which, I wanted to let you know that I've done some work with foster systems in the past when I was practicing as a pediatrician."

Charlotte looked confused.

"Children whose parents die are entitled to dependent social security payments. Sometimes the state tries to keep the money, but several legal cases have ruled against this confiscation. You're entitled to money that you should have gotten from when your parents died until you were adopted. Foster is entitled to money from the time of their deaths until age eighteen."

"You're kidding, right?"

"No. It's frequently several thousand dollars. I spoke to an attorney friend of Chris, and he said he would investigate it for you. Pro bono."

"Oh Marnie, that is so nice of you. It would be great for Foster to have something good happen in his life now."

Marnie smiled. "Glad to be a bearer of good news. I'll let you know when the baby comes. Maybe you can come over then."

"Thank you, Marnie. Please let me know."

At the door, Marnie reached over and pulled Charlotte into a hug. "It's all going to work out. I'll be fine. You and Foster will have a fresh start."

With tears in her eyes, Charlotte hugged Marnie back.

***

Taylor looked through the MacFarland's bay window. He had met Yvonne and Betty at the house at noon. Yvonne had signed a realtor contract for the sale of her house. She had decided to move in with Betty for the time being. Taylor had helped the women load up Betty's Subaru with personal belongings to take to Matagorda. Betty's parole allowed her to travel home with her ankle monitor system. He planned to inspect the MacFarland's house and make a list of repairs before meeting with Foster and Charlotte at 1:00.

When Foster and Charlotte arrived, Taylor led them into the small kitchenette where they took seats around the table. Taylor felt their anxiety. "I wanted to meet somewhere neutral, but timing was difficult. I've been contracted to sell Yvonne's house, and she said I could use it as much as I needed. How did it go with the police?"

Foster looked at Charlotte who gave an encouraging nod. "Pretty well overall. We confirmed that Kevin Small was the man who um, did what he did to your father's body."

"You mean hacked him up like a slaughtered animal?" Taylor asked.

Foster nodded and met Taylor's gaze. "Yeah. It's just hard to say it out loud, but you're right. The detective said that at this point the review of the autopsy supports my story. She said that what happens next would depend on what you wanted."

Taylor gazed out the small window in the kitchenette. *What do I want?* He took a deep breath. "I've thought a lot about that. After the shoot-out with Kevin, EJ and I went to the police station. Chris told Detective Sudhan what we learned from you. He tried to keep your names out of it, but Sudhan said she needed to interview you."

Charlotte put her hand on Taylor's arm. "We are so sorry that this cover-up expanded to you and your friends. We were trying to avoid harm coming to you."

Taylor nodded. "Cover-ups rarely seem to work out. But after my encounter with your uncle, I do understand the difficult position you were in." He looked from Charlotte to Foster. "I don't need or want any more suffering on your part. I find myself increasingly furious with the police. Detective MacFarland and Dr. Melvin hid and altered the evidence in my dad's case right under their noses. Apparently, the racket between the cartel and those two went on for years."

Foster looked at Taylor expectantly. "Is our ordeal over?"

Taylor smiled. "I imagine there will be rumors about who the 'minor' was, but they'll die down. I want a full report of my father's death, and the desecration of his body released. And a formal and public apology from the police for the hell they put my mom and me through. The Daily will be running several articles about it. I'm sure I'll have several meetings with Detective Sudhan. I've decided to tell her that pursuing charges against you is unnecessary from my point of view."

Charlotte's and Foster's relief was palpable.

Taylor looked around the room and gestured broadly, "As you can see, if I'm going to get this place ready to go on the market, I'm going to need a lot of help."

Foster smiled for the first time as he stood up. "Let me know what I can do. I'm familiar with the place."

Charlotte stood and took Foster's hand. Then appeared to take in the crazy Italian murals covering the walls. "This place deserves a fresh start, too."

* * *

Giles looked at Anita's empty office. Rumors had it that she was done at the hotel. Should she get out of the hospital, she was going to prison for a long time. *Might as well make use of the situation.* He was mad that she had nixed his little money-making scheme. The thought of that pompous 'upstanding citizen' getting away without any penalty grated on him. He could still feel that man's sweaty hands touching him.

I don't really need this minimum wage job. I can hitch a ride out of town and use my savings and anything I gain today to set up in Florida. Giles went into Anita's office. He had watched her get money out of the safe to pay him for two tasers. Looking over her shoulder, it had been a cinch to memorize the code. He opened the safe on his second try, grabbed a flash drive, and a couple of stacks of twenties. He uploaded the flash drive on Anita's computer and made sure it contained his tryst with Mr. Parker Dodge. Giles doctored the video so that his face was obscured. Then he sent the pictures to a fake account of his on a social media site. *I wonder how long before this is the talk of the town. Payback is great.*

Chapter 34

Saturday, February 22, 2020

2:10 a.m.

Marnie sat in her adjustable bed. Braxton Hicks contractions had been waking her up for the last few nights. This time, they didn't stop. She had a twenty-four-hour news program playing on the TV. This new virus was sweeping through the world. Italy seemed to be having it the worst.

Come on baby, let's get the show on the road.

As the contractions became stronger and more regular, she called Chris in the upstairs bedroom. "It might be time to go to the hospital."

"Be right there!"

When Marnie went into the bathroom, her water broke.

Chris entered the bedroom, dressed and ready-to-go.

Marnie looked at the wet floor. "At least it's on the tile."

"No worries." Chris went to her. "How do you

feel?"

She bent over the sink as a strong contraction hit. "Like I'm going to have a baby."

Chris grabbed her go-bag. "Can you make it to the car?"

When the contraction eased, she said, "Yes." She pulled on the sweatpants and shirt that she had been keeping at the ready, slipped on her shoes, and leaned on Chris's arm. "Let's go."

Chris had parked in front of the house and helped Marnie into her seat which already had a towel on it. They had been prepared for this trip. Last time stretching the seat belt over this bulk. She smiled. Then another contraction hit. "I wouldn't waste any time."

"Got it," Chris said.

They pulled up to the ER entrance. An attendant came out with a wheelchair.

"We're headed to labor and delivery," Chris said.

"Ahh, this is the ER. Labor and delivery is around the corner."

Marnie leaned on Chris and moaned as another hard contraction hit her. Chris looked at the attendant with disgust, grabbed the wheelchair, and helped Marnie into it. He pushed it straight through the ER door and headed to labor and delivery.

Marnie was taken to her room and several nurses surrounded her for vital signs. They placed a monitor and started an IV. Chris stepped out of the way.

The head nurse put a reassuring hand on Marnie's shoulder. "Hi, I'm Julie. I think we have a mutual friend, Garrett Mancinelli. He told me to keep an eye out for you. All your vitals look stable."

Marnie was trying to relax between contractions. She smiled at Julie. "Always good to see a friendly face at a time like this."

A young female resident came in to check her out. "Hi, I'm Dr. Brown. I see from your chart that Dr. Ramirez wanted to be called when you came in. Let me check your cervix and see how far along you are. When did the contractions start?"

"About two hours ago. At first, I thought they were just Braxton-Hicks, but they've become stronger and more regular."

Dr. Brown smiled. "You should still be early in the process then."

A strong contraction hit Marnie. *Bullshit. This baby's head is about to come out.*

Julie quickly examined her. "You're crowning! Delivery in 202, STAT!"

The bed was reconfigured for a delivery. Chris went to the head of Marnie's bed and touched her shoulder. "I texted EJ and Dr. Ramirez before we left home. They're on their way."

"BP elevated. 190/100," said one of the nurses.

"Push twenty milligrams of labetalol!" Dr. Ramirez ordered as she entered the room.

A wave of relief washed over Marnie when she saw her doctor. *Someone who knew her complicated history. Someone she could trust.*

Another contraction hit. "I want you to pant through this, Marnie. Try not to push." Dr. Ramirez was throwing on a delivery gown and gloving up.

Chris squeezed Marnie's shoulder.

Marnie resisted the urge to scream, "Keep your

hands off me!" Instead, she continued to pant.

"Marnie, you're one hundred percent dilated and effaced. With the next contraction I want you to bear down and push. We're going to have a baby."

We are. Marnie took three slow deep breaths. She pictured herself climbing the last five hundred feet to the top of a mountain pass. As the contraction started, she took a deep breath and pushed for all she was worth. She could feel the baby's head slip through the birth canal. It felt like her pelvis was splitting apart.

She screamed as the contraction ended.

"Don't push, let me suction his mouth," Dr. Ramirez said.

Marnie started panting again.

"Ok, let's see this young man," Dr. Ramirez said.

Marnie smiled at Chris then grabbed his hand in a vice-like grip as she gave one final push. Jon slipped into this world. She heard him whimper. Dr. Ramirez laid him on Marnie's chest. She clipped the umbilical cord.

Jon looked up at Marnie's face, with a bewildered expression.

"You're finally here," Marnie said.

Chris reached over and touched Jon's fingers. "It's truly a miracle." He had tears streaming down his face.

Marnie gently rubbed Jon's back with a towel. After a few minutes the nurse took Jon to weigh him. She wrapped him up and brought him back to his mom. "He's six pounds eight ounces. Good size for a thirty-five weeker."

Marnie loosened the blanket so that she and Jon were skin-to-skin. She guided his mouth to her nipple. She shuddered as the placenta was delivered. She could feel her blood run out of her body bringing back horrible memories. Then it started to slow down.

"The placenta is completely intact. Your bleeding is slowing. Everything looks normal. Your BP is down to 130/80. You're going to be fine," Dr. Ramirez said. "But we need to keep an eye on you and monitor your blood pressure for a few days."

Marnie took her first relaxed breath in eight months. She squeezed Chris's hand and smiled up at him. *It's over. We're all still here.*

Chapter 35

Monday, February 24, 2020

Marnie had forgotten how the days and nights blurred after giving birth—especially in the hospital. Her blood pressure was fine with the labetalol. Jon was sucking well, and her milk was starting to come in. Despite the attempts not to awaken her during the night, someone always came in just as she and Jon fell asleep. She was tired and wanted to go home.

Louise, EJ, and Rosa had come by the day before. Louise said that she would be more than happy to make house calls once Marnie went home.

When Dr. Ramirez came in for rounds at 6 a.m., Marnie was ready. "I want to go home. I have lots of help and would be much happier there. I won't be left stranded by myself like last time should anything happen."

Dr. Ramirez nodded. "As long as you can check your blood pressure and let me know if it's not controlled, I think it's fine if you go home. It's probably for the best. The hospital is preparing for a public health disaster with this pandemic on the horizon."

"I saw that Italy was locked down yesterday. It's

terrifying," Marnie said.

"After years of speculation, it appears that we might have a pandemic."

Marnie looked at Jon as he nursed. He had a full head of soft curly brown hair. Just like his dad. "We may go on shutdown early."

"Call me if anything changes. Twenty-four/seven. I've enjoyed guiding you through this pregnancy. Jon is a beautiful baby. See you at your two-week follow up."

Marnie used her free hand to grab Dr. Ramirez's. "Thank you for everything, Linda. We'll see you then."

***

On Monday, Louise was back at work in the clinic. She was gratified that the staff and her patients had missed and worried over her. When her medical assistant knocked on her office door, she was busy finishing her notes for the day.

"Dr. Finnerty? You have two visitors up front who want to speak to you," Katia said. "One of them is Yvonne MacFarland. I don't recognize the lady with her."

Louise hesitated for a minute. An image of tasers and syringes came to mind. "I'll come up front." The waiting room would be empty at that hour, but staff would be nearby. She preferred to meet the sisters away from the sanctuary of her office.

When Louise entered the room, Yvonne and Betty stood up from the couch they shared. Yvonne looked frail after her heart attack, but Louise was glad to see she had dressed with care in lightweight denim pants and a colorful top. The only aspect of Betty's attire to catch

Louise's eye was her ankle bracelet. The bulky plastic strap and monitor rested above her sensible walking shoe. Louise had heard that Betty's plea deal had been accepted and her sentence had been reduced to time served, albeit under the strict parameters of her parole.

Yvonne began. "Dr. Finnerty, we couldn't leave without seeing you one more time and apologizing again."

"And to thank you," Betty said. "It was your words of support that helped my case."

Louise wasn't prepared for the emotion that flooded her as she thought about the tragedy that had touched so many people. *I'm not going to cry.* She asked them to sit, and she pulled another chair close to them. "I'm glad you came. I don't want the scene in Matagorda to be my last memory of you two. Where are you going?"

"Back to my place," Betty said. "Yvonne agreed to come live with me."

"It's just the two of us. We need to take care of each other now," Yvonne continued. "And I don't want to live in the house I shared with Bruce for all those years, never suspecting…"

Betty patted Yvonne's leg. "On a brighter note, we plan to sell the house on M Street and donate as much as we can afford to the fund for victim relief at the police department."

Yvonne broke into a smile. "I've asked that nice young man from Sand Dollar Estates to manage the sale. He said he would take care of the painting and renovations. I even agreed to let him stage it."

"It sounds like a new start for both of you," Louise said, grateful that the women were rebuilding what was left of their lives. Apparently, Yvonne had made peace with the fact that her sister had briefly considered killing Bruce. *Then again, he had treated Yvonne badly enough that she might have been relieved.* "Give Randy some primo cat treats to thank him for saving us."

They laughed and chatted for a few more minutes about Yvonne's recovery. Louise walked them to the clinic door and watched as they drove off in the same Subaru she had traveled in on that horrible night. She touched the scarf around her neck. She realized she hadn't acknowledged their apology and wondered if they'd noticed.

Her phone chirped with a text. She smiled. Didier had arranged for a sitter and made reservations for dinner. She smiled and returned the text "Making a quick stop at Marnie's. Home by six thirty."

When Louise arrived, Chris, Marnie, and Jon were in the downstairs bedroom. Jon was sleeping soundly despite the headlines on the TV news playing in the background.

"Thank you for stopping by," Marnie said to Louise. "We're doing well."

"I had to cuddle this new baby one time today."

Chris reluctantly handed over the sleeping baby. "What's the word at the clinic about Covid-19?"

"We're so overwhelmed by the day-to-day that we haven't really discussed it. Our director reached out to the health department but didn't hear back yet."

"I called Allison from the VA in Aurora to tell her about Jon's arrival. She feels strongly that a true pandemic is coming based on the communications she's getting from the government," Marnie said. "The VA is already planning ways to do telemedicine for all but the most critical illnesses."

Louise shook her head as she handed Jon back. "Mardi Gras is in full swing. Perfect way to spread disease."

"Speaking of Mardi Gras, Rosa asked me last Friday about your plans for a party this coming weekend," Marnie said.

"OMG, I totally forgot. We could celebrate Jon's arrival. Maybe just a small leap-year party on the twenty-ninth. My folks, Sudhan, Bob, and Ben, our two families and Rosa. Taylor and Garrett and his new squeeze? Potluck?"

***

After Louise left, Chris asked, "Do you want the good news or the bad news first?"

Marnie looked at him. "We have bad news already?"

"My parents are coming to meet Jon on Wednesday."

Marnie laughed. "Well, that's expected news anyway. What's the good news?"

"Their friend, Parker Dodge, was outed on social media as batting for both sides."

"That's hilarious! It must have been quite a shock for your mom. I think he just lost his invitation to the non-existent baby shower."

Chris looked at Marnie. "I think we need to talk about my parents. I know we both struggle with them."

Marnie interjected, "Actually, we only struggle

with your mom."

Chris sighed. "Yep, my mom. But look, Marnie, they are Jon's only grandparents. Do you remember how important your relationship with your grandparents was?"

Marnie looked lovingly at Jon. "Yes, both before and after I lost my parents. What are you suggesting?"

"I had a long talk with my parents. They want to be a part of Jon's life—and that's a great resource for the two of us with our careers. Mom promised to tone down the MAGA stuff around us. Both will follow our lead on parenting issues."

Marnie smiled at Chris. "Thank you for that. I'll give the relationship another chance."

Chapter 36

Wednesday, February 26, 2020

Torres had made several trips to Matagorda tying up loose ends in the MacFarland case. At least it took his mind off the shooting. It had been twelve days since he shot and killed another person. Firing the bullet that killed Kevin Small was justified. Nobody questioned that. *Nobody said being a police detective would be easy either.*

He pulled in front of the regional hospital. An attendant was waiting with a patient in a wheelchair accompanied by an officer from the sheriff's department. Torres stepped out, signed several forms, and shook the hand of the deputy.

"Thanks, I've got her from here," he said. Then to Anita, "Let me help you get into the car."

Torres settled her in the back seat. Anita was dressed in hospital scrubs. A neck collar, plastic jail issued slip-on sandals and handcuffs completed her ensemble. He pulled out of the hospital's circular drive. When he glanced at Anita from his rear-view mirror, her head was turned to the window. He held up a turkey sub wrapped in paper. "Are you hungry? We have a long ride."

"Yeah, I am. The hospital food's been awful. Not that I can expect much better where I'm going."

He handed her a sandwich which she grabbed with her cuffed hands and passed her a bottle of water. He opened his and ate while he drove.

Anita had been charged with aggravated assault with a deadly weapon. Plus, kidnapping. With the evidence they had, Torres knew she would be going away for a long time, no matter what kind of fast-talking lawyer she or her family could hire to defend her.

Anita put down her sandwich and sighed.

"You don't like it?" Torres asked.

"It's not that. And thanks. It's the first nice thing anyone's done for me since this whole mess got started." She took another bite. "You wouldn't understand what it's like to grow up under the black cloud of a family like mine. Shit, I didn't have a chance from the day I was born."

Torres let out a laugh. "You think it's easy for everyone else? How about being a gay Brown man trying to get ahead in a straight White police force?"

When he glanced back at her again, Anita looked chastened. "I got into this for my daughter's sake. Do you have kids?" she asked.

No, not yet anyway." Maybe someday, he hoped. "Where's your daughter now?"

"Harper's living with her father in Houston. At least she's off this inbred island even if that wasn't the situation I would have chosen for her. I wanted to get away with her."

Torres drove on in silence. He smiled grimly as he drove across the bridge to the island. He knew that Anita would be granted part of her wish. She would get a ticket out of Galveston—to a women's prison on the mainland.

After he pulled up to the police station, he helped Anita out of the car. As they entered the station, Sudhan met them. "We're going to interrogation room number one. Betty's lawyer, Megan Emerson, is back again. She wants to confer with Anita before we get started."

Anita said, "I can't hire a lawyer. I'm broke."

"Ms. Emerson said she was doing this as her pro bono work for the court. She's familiar with the case and doesn't feel you should be left shouldering all the guilt unless you choose to do so."

After an hour, Ms. Emerson alerted the guard that they were ready to talk. "Ms. Martin would like to discuss a plea deal. She's willing to trade information for a reduced sentence. She can provide the identity of the person who hired her to retrieve the files." Megan paused. "At no time did she plan to kill anyone nor was she instructed to do so."

"We're listening," Sudhan said.

Anita said, "I agreed to do two jobs for my cousin Crawford Pappalardo. One was about a compromising hotel video that was being used to blackmail a prominent Galveston citizen. No problem getting rid of the video, but I ran into some complications when I had to give Crawford the name of the blackmailer. I pinned it on that real estate agent at my hotel. Taylor Wood."

Torres and Sudhan exchanged glances. "That explains a few things," Torres murmured.

"In case you don't know, the video was leaked anyway," Sudhan said. Anita shrugged.

"The second job was to retrieve an evidence file in the possession of Bruce MacFarland. He had been holding on to notes and evidence about some of our family members. The kind of evidence that could cause a lot of problems for them if it made its way back to you guys. The situation got out of hand when I approached Yvonne and Betty to get the folder. Dr. Finnerty was unfortunately there, and Yvonne was having a heart attack...."

Megan interjected, "Ms. Martin will claim diminished capacity due to alcohol intoxication which has already been corroborated by others at the scene."

Anita winced.

Sudhan said, "I'll discuss this offer with our DA. You've given us a lot to think about."

When Anita had been escorted back to her cell and Megan had left, Torres and Sudhan retreated to her office.

"What did you think about all that?" Sudhan asked him. "Anita's testimony is valuable. It could right quite a few of our predecessors' wrongs. Not to mention providing an explanation for the attempted kidnapping of Taylor Wood."

"It's a lot to take in. A lot of people could be going down." Then Torres smiled. "I bet the prominent citizen she mentioned is Parker Douglas. Didn't really work out for him either, did it?"

Chapter 37

Friday, Morning February 28, 2020

Sudhan was looking at her phone as she walked through the lobby of the police station. She smiled as she opened a text from Louise with a picture of baby Jon. He was holding his tiny fist under his chin in a thinker pose.

"Morning, Detective Sudhan," said the duty sergeant at the desk. "There's a fellow here who says he needs to talk to you. He has one of your cards."

Sudhan followed the sergeant's gaze to the waiting area. Her smile faded as she recognized Dr. Mark Melvin. He had a carry-on suitcase with him. He nodded to her.

As Sudhan approached him, she noticed that he appeared worn out. "Good morning, Dr. Melvin. Let's go back to my office."

Sudhan closed the door as he took a seat and parked his suitcase next to it. "It looks like you're on your way out of town," Sudhan began.

"Yes, I was notified that the police had completed

their search of my father's condominium and possessions. I want to explain a few things before I begin." Sudhan tilted her head slightly to encourage him to finish his thought. He straightened his shoulders and continued, "I wasn't completely forthcoming with you at the hospital. The heartache he caused has been gnawing at me."

"Are you referring to his assault on Dr. Liccione?"

"Yes, of course. But it's clear that there were other people he hurt over the years. I've been following the news."

Sudhan sat back and folded her hands on her desk. "Go ahead."

"I told you that my father had been very generous in his financial support. And he alluded to a lifestyle that exceeded the salary of a small-town medical examiner. He never volunteered an explanation, and I never asked." Mark shifted uncomfortably in his seat. "Then, a few weeks ago, my father called me and said he wanted to warn me to be careful who I talked to. I had no idea what he was talking about."

"A warning? Did it involve a threat to him or to you?"

"That's what I couldn't understand. I thought he might have been drinking. At that point, I attributed his change in demeanor to the loss of his good friend, Bruce MacFarland. Man, was I off base there." He shook his head and cleared his throat. "I pressed him for more information."

"Was he more specific? Dates or names?" Sudhan asked.

"He said something happened in 2002. MacFarland and he were asked to make the case of a brutal dismemberment look accidental. Powerful people in Galveston didn't want the public to think it was a copycat of the Durst murder. For some reason the two of them decided to make it look like a shark attack, of all things. I thought he was rambling and none of it made any sense to me. Until I got down here and saw the news coverage about the teacher who was found dead and mutilated."

"Sadly, yes."

"Then it finally dawned on me that he and MacFarland were paid off to tamper with the evidence and provide bogus autopsy results. Subsequent payoffs must have financed my education and his lifestyle."

"You said he warned you?"

"Yes. That was how the conversation started before he told me about the events in 2002. He told me these powerful people, his clients or bosses, call them what you will, recently came after him for some files MacFarland had kept on their operations. My father said that they would come after me if he didn't produce them."

"Have you been approached or threatened?"

"Not yet. But as I learn about my father's life in Galveston, I find myself looking over my shoulder. I feel like it's just a matter of time."

"Did your father indicate who these people were or currently are? We searched his condominium thoroughly and didn't find any records, written or on his computer, that would identify his clients. Have you found anything?" Sudhan asked.

Mark pulled a folded piece of paper out of his shirt pocket. "Here is a list of names he gave me the last time we spoke. At the time, I thought he was being paranoid. Not anymore." He handed Sudhan the page of handwritten names.

As Sudhan perused the names, some were familiar. She recognized names of long dead island Mafia and cartel figures. Several names were new to her. A few names registered as being members, past and present, of the Galveston Hotel Consortium.

She looked up. "Thank you. This information is extremely helpful, Dr. Melvin. I'd like to ask you to make a formal statement." She was eager to review the list with her task force. Cross referencing these names with cold cases should expedite the process. Or open new avenues to pursue.

"I understand. I think that will be a relief." He sighed. "You read the list I gave you. Do I need police protection? I have a family, detective."

"Based on several of the names you've provided, yes, you will need police protection. At least for a time. I can reassure you that the files in question are now in our hands. Any incriminating evidence will soon be made public. At that point, there will be no reason for anyone still alive and named on the list to pursue you," Sudhan said as she stood. "I'll reach out to your local police department."

"One more question, Detective," he said as he stood up. "How is the woman my father attacked, Dr. Liccione? Is she still in the hospital?"

Sudhan decided he deserved a bit of grace for having come forward. *Better late than never.* She picked up her cell phone from her desk and showed him the picture of Marnie's baby.

"Mother and baby are doing fine."

***

Chris was at his office at the Daily early Friday morning. It was his first day back. He had always heard that having a baby changed everything. Now he understood. He was exhausted and exhilarated at the same time. Not to mention relieved that Marnie and Jon were healthy and safe.

The events of the last month, since the arrival of Taylor's letter to the editor, had kept him on constant alert. He shook his head as he remembered regaling EJ and Ben with anecdotes about the island Mafia. He never gave a thought to the reputational burden their descendants lived under. He felt sorry for Anita, despite the mayhem she created.

He wanted things to get back to normal. He sat at his desk, ready to pull up that letter and proceed with the ideas he had been mulling over for the last few days. He had to laugh when he saw his computer monitor lined with post-it notes. Willa! He knew he would have to deal with them before he could proceed. He began peeling the notes off his screen.

"Caught you!" Willa said as she came in with her spiral notebook in hand. "I've been going easy on you while you were off. But before we start, show me your most recent photos of Jon. I know you have hundreds."

Willa scrolled through the album on his phone while Chris gave a commentary. Soon, they were joined by Tom Assan. "Welcome back, Dad!"

They worked their way through the tasks that Willa had prioritized. Tom reported that he had assigned a reporting team to address Covid 19. "We're getting emails from our readers wanting up to the minute local information about the virus. We're renewing friendships with our county and state health departments, the medical school, and the Gulf National Lab. Lots to consider with how to display the data and provide accurate recommendations."

"Good. While I've been working from home, I've had discussions with IT. We've been working the kinks out of remote work. They'll be meeting with our staff. A period of remote work for all looks likely. Have you heard about a program called Zoom?"

When Tom and Willa left, Chris turned his attention to Taylor's letter of January 21. He looked up when EJ and Ben came into the office for their meeting. They had three cups of coffee between them. "Ready to get back to it?" Chris asked them.

"Raring to go!" said EJ. "But you look like you're flagging. I can hear my brother hollering at all hours from all the way over in the garage apartment. Here." She handed him a cup.

"How's your mom doing down at police headquarters?" Chris asked Ben. "She told me about the task force she's heading up. They'll be looking at all the convictions that came out during our time frame. She said that similar corruption was being uncovered all over South Texas. We have a great story here for a small independent newspaper."

"It sounds intense. At least from what she tells my dad and me, which isn't much," Ben said.

Chris handed each of them a copy of Taylor's letter. "It's hard to believe how much has happened in the last month," he began, shaking his head. "I've decided that it's time to give a formal answer. I'll write a response to run in the editorial section. In that piece, I want to let 'T. Wood' and our readers know what we discovered. I cleared it with the police. Sudhan said she was working on a formal apology from the department to print alongside it."

EJ smiled and nodded. "That will mean a lot to Taylor."

"I spoke to your mom, Ben. She put me in touch with the police communication liaison. I want you two to work with this person and put together a weekly update from the task force. With everything you two have dug up on MacFarland and Melvin, you should be able to create some great copy."

"And get the bylines?" Ben asked.

"Let me think that one over," Chris said. "This kind of reporting will get some folks riled up. I'm not sure it's fair to make targets of my interns. Let's see the initial response and take it from there. Okay?"

When the interns left, Chris got up to stretch. He yawned, despite the coffee. Looking out at the parking lot, he saw employees coming and going for lunch. Normal life never looked so good. He decided to banish thoughts of lawsuits claiming slander and threats of retribution when the Daily put this seamy chapter of the island's history in print.

Instead, he texted Marnie: *I miss you two. FaceTime?*

***

EJ walked slowly from her apartment to the quiet restaurant downtown where she was meeting Taylor. They thought they would sneak one more meal out before Covid came to Texas. The stories out of Italy were scary. The restaurant was hopping. *Might not be the only ones with this thought.* Taylor had reserved a table in an alcove. He was waiting there when she arrived.

EJ leaned over and gave him a kiss. "How was your day?"

"Busy. I took a decorator over to the MacFarlands'. She had some good ideas. I have some more estimates coming from a kitchen and bathroom remodeler. How was your day?"

"Ben and I had a meeting with Chris. He's given us the assignment of being liaisons for the police task force on the reinvestigation of cases handled by Melvin and MacFarland. We went to the department and made introductions. After tidying up work, I got back to my thesis. It's the last requirement I need to graduate with my BA in history.

"Your thesis? Tell me about it."

"I'm contrasting how newspapers continued to flourish in America during the twentieth century, despite the addition of radio and TV reporting. More recently they've done less well against the tide of corporate buyouts. But the biggest change in status appears to be the internet."

"That's a big topic. You have a ringside seat."

"Thinking about graduation made me realize that I need to plan what to do with the rest of my life."

"Whoa. I think it's a good time to just think about what you're going to do after celebrating your graduation."

"So, take life one step at a time—the rest of my life is too long a time frame? What about you? Are you planning to stay in real estate?"

"I've enjoyed doing it for the last few years and I've been able to build a rainy-day fund. But no, I don't plan to do it for the next 30 years. I minored in computer science, and I've been looking for tech jobs where I can combine my experience in business and sales with the coming wave of AI."

"That sounds complicated. I get the feeling that all fields are related to the internet. I've heard my mom complaining about IT and the electronic health records for 10 years." EJ smiled. "You are a good salesman. I've seen you in action."

"Have your musings about the future dwelt on us at all?" Taylor asked.

EJ blushed. "Of course. But I don't sit around writing my first name with your last name."

"What are you talking about?"

"Oh, in old romance novels that's what young maidens did when they fell in love. Don't worry, I'm not thinking about marriage. Nor, when I do, do I plan to change my name."

"I'm still thinking about your indirect way of telling me you're in love with me," Taylor said as he took EJ's hand. "I've been thinking about it some. I'm hoping there is a long future for us."

Now EJ turned very red with her dad's fair bloodlines overcoming her mom's olive complexion. "I really hadn't gotten there yet."

"It's probably the five-year difference in our ages.

Maybe at thirty, it comes to mind more easily. I love you EJ. I would like to see where our relationship takes us and hope we both get to the point that marriage is the next step."

Taylor stood up and slid into the EJ's side of the booth. He took her face between his hands and gave her a deep kiss. EJ responded, drew him close and whispered. "I want to see what the future has in store for us too."

Chapter 38

Saturday, February 29, 2020

Louise was excited about her party. Bad news about Covid 19 was coming in fast and furious. This may be the last time they could get together for a while. There was no community spread in Texas, but it only seemed a matter of time.

Didier was cooking jambalaya. His Creole roots made it a favorite party food. Rosa was bringing multiple Mexican dishes. Louise's mouth watered at the thought. Garrett was bringing appetizers and his new friend, Julie Diaz. Iliana had asked Bob about her, and he confirmed she was an excellent nurse and a good person. Noah and Cora had done the decorations, both Mardi Gras and new baby themes. They were especially excited to meet Jon.

The first people to arrive were the Liccione-Hills with EJ, Taylor, and Rosa.

"Jon is looking great!" Louise exclaimed. "You'd never know he was a preemie."

Marnie beamed. "He's gained half a pound this week. I can't believe how much milk I have.

Breastfeeding EJ was so difficult."

"That's great news. We're starting this party on the veranda. We have the heaters on and it's such a warm February day. We dug out my old rocker for you and Jon and plan to move it during the evening to wherever you need it."

Within the next thirty minutes, the rest of the crowd arrived. Conversations varied from group to group. Bob was discussing the plans for pandemic protocols at the hospital with Julie.

Didier asked Garrett if he was making any plans for the pandemic. "I've heard there are plans to close all non-essential businesses for two weeks to two months," Didier said.

Garrett shrugged. "We're reworking our takeout menu but not much else. I have weddings booked every weekend from now to September. I wouldn't have any way to change the dates for them."

Nancy laughed. "I have friends whose grandchildren are getting married in the fall and they're happy now that they were unable to get summer wedding dates."

"What do you think we should be doing before this virus hits Texas?" Nancy asked Marnie.

"I'm taking my cues from my mentor in Colorado. Allison said that we should stock up on everything we need for two months. She's been following the virus's impact in Europe with her veteran and military connections. They said they're having trouble finding toilet paper and soup, much less staples like pasta, canned goods, and baking supplies."

EJ joined the conversation with Taylor at her

elbow. "On this note, I want to tell you that Taylor is moving into the garage apartment with me. The move will reduce his exposure to the virus."

Marnie smiled. "What a smart and convenient plan."

EJ gently nudged her foot. "Don't be a smart-ass, Mom."

"Chris said that you talked about graduation plans—and after graduation plans. Do you think we should buy tickets for the trip?" Marnie asked.

"I'm glad we made the hotel reservations at the start of the year. Everything is sold out now. Do you think the pandemic will have died down by then?" EJ said.

Marnie shrugged her shoulders. "Could be. No one has any idea how this plays out, but I think we make our plans and cross our fingers. Other scares like SARS calmed down soon. What about after graduation?"

"I'd like to continue working on the newspaper— at least for a while. Taylor and I talked about taking several weeks off after he sells the MacFarland house and taking a safari in Africa. All of this depends on the pandemic being mild. Anyway, I'm looking forward to spending some time with my baby brother before taking off somewhere."

Marnie smiled. "I just want you to be happy, EJ. But if your plans keep you in Galveston for a while, it would be wonderful."

Louise said to Taylor, "I hear you're taking on the remodeling and sale of the MacFarland house."

"I am. I was planning to hire a lot of it out with Rosa's help. EJ told me that Rosa basically oversaw the remodeling of the 18th Street house for Chris. I may do as much as I can by myself."

EJ turned to Chris. "What's the plan for running the paper?"

"I'm making sure that everyone has a home office with adequate internet connection. We've ordered masks and other protective gear for when we need to be in the field."

"That's going to take a lot of organization. Let me know if I can help."

"I will. The Daily has been in continuous publication since 1842. If the Great Storm didn't make us miss a day in 1900, this virus sure as hell won't either."

After a second round of eating, it was time for the crowning glory of the evening. Rosa brought out her tres leches cake and Garrett his chocolate mousse cake. People who thought they couldn't eat another bite found room.

Didier and Louise offered a champagne toast to their friends and family. "May we all meet here again in a year with this threat safely behind us and a toddling Jon tipping over our plates."

"Here! Here!" echoed around the room.

"We have a surprise for you, Marnie—baby gifts!" Louise said.

"Oh no! I didn't want any!"

"You'll like this."

Noah and Cora wheeled out a little red wagon stuffed with paper towels, toilet paper, diapers, and wipes that all the guests had contributed to.

The whole room burst out laughing! Marnie had been telling everyone to stock up on these supplies for three weeks.

"Okay, okay," Marnie giggled. "But I may get the last laugh. I'm going to charge you double when you come knocking on my door in a few months."

Epilogue

Published in the Bay City Daily, Thursday December 31, 2020

A letter from the editor:

As the managing editor of the Bay City Daily, along with my team, I wish everyone a safe and happy new year. None of us are sad to see the end of 2020. The world-wide devastation caused by the Covid-19 pandemic has touched us all.

At the beginning of the year, I thought the most important personal event would be the birth of my first child. That was certainly the best part of 2020.

Next, I thought our investigation of Luther Wood's murder which exposed police and cartel collaboration throughout Texas would be the biggest story of 2020.

I was wrong. My physician wife had concerns about how bad this epidemic might be but none of us foresaw the magnitude of lives lost to Covid-19. At a gathering last winter, we joked about stocking up on supplies and, at worst, a two-month shut down of non-essential businesses. Instead, life as we knew it stopped. Graduations were canceled. Schools and daycares closed.

Weddings were postponed. Family celebrations were followed by family funerals. Below is a quick review to clarify the fog of last year.

On March 4, the first case of community acquired Covid-19 was confirmed in Texas.

One week later the World Health Organization declared a pandemic. Four days later the country went on a voluntary national shutdown for six weeks.

On April 30, Operation Warp Speed funded six candidates to produce a vaccine for Covid-19. By May 28, 100,000 Americans had died from this virus. By the end of the year, the number was three times that amount. Worldwide, the estimated toll is 1.5 to 3 million people.

Health care workers were decimated by infection, death, and burnout. The unemployment rate soared to 13.7 percent as businesses closed.

What the future will look like none of us can predict. Will this devastation bring us closer together or further our political and social divides? Will we continue to work from home and become more isolated or regroup again?

Our grandparents tell us that they faced such uncertain futures during World War II. Since I know how that turned out, I forget that at the time they did not. Let's hope that the war against this virus brings us closer together and united in our similarities and forgiving of our differences.

This is the season of hope. And hope appears on the horizon. On December 11, the FDA issued an emergency use authorization for the Pfizer-BioNTech Covid-19 vaccine. Early results report a large degree of protection from serious illness and death. We all believe that this vaccine will turn the tide of this pandemic. You can count on all of us at The Daily to keep you informed and up to date.

May peace and grace be yours in 2021 ---
Chris Hill

Acknowledgements

Returning to Galveston for our third book was exciting. We were able to dive deeper into its history as well as explore the Galveston of today. We wanted to honor the difficult work of local newspapers and their importance in reporting local news and maintaining a search for the truth. Galveston County's The Daily News is a prime example. Our digital subscription was an excellent and colorful source.

It was fun to return to our characters and intersect with them right before the Covid epidemic. Four years after its start, it is hard to remember how naïve we were about the impact it would have on our communities, our country and the world. We used many resources to review this event, Center for Disease and Prevention, National Institutes of Health, the National Library of medicine, and the World Health Organization. These institutions do not have all the answers. But they attempt to provide the facts and truth as it's known at the time, uncorrupted by politics and biases.

The biggest addition to our writing team was Caitlin

Cieslik-Miskimen, our editor. She brought a clear eye to the central themes of our book and kept the action moving. Many thanks to Janice Ricciardi for an early read by younger eyes. Greg Cantrell shared helpful references about Galveston's history and recollections from his time on the island.

Support for our writing came from family, friends, book groups, and fans of our first two books. Thanks to our local chapters of Mystery Writers of America, NorCal and Rocky Mountain, for support and inspiration.

Mary Rae and Wanda Venters

Authors' Note

Enthusiasm from our readers inspired us to continue the Finnerty-Liccione series. Marnie and Louise are back in Galveston and find themselves making life and death decisions once again. Complications in their personal lives demand that they grow and change.

With our first two books garnering recognition, Break Bone Fever as a finalist in the Colorado Book Awards, mystery division, and Breaking Apart winning the Killer Nashville Silver Falchion Award in Thrillers, we were emboldened to create our third book, Breaking News.

Our fourth book is in its early stages but should get published in 2025. We are maintaining our characters but will shift some of the focus to the next generation.

Mary Rae, MD and Wanda Venters, MD

About the Authors

A native of Oklahoma City, **Wanda Venters,** attended Yale for her undergraduate studies and returned to Oklahoma City for her medical degree. She completed her pediatric residency in San Antonio with the US Army.

Retiring from her pediatric practice after three decades, she began her second career as a writer in 2019. She lives in Colorado with her husband, two labradoodles and a Siamese cat. She has three grown children and four grandchildren. She is an avid gardener, golfs with more enthusiasm than skill and enjoys craft beer.

Writing and publishing the Finnerty Liccione Series has been incredibly rewarding. All authors struggle with self-doubt. Being a finalist in the Colorado Book Awards and a winner of the Killer Nashville Silver Falchion Award for a Thriller in 2024 has bolstered our determination to share our work with the public.

Mary Rae grew up in the New York City suburbs. She graduated from Colgate University before attending the University of Oklahoma College of Medicine. After residency, she moved to Texas where she practiced Emergency Medicine for twenty years. She then changed course to practice Primary Care until her retirement in 2020. Soon after her retirement from medicine, she and her husband moved to Oakland, California. Mary spends time with her two grandchildren continues her lifelong quest for proficiency in Spanish and French, and, of course, writes

While living in Houston, she enjoyed exploring the Gulf Coast. Her fascination with the area led to the idea of writing a murder mystery set in Galveston in collaboration with her friend, Wanda Venters.

In 2019, Mary and Wanda began writing the Finnerty/Liccione Mystery Series. Their first book, **Break Bone Fever,** was a finalist for the Colorado Book Award in 2022 and they were winners of the Killer Nashville Silver Falchion Award for best thriller for **Breaking Apart** in 2024